2 5

'í0

13

24 ↑

Plea:

V

LS 1636a 6.11

Dead Ends

CRIME FICTION
The 'Carnaby' series (1967–84)
Carnaby and the hijackers
Carnaby and the gaolbreakers
Carnaby and the assassins
Carnaby and the conspirators
Carnaby and the saboteurs
Carnaby and the eliminators
Carnaby and the demonstrators
Carnaby and the infiltrators
Carnaby and the kidnappers
Carnaby and the counterfeiters
Carnaby and the campaigners
Fatal accident (1970)
Panda One on duty (1971)
Special duty (1971)
Identification parade (1972)
Panda One investigates (1973)
Major incident (1974)
The Dovingsby death (1975)
Missing from home (1977)
The MacIntyre plot (1977)
Witchcraft for Panda One (1978)
Target criminal (1978)
The Carlton plot (1980)
Siege for Panda One (1981)
Teenage cop (1982)
Robber in a mole trap (1985)
False alibi (1991)
Grave secrets (1992)

Written as Christopher Coram
A call to danger (1968)
A call to die (1969)
Death in Ptarmigan Forest (1970)
Death on the motorway (1973)
Murder by the lake (1975)
Murder beneath the trees (1979)
Prisoner on the dam (1982)
Prisoner on the run (1985)

Written as Tom Ferris
Espionage for a lady (1969)

Written as Andrew Arncliffe
Murder after the holidays (1985)

Written as Nicholas Rhea
Family ties (1994)
Suspect (1995)
Confession (1997)
Death of A Princess (1999)
The Sniper (2001)

THE 'CONSTABLE' SERIES
Constable on the hill (1979)
Constable on the prowl (1980)
Constable around the village (1981)
Constable across the moors (1982)
Constable in the dale (1983)
Constable by the sea (1985)
Constable along the lane (1986)
Constable through the meadow (1988)

Constable at the double (1988)
Constable in disguise (1989)
Constable through the heather (1990)
Constable beside the stream (1991)
Constable around the green (1993)
Constable beneath the trees (1994)
Constable in the shrubbery (1995)
Constable versus Greengrass (1995)
Constable about the parish (1996)
Constable at the gate (1997)
Constable at the dam (1997)
Constable over the Stile (1998)
Constable under the Gooseberry Bush (1999)
Constable in the Farmyard (1999)
Constable around the Houses (2000)
Constable along the Highway (2001)
Constable over the Bridge (2001)
Constable goes to market (2002)
Constable along the River-bank (2003)
Heartbeat Omnibus I (1992)
Heartbeat Omnibus 11(1993)
HEARTBEAT TITLES
Constable among the heather (1992)
Constable across the moors (1993)
Constable on call (1993)
Constable around the green (1994)
Constable in control (1994)
Constable along the lane (1995)
Constable versus Greengrass (1996)
Constable in the dale (1996)
Constable about the parish (1997)

THE 'MONTAGUE PLUKE' SERIES
Omens of death (1997)
Superstitious death (1998)
A well-pressed shroud (2000)
Garland for a Dead Maiden (2002)

Written as James Ferguson
EMMERDALE TITLES
A friend in need (1987)
Divided loyalties (1988)
Wives and lovers (1989)
Book of country lore (1988)
Official companion (1988)
Emmerdale's Yorkshire (1990)

NON-FICTION
The Court of law (1971)
Punishment (1972)
Murders and mysteries from the North York
  Moors (1988)
Murders and mysteries from the Yorkshire
  Dales (1991)
Folk tales from the North York Moors (1990)
Folk stories from the Yorkshire Dales (1991)
Folk tales from York and the Wolds (1992)
Folk stories from the Lake District (1993)
The Story of the Police Mutual Assurance
  Society (1993)
as Nicholas Rhea
Portrait of the North York Moors (1985)
Heartbeat of Yorkshire (1993)
Yorkshire days (1995)

DEAD ENDS

Nicholas Rhea

Constable • London

First published in Great Britain 2003
by Constable, an imprint of Constable & Robinson Ltd
3 The Lanchesters, 162 Fulham Palace Road
London W6 9ER
www.constablerobinson.com

ISBN 1–84119–698–3

Printed and bound in Great Britain

A CIP catalogue record for this book
is available from the British Library

Chapter One

'Adults who have simply left home aren't usually our concern.' Detective Superintendent Mark Pemberton had a buff-coloured file on the desk before him. 'But this one's different, Paul.'

Detective Inspector Larkin was standing near Pemberton's desk with a pile of crime reports in his arms along with the rest of the Monday morning mail. 'You mean we've a suspected murder, sir?'

'We've no idea what's happened to him. The file's been sent up by Crime Intelligence, they want us to take it on board. The missing man is Darren Mallory from Dovedale. He's twenty-four, old enough to leave home if he wants to, but the reason for our interest is that he's been under police surveillance – mainly outside our area. On top of that, the probation service has been keeping tabs on him. Just over a month ago he got two years' probation for ABH, he attacked a man, hit him in the face with a brick. He made a mess of the fellow's nose and eyes and knocked some teeth out.'

'And is that all he got? Probation?'

'There wasn't enough evidence to do him for GBH and there were mitigating circumstances, so the court believed, otherwise he'd have been sent down,' Pemberton told him. 'These notes don't say what those circumstances were.'

'How much do we know about him?'

'Quite a lot. He's from a criminal background, a Mallory family trait. As a juvenile, he got himself into bother almost as soon as he could walk, vandalism, shoplifting and so on, then he graduated to burglary, robbery and car crime – the usual stuff kids get up to. As he got older, he started to use his brains and considerable charm, then found he could con people. He started a string of deception offences. One was to trick pensioners into giving him money, pretending he was going to arrange home deliveries of meals. He's a bright lad, the brightest of the Mallory Mob by a long way, and not usually violent. There's no doubt he lives by crime, and the more experience he gets, the more skilled he is at not getting caught.'

Pemberton passed the file to Larkin who opened it, saw it contained some photographs of a dark-haired, rather handsome young man, then glanced at Form 32, the first sheet. 'I see the person initiating this report is a senior probation officer, James Dent. From Port Haverton on Greater Balderside. That's not in our patch either, sir. Hasn't Mallory anyone to bat for him? Wife? Parent? Relation of some kind?'

'His father won't co-operate, Paul, not with the police or any of the support services. Jack Mallory's against everything and anything to do with authority. The probation service tried to persuade him but he didn't want the police or anybody else snooping into his affairs and poking around his private life. His attitude is that if Darren wants to clear off it's got nothing to do with the law or anybody else. Jack Mallory says he's not worried about Darren's disappearance.'

'It happens all the time, sir, young lads flying the nest.'

'Darren's gone off before, sometimes for a few days or even a week or two, but because he always comes home his father has no intention of reporting him missing. He doesn't want the police involved, he's adamant about that.'

'Understandable, in view of the family background.'

'Quite, and on top of that, he regards Darren's probation as little more than an occupational hazard.'

'So why are we bothering, sir? He's just a villain who's doing his own thing.'

'Darren's supposed to keep his probation officer

6

informed of his whereabouts. He hasn't done so. He's not said a dicky bird to anybody about going away. That makes us curious.'

'I can understand that, but surely it's the probation service's worry, not ours? It's a common enough problem, we've enough on our plate without this kind of thing. Besides, Uniform normally deal with Missing From Homes.'

'It was Port Haverton's Criminal Intelligence Unit who persuaded Dent to make the missing person report because Darren's family wouldn't do it, his mother left home years ago. Darren still lives at home, by the way, with the rest of the Mallory clan. At Dovedale. That is on our patch. Talk about a nest of vipers!'

'I remember the Mallorys coming to Dovedale, sir. The family from hell! Am I right in thinking this is really a ploy to provide us with a lever to start probing? We can disturb some criminals' cosy routine, make a legitimate nuisance of ourselves among villains who think we've lost interest in them. Is that the idea?'

'Something like that, Paul. We're involved because Darren's family home is on our patch. Port Haverton's own officers are asking around Greater Balderside's force area because that's where the Mallorys operate most of their time. With a gentle nudge, the probation service has provided a starting point. It's clear this is more than just a yobbo missing from his haunts but Crime Intelligence aren't saying anything. They just want us to make a few enquiries in our area.'

'This file doesn't tell us much. Is there anything else I should know?'

'Background stuff mainly,' said Pemberton. 'You know the Mallorys are a dysfunctional family – and that's putting it mildly. The dad – Jack – is an out-of-work docker, very antagonistic towards the police, very anti-authority and violently left wing. He was one of the loony left in his younger days, although he's mellowed with age. I don't think he's politically active any more but he was a trouble-maker at work, causing strikes and fomenting internal strife on the docks just for the hell of it. The company managed to get rid of him and he's been living on state handouts ever since. His wife, Elsa, disappeared about ten years ago – there were no suspicious circumstances. Word was she just wanted to be clear of them, she'd stuck it long enough. She rang a friend to say she'd gone but daren't tell the friend where she was in case the mob tried to find her.'

'A brave woman!' smiled Larkin.

'Very. She's never been home but Port Haverton Criminal Intelligence Unit knows she's alive and well. There's five sons, most of them not the sort you would want to cross on a dark night – Damon, twenty-six, Darren, twins Neil and Max, twenty-two, and the baby of the family, Garry, who's twenty. All with form, all villains, all ruthless. Like father like son. They're into all sorts – car thefts, burglaries, scams of various kinds, protection rackets, fencing stolen property, smuggling stuff in and out of the country, but it's said they never touch drugs. Word is they've never done drugs because Jack hates drugs and druggies. And they've never murdered either. That's Jack's ruling – no killings, no drugs. He's still boss of the family firm – if he says no drugs and no killings, then that's how it is. That's the Mallorys, all living off crime, all professional villains. Darren's the brightest, as I've said, a charmer who tends to use his brains rather than muscle. He has taken jobs at times, often to acquire inside knowledge so he can commit more crimes – a spell as a postman, for example, railway porter, dock worker, supermarket shelf stacker – he's a dab hand at all sorts. With that sort of background, you can understand CI's continuing interest in this bunch, especially with Darren doing a vanishing trick.'

'Fair enough, sir, so if Criminal Intelligence are so concerned about Darren, why aren't they doing the digging? Why pass it to us?'

'Port Haverton's CI are making enquiries on their own patch, over the whole of Greater Balderside in fact. It's our job to do likewise in our force area. In simple terms, they want us to find out if Darren is up to something on our patch and they want to know where he is. The two things might be linked.'

'I guessed there'd be trouble when we inherited those scumbags from Port Haverton. How long ago was it?'

'Nine or ten months ago, Paul, a couple of months before Christmas. They were kicked out of a council estate and dumped in one of our nicest areas. They were evicted because of incessant complaints over the years. It was one of those God-awful council estates in Greater Balderside – and they were one of the worst families living there.'

'Are the council allowed to do that? Dump their rubbish on our patch?'

'They are, but we've got to be careful what we say in public – political correctness and all that. Political correctness is a wonderful way of hiding the truth.'

'I remember when they came out here – we got a note from Greater Balderside CID complete with photos and a card saying "A Present from Balderside". Somebody's idea of a joke,' laughed Paul.

'There's no doubt they were glad to see them go. Everybody was glad to be rid of them. Council, probation service, neighbours, the lot. It was the neighbours from hell syndrome, loud music, fighting, verbal and physical abuse to objectors, never paying rent or keeping the house clean, and having a garden like a scrap yard. They were several families from hell, all rolled into one.'

'I can understand the authorities wanting rid of them, but it seems wrong that the decent folk of a peaceful moorland village like Dovedale should be landed with a bunch of unwanted nasties like that,' Paul said.

'There was no council house big enough to take them all, but apart from that there were protests whenever other tenants discovered who their new neighbours might be. The protests continued even if there was talk of the Mallorys being split up – nobody wanted any of them living nearby. Then a council official had a bright idea. He knew of a remote house on a hilltop in Dovedale. It was owned by a religious trust of some kind, happy-clappies of some sort, but it was empty and the owners wanted to put it to some worthy use. Being very trusting, and thinking there was good in all people, they agreed the Mallory Mob could use it. It was once a retreat house but fell into disuse and it's been empty for a few years because no one would live there. It's miles from anywhere, very remote, a mile or so along a disused ironstone mine railway track with only the most basic facilities; it's four former ironstone workers' houses knocked into one. Very desirable if it was closer to civilization.'

'And so they were dumped in the middle of nowhere? Like somebody getting rid of their unwanted rubbish by dumping it in a beauty spot?'

'Yes, but in many ways it's ideal, Paul. There are no neighbours for them to upset. I don't think they'll look after the house, though, they'll probably chop the doors up for firewood and keep coal in the bath but the odd thing was that no one complained when they moved in. I don't think anyone in the village realized who the new inhabitants were but they were far enough away for no one to be unduly bothered, over a mile as the crow flies.'

'Rather like sending all our unwanted rogues to Australia?'

'Similar logic, Paul, but it did solve a local problem – it got rid of the Mallorys.'

'It didn't get rid of them, sir, it just transferred the problem somewhere else, to our doorstep as it happens. What I can't understand is why those hardened townie villains agreed to the move. It's very strange they allowed the authorities to place them on a remote and windy Yorkshire moorland hilltop when they were used to a dole-funded life of crime on a less-than-pleasant inner-city type of council estate. You couldn't have more of a contrast.'

'It amazed everybody, but because they agreed, Port Haverton CID smelt a rat and told us. We've always been aware of their presence amongst us.'

'Even so, I haven't seen any reports of their criminal behaviour since they arrived. You're not telling me the country air and rustic lifestyle have changed their behaviour? Made honest citizens of them?'

'They have been uncharacteristically quiet, Paul, but it must be said most of their activities and crimes are in Greater Balderside, well beyond our boundaries. They haven't come to our notice as local suspects because they travel across the moors and into town to continue their villainy. The sons are very mobile, by the way, either by nicking cars or owning them, and seem to spend most of their time in their old haunts. Crime Intelligence have quite a detailed log of their cars, their journeys and their movements in and out of our patch.'

'All good background stuff. So is the official line that Darren's disappearance might be connected with whatever racket they're currently involved in? Some scam being master-minded from their new home? Could our hero be away on a business trip perhaps? On behalf of the family firm?'

'It could be anything, Paul. He could have vanished deliberately to throw the police off the scent of whatever the Mallorys are up to, a diversion perhaps, a ploy to take our minds off something more serious. The Mallorys know they're under regular surveillance – it's not twenty-four hours a day, but it's fairly constant.'

'For a simple Missing From Home enquiry, sir, this is beginning to sound very interesting!' smiled Larkin.

'You'd be wise to liaise with DI Kirkman if you intend making personal contact with the family. Apart from anything else, they're very anti-police.'

'Does this development mean Crime Intelligence have some undercover operation afoot?'

'If they have, it doesn't involve our force, Paul, otherwise you'd have known about it. I don't know what Greater Balderside Police are up to either, but whatever they're doing it's no concern of ours. Ours is a very simple task, one that a rookie cop could do. A Missing From Home enquiry, that's all.'

'Right, sir. I'll have words with Roger Kirkman to see if there's anything or anyone I should avoid,' Paul agreed.

'Now, what do we know about Darren's actual disappearance? When was he last seen, and where?'

'It's all in the file, but he was last noted nine days ago. Saturday the twentieth. He went to the Blue Raven, that's a night-club in Sidlesbrough, one of the boroughs in Greater Balderside. It's not a dive, in fact it's quite a decent place, not the sort of club his brothers or father would visit.'

'So Darren has ambitions above his real place in life?'

'He has. He dresses smartly, dark suits as a rule, he's got brains, charm and ambition. If he'd had a different upbringing, you could see him with a decent career, I'm sure. He's not into violence like his brothers.'

'Except for clouting a man with a brick!'

'We're sure that was a one-off incident. Anyway, that night – the twentieth – he met a girl in the Blue Raven. Julie Carver, she's a year younger than Darren and works in the offices of the Sidlesbrough Building Society.'

'Building society, eh? Is he after inside information? Another of his ploys?'

'It's always a possibility.'

'A decent girl, is she?'

'So it seems.'

'That's often a problem. Nice decent people don't always recognize villains for what they are. They trust everybody.'

'She's a receptionist, Paul, nothing more than that. We've run a check, we know she's not into drugs, crime or prostitution, but suspect she has no idea of his background. He's charmed her, we're sure of that! He spent the later evening with Julie – they didn't spend the night together, she's not into that kind of relationship.'

'She sounds very sensible!'

'Outside the club, Julie took a taxi home and Darren had a car – a Vauxhall Omega. That's his own vehicle, he bought it new, so he got the money from somewhere. It was parked in a side street and he drove off in it. Greater Balderside's man saw him leave about midnight.'

'To go home? To Dovedale?'

'So it was thought – it's about an hour's drive, much of it over open moorland once you leave suburbia. He didn't go to Julie's but he didn't get home either. He's not been seen since. He wasn't followed from the club, not by us or anyone else. There were limited police resources that night with no mobile back-up, the observer was on foot, so we don't really know where Darren went – except he took the road towards Dovedale.'

'And his car? Has it been located?'

'Vanished without trace as well, Paul.'

'Julie's been interviewed, has she?'

'Discreetly. All she could say was that when Darren left her that night, he told her he hoped to be in the club the following Saturday. If he was, he'd see her there, so he told her. He didn't make a firm commitment but seemed keen enough to meet her again. She's not heard from him since, but she didn't reveal her home address or phone number – she doesn't believe in giving away too much too early, something to do with the nature of her work.'

'She seems a very wise young woman!'

'I think she is, Paul. However, Darren didn't turn up at the Blue Raven the following Saturday, the Saturday just gone that was. The twenty-seventh. She did – with a girlfriend – and she confirms Darren wasn't there. He's made no attempt to contact her at work. She wasn't questioned too closely about all this and she didn't realize she was being quizzed by the police. She thought she was talking to a young woman who'd seen her with Darren, one girl quizzing another about boyfriends, that sort of thing. Greater Balderside have some very good operators.'

'Do you think Darren realized he might not get to the Blue Raven that Saturday?'

'It's possible, it might explain why he didn't make a firm commitment.'

'If his disappearance is unaccountable, perhaps he could have upset some local villains? Some of the Balderside hard men? How far is Sidlesbrough from Port Haverton, for example?'

'Three or four miles, all built-up and some of it industrialized. They're both boroughs within the Greater Balderside conurbation, with Sidlesbrough being more upmarket that Port Haverton. As the name suggests, Port Haverton is the dockland region.'

'So in a place that size, sir, there must be other criminal gangs, all competing with the Mallory Mob. Can we think he's been given "advice" to leave the town? Or worse?'

'There is another prominent gang, north of the River Balder. The Clarksons. We can't ignore the possibility there's been some kind of showdown but from what we've gleaned so far, we've learned absolutely nothing along those lines. I've had words with Sidlesbrough CID, Port Haverton CID and Greater Balderside Criminal Intelligence Unit and to their knowledge, there's been no recent feuds or battles between the gangs, certainly not involving Darren Mallory. He's not the sort to get into gangland fights and feuds, he prefers to operate alone, he keeps out of that kind of trouble. He leaves the rough stuff to his brothers. Even if they never kill, they can make a nasty mess of someone.'

'So how detailed a search has been made for him?'

'Because it was Dent's office who originally thought he might have gone missing, both ourselves and Greater Balderside Police made preliminary enquiries. Airports and seaports were checked, along with all his known haunts, his home, garages where he got his petrol, betting shops he used, his known contacts – but we got nothing. He's not drawn his dole and no cash has been taken out of his building society savings account. He's with the Halifax, not the one his girlfriend works for. Car parks both on Teesside and in our patch have been searched for his car, garages too, in case it's being left for repairs or offered for sale. Nothing. As I told you, his father says he's not worried – Greater Balderside Police have managed to get a slight response from Jack – but we haven't quizzed the brothers yet. There's no point at this stage, they'll say nothing. But as each day passes without any sign or word from Darren, there is increasing concern. Hence this file, Paul.'

'You say "we" from time to time, sir!'

'I do, because I include the police in general, ourselves and Greater Balderside Police, especially in Sidlesbrough and Port Haverton Divisions. They've all made initial enquiries on their own patches, as well as Criminal Intelligence Units from both forces. We're working together on this.'

'Is there any reason for thinking he might have been harmed?' asked Larkin. 'I still think it's most unusual for us to take this kind of interest in a villain who's done a runner. Normally, we're glad to be rid of them!'

'Darren doesn't go away much. As I said, he has been on holiday sometimes, but generally he's a home bird – rather surprising when you consider the sort of home he comes from. He spends most of his free time there, when he's not conning people out of their money or snatching cash from tills. To vanish like this is out of character. So yes, there is concern for his safety even if his family doesn't seem worried, and we can't lose sight of the fact that the family could be up to something. Either them or their villainous pals. Someone might have set up Darren deliberately to mislead us, to distract us – all of us, I mean – from something more important. Villains tend not to worry about police force boundaries. We do. So, taking all these considerations into account, can we afford to ignore his disappearance? That is the question.'

'If that's the case, we can't ignore it, but do you think the Mallorys have enough brains to think of setting up a diversion plot?'

'Darren has, the rest of the bunch have got animal cunning, Paul. So yes, it's a possibility, perhaps with Darren doing the thinking and planning. It's the sort of thing that might have been suggested by Darren – or someone else, of course.'

'All right, sir, you've convinced me. I'll get things moving.'

'Good. I'll let you get on with it. Put a good team on to it, a DS and a DC, choose someone with brains and intuition. Give them until Saturday to come up with something, dig as deep as you can during that time, then we'll have a rethink. The local police – uniform branch, I mean – have been informed and they will be making their own enquiries. I know we've more important things to worry us, but I promised we'd do our bit.'

'Fair enough, sir.'

'Right, it'll be interesting to see what our enquiries turn up,' smiled Pemberton. 'Make sure you're equipped with mobile phones and keep them switched on. Now, what else have we to entertain us this morning?'

'That series of raids on off-licences . . . we've a good description of a suspect vehicle . . .'

And so began Pemberton's week.

Chapter Two

'I've been allocated the Darren Mallory action,' Detective Constable Lorraine Cashmore told Pemberton over lunch that Monday lunchtime. 'With DS Williams.'

'I thought Paul might drop that one into your in-tray,' smiled Pemberton. 'Don't spend too much time on it. Mallory might have gone on holiday or taken a girl away or gone off to settle some crooked business deal. He might even have gone to live somewhere else; his mother did. Having said that, give it your best shot, Lorraine, ask around, dig deep in the time available. We want to show Greater Balderside we're as good if not better than them! It would be nice if we could produce some kind of positive answer. You'll liaise with Sidlesbrough and Port Haverton CID? We need to be aware of the latest information they've got on him.'

'Andy Williams has set up a meeting for this afternoon,' she told him. 'With Detective Sergeant Probert and DC Baxter. It's the earliest we could arrange.'

Pemberton and Lorraine met for lunch away from the office whenever possible. He was a firm believer that one way of countering stress was to have a short but complete break from workaday pressures during office hours. He did not want his break to be in the canteen or a place frequented by his fellow officers where everyone talked incessantly about work. He preferred somewhere discreet and comfortable where work could be relegated, however temporarily, to the back of his mind.

Rainesbury, where he was in charge of the Divisional Criminal Investigation Department, was a popular seaside resort on the spectacular Yorkshire coast. It had an excellent selection of hotels and restaurants along with some delightful small inns and restful tea shops or smart coffee bars. There was also a McDonald's, a pizza palace and a few garish eating establishments designed to woo tourists. There were times, though, when even a brash and noisy place full of cheap and cheerful holidaymakers could provide comfort to a busy detective – you could lose yourself in the crowd and listen to their happy, inconsequential and at times hilarious chatter rather than the waffle of officialdom. As both Pemberton and Lorraine worked in civilian clothes, they could mingle with the visitors and appear just like any other office workers having a lunch break – except that Pemberton's smart appearance inevitably set him apart. Even in the height of summer he looked cool, immaculate and confident. But it was a rule that he and Lorraine did not talk about work at home or during these interludes, although on some occasions that rule had to be broken. Like today.

'We shouldn't be talking shop, Lorraine, not during lunch,' he reminded her.

'I'm starting my enquiries straight after lunch,' was her response. 'I just wanted to tell you I might be a little later home tonight.'

'Fair enough. If nothing urgent crops up, I'll get supper organized. Paul Larkin's on call this week so it looks as if I might be blessed with a few days of normal office hours with a tolerable finishing time. So what do you fancy tonight?'

'Apart from you, you mean?' Her eyes twinkled.

'Apart from me and a bottle of red wine.'

'Something beefy,' she suggested. 'With a hint of strongly scented herbs, all nice and hot, with an air of mystery, a surprise . . .'

'I'll do what I can,' he laughed. 'Any idea what time you'll be home?'

'The meeting's been fixed for four o'clock,' she told him. 'Midway between Greater Balderside and Rainesbury.

Howe Rigg. It's a vantage point and picnic area on the moors, close to the county boundary.'

'I know it. You'll not be overheard and overlooked up there!' The venue was surrounded by open heather, boundless space and endless views. 'So I'll expect you when you arrive, as they say. Eat at eight, shall we?'

'We'll make a few enquiries after our meeting, but I should be home well before eight,' she smiled. 'But thanks, it'll be nice to eat in the comfort of our own home.'

After lunch, Lorraine, so tall, slender, dark-haired and gracefully beautiful, returned to her duties while Mark Pemberton retreated to his office. In spite of a temporary lull in serious criminal activities, there was enough accumulated office work to keep him busy for a day or two. Indeed, an occasional full day in the office was vital if he was to keep abreast of the ceaseless routine paperwork which accumulated in his in-tray, not to mention the more urgent stuff like quarterly crime returns, reports for police authority meetings, requests from the Home Office for statistical data, queries and pressure for results from the Chief Constable and a host of other immediate administrative matters. The advent of computers had generated a hope that paperwork would be greatly reduced but that had not happened. Indeed, computer-generated paperwork had multiplied to produce even greater mountains of files and more bins full of waste paper. The police service seemed to be sinking in a sea of unwanted and unnecessary paperwork. New Labour wasn't helping either – it was creating a bureaucratic nightmare, a world of yet more forms and returns to complete for every tiny and trivial matter.

In addition to his ongoing enquiries, there was the Muriel Brown investigation. It was the only unsolved murder on the force records, a brutal murder and rape committed more than sixteen years ago and undetected in spite of repeated and renewed attention to the case. As with all such investigations, the file was never closed but now, with DNA proving so useful in old, unsolved cases of rape and murder, there was every chance the crime might be detected – all that was needed was a suspect with whom to compare the DNA sample retrieved from the semen found on Muriel's underclothes. If only DNA had been available at the time! He scribbled a reminder in his diary to allocate a new team to Muriel Brown once the existing one had finished its enquiries into taxi owners known to have been operating at the time of her death. Much as he wished to solve that crime, however, he didn't want the press complaining he was allocating precious resources to a near-forgotten crime when there were more recent ones demanding attention. For all that, however, he fully intended finding Muriel's killer before he retired.

At the moment, though, his detectives were busy with a spate of raids on off-licences and building societies, never-ending car crimes including two cases of violent car-jacking, professional shoplifting cases and a man who was stalking women in the town's parks but who, to date, had not assaulted or even approached any of them. The fellow seemed able to dodge the surveillance teams. In some cases, the good old-fashioned system of routine enquiries supplemented by careful observations was being utilized; in others, crime intelligence gathering was thought a better approach. Intelligence-led investigations were considered the way forward because there was much merit in assembling irrefutable evidence of guilt, even by covert means, prior to any arrest or court appearance. Positive evidence supporting several charges meant a custodial sentence for some perpetrators. Although Pemberton was not directly involved in these cases, his officers were kept fully occupied – it was all a matter of keeping the detection rate high by maintaining a continuing sense of purpose among his busy and hard-worked staff.

Most would be too engrossed in their work to concern themselves with a criminal who had done nothing more than leave home without explanation. As his thoughts turned to Darren Mallory, he grew keen to hear Lorraine's account when she returned from her meeting with detectives from Greater Balderside CID.

Pemberton's afternoon passed without incident and his efforts to reduce the pile of paper in his in-tray were successful. At five thirty, after he had dictated the final letter to his secretary, he decided to go home. For him, this was an earlier-than-normal finish, one which could be celebrated with a malt whisky before preparing a meal for himself and Lorraine. In relaxing with good food and drink, Pemberton had to be aware of the likelihood of a call-out, consequently most evening meals had to be enjoyed with no alcohol intake. Tonight, though – and all this week – he was not on call. It was Detective Inspector Larkin's turn! That meant he could relax – and hopefully Lorraine would be off duty too. Cosy togetherness was the order for this evening!

And so, when he returned home, he lit the fire and changed out of his dark suit. His instinctive dress sense and natural style had won him the accolade of smartest man in the entire police service – it was said he could walk across a wet ploughed field without staining his shoes or trouser bottoms. He showered and put on a light T-shirt, slacks and casual shoes, then poured himself a generous helping of The Macallan before settling down to study a recipe book. For a starter, he decided upon button mushrooms marinated in herbs and white wine followed by beef cooked in red wine and accompanied by new potatoes and crisp green beans. The sweet would be a fresh fruit salad followed by cheese and biscuits – all helped down with a bottle of Burgundy.

It was quarter-past six when Lorraine returned. While she was showering and changing into something relaxing, he concluded the preparations, laid the table, opened the wine and selected some easy listening classical music. Then he settled before the fire as the fine-smelling casserole simmered in the oven. After her shower, Lorraine kissed him and settled down on the fireside rug with a glass of sherry, her slim legs encased in soft smooth leggings and a light T-shirt highlighting the shape of her neat breasts and slim stomach. She rested her back against the chair in which he was sitting and he touched her hair. Even from where he was sitting, he realized it was scented and it still felt rather damp after her shower.

'It's nice to be home,' she murmured. 'You're not on call, Mark, are you?'

'Not tonight.'

'Good,' was all she said.

There were long moments of silence as the fire flickered over the logs and the music filled the room and then, in one of those quiet periods he couldn't restrain himself and asked, 'How did it go, then? The meeting?'

'That's work, Mark. We're not talking about work tonight.'

'I just wondered . . .'

'Then keep wondering. I'm not going to spoil this by talking shop!'

'Oh.'

Another long silence. 'How are you feeling now?' he asked. 'In general I mean.'

'I'm fine.'

'No more lumps?'

'Do you want to have a look?'

'Love to,' he murmured. 'But seriously, you've no more lumps in your breasts?'

'No,' she said firmly. 'I got the all-clear as you know, and for which I am eternally grateful, but as the doctor advised, I've kept a careful check ever since. Nothing, Mark. I'm clear, I'm confident about that. I'm not a cancer sufferer any more, and I believe what the experts tell me.'

'Good,' he said, not reminding her that it could take five full years to be completely sure.

He lapsed into another silence, wondering whether the invitation to examine her had been genuine or whether he should go and check the progress of the meal. She made no further comment and sat gazing into the flames as the shadows flickered across her silken skin. She was a picture of relaxed loveliness and he had no desire to interrupt those precious moments.

'If you're getting up,' she said, 'I wouldn't say no to another sherry.'

'I'll check progress in the kitchen.' His moment of anticipated passion had evaporated. 'I'll fill your glass.'

The meal was delicious. They savoured every mouthful, and when it was over, they adjourned to the fireside where they settled on the huge settee wrapped in each other's arms.

'I do love you,' he whispered as her scented hair brushed his face.

'Me too . . .' She turned in his arms and kissed him. 'This is nice, Mark, so very nice . . .'

'I want it to last for ever,' he said.

'You'd get bored!'

'Not with you,' he promised and so they stayed on the settee as the firelight withered and died and the heat of the flames dwindled, then they went to bed.

There was a massive temptation to remain in bed the following morning but both were on duty at nine and so each had to clamber from the sheets, wash, dress, have breakfast and then drive to work in separate cars – in case either was called out to a crime. At work, they were segregated – she was a detective constable which meant she could not eat in the officers' mess with Detective Superintendent Pemberton; after all, he was the boss. At home, though, they were equals even though there had been no formal wedding ceremony.

Because they travelled separately to Rainesbury Divisional Police Headquarters, Pemberton could not quiz Lorraine about yesterday's meeting. She had steadfastly refused to talk about work during that lovely evening and had continued her refusal over breakfast. As the first hour in his office would be frantic while his admin staff demanded his immediate and complete attention, he realized it would be some time before he could talk to Lorraine about her meeting with Greater Balderside. The moment he sat in his chair, therefore, he pressed the intercom button and said, 'Pemberton here, Paul. Ask Lorraine to come and see me, ten o'clock. Over coffee. To discuss

Darren Mallory. You'd better come too, and Detective Sergeant Williams.'

That achieved, he settled down to cope with the morning's events. Promptly at ten, there was a light knock on his door. Lorraine entered to his call of 'Come in.' Paul Larkin and DS Williams followed and they settled on chairs before his desk as coffee arrived courtesy of his secretary.

'So, Andy.' He smiled at Williams. His vivid recollection of last night's happiness made him want to concentrate upon Lorraine, but he steeled himself to focus upon his work. 'Darren Mallory. Tell me what you learned yesterday.'

Detective Sergeant Andrew 'Andy' Williams, in his early thirties, looked like a well-heeled country gentleman in his cavalry twill trousers, tweed hacking jacket, brown brogues and red waistcoat. Well over six feet tall with a handsome square face, a mop of curly light brown hair and ready smile with sparkling white teeth, he wouldn't have been out of place driving a vintage E-type Jaguar, attending race meetings or taking part in any major rural event. He had the right accent too – he looked as if he would be totally at ease in a large country house or riding to hounds. That was by no means impossible. Titled gentlemen were joining the service – in recent months, there'd been lords in both the London Metropolitan Police and West Yorkshire. Whatever his background, he did not boast about it or even talk about it but he was a very good detective. That was why he was in Pemberton's department.

Williams said they'd had a useful meeting with DS Probert and DC Baxter of Greater Balderside Crime Intelligence Unit, both stationed at Sidlesbrough. They had provided a lot of background information after confirming what was already known about the Mallory family. They added that the father, Jack, now tended to remain in the background, albeit still a powerful presence in the Mallory Mob. In his early fifties, Jack Mallory was not as criminally active as he had been in his thirties and forties and now spent most, if not all, of his time at his new home.

One surprising fact was that Jack Mallory did not drive. He'd always considered car ownership to be elitist and believed public transport should satisfy everyone's travelling needs. As there was no regular bus service in Dovedale, however, he'd found himself somewhat isolated. Another remarkable happening since moving to Dovedale was that he had taken up woodwork as a hobby and had surprised everyone with his skills. He'd furnished the entire kitchen with handmade pine units even though he'd never done a stroke in his council house; his long-suffering wife had never experienced that kind of useful home-making talent.

In his past, though, he had accumulated a long list of convictions, often associated with violence – robbery with violence, assault occasioning actual bodily harm, and grievous bodily harm were listed alongside others like housebreaking, burglary, receiving stolen goods and demanding with menaces. From what the police knew about Jack in more recent times, he'd resorted to the occasional bout of shoplifting, usually groceries and food, and in some ways he was turning prematurely into a sad old man who was turning to 'soft' crime. His current lifestyle meant he'd been removed from all such temptations; opportunities to commit crime were almost nil in Dovedale. It was very doubtful whether he was currently committing crime; certainly, he was not suspected of any.

By contrast, all five sons were criminally active in Greater Balderside, even if it was difficult obtaining sufficient evidence to justify a prosecution. At one stage, they had run a very successful protection racket involving ladies' hairdressers, demanding money from the owners to 'protect' the premises against raids on their tills. They'd had a similar scam in bingo halls – the Mallory insurance scheme, it was called. Both had come to an end after the police installed surveillance cameras. Another enterprise was 'steaming' – four of the five hurtled the length of commuter or tourist-filled railway carriages armed with knives and terrifying the passengers into handing over purses, wallets and other valuables. Darren had not taken part in that. The twins, Neil and Max, had had a long run of successful raids on pensioners' bungalows in Sidlesbrough, one of the smarter areas of town. They'd operated separately while pretending to be water pressure inspectors to gain access to the pensioners' homes and then they'd stolen cash, often the life savings of their victims. As they dealt in cash, and as the victims had poor recollections of the precise details, proof of guilt had been difficult to obtain, more so because the twins looked very much alike and used their similarity to create alibis – as they had with lots of other criminal stunts. Several prosecutions had failed because one twin had claimed he'd been mistaken for the other. They were into car crime, stealing vehicles to order for a local exporter of stolen cars, and had also taken to stealing statues and large garden ornaments.

The youngest Mallory, twenty-year-old Garry, was a skilful burglar, specializing in detached houses in suburbia, especially those not overlooked from the rear, but taking only cash or other portable objects which could not be readily identified. He made a point of rapidly disposing of his ill-gotten goods, often before the owners had even discovered their loss.

'They're into much more, they can't walk into a shop, garage or house without removing something illegally,' Williams added. 'Even if they buy an item, they will steal another. Security cameras once caught Damon stealing a *Daily Mirror* from a display just after he'd bought a copy of the *Sun*. That's how they are all the time – they just can't help it, it's their way of life. They live off crime, they're cunning and they're ruthless, even if they can switch on the charm. Thanks to modern surveillance techniques, their activities have been curtailed, but it doesn't stop them. The local police have managed a few prosecutions, often for very minor stuff; on some recent occasions, goods stolen by the Mallorys were found and confiscated even if it was never proved they had committed the thefts. They blamed rewards which were published in newspapers, the money persuading people to volunteer information anonymously. It seems the police are now receiving more information from this source than from their regular informants.'

'So out of all this, Sergeant, it seems Darren isn't working hand-in-hand with the rest of the Mob?' put in Pemberton. 'He's a bit of a lone warrior.'

'That's the impression we've gained sir,' agreed Williams. 'Whereas the other brothers often work in teams, either together or in twos and threes, Darren is a loner. That's become more evident in recent months, although he has been known to give his siblings a helping hand – acting as driver, being a lookout and so on.'

'So what's the latest intelligence?'

'Darren has bought a new car, the Vauxhall Omega, a two litre GLS automatic, silver-grey coloured. £14,000 or thereabouts. He paid cash. When Sidlesbrough Divisional CID checked at the garage where he bought it, they learned he didn't use a cheque or bother with any kind of purchase scheme. Dressed in a smart business suit, he walked in with a briefcase and produced the payment, in cash.'

'Has he been quizzed about his sudden wealth?' Pemberton asked.

'No. Because Greater Balderside Crime Intelligence Unit is keeping tabs on the whole family, with Probert and Baxter targeting Darren as their special task, it was thought best not to draw attention to their increasing interest in Darren. They hoped he might lead them to his honey-pot of gold. It was that act, the production of all that cash, which prompted CI to put him under tighter surveillance. There were no reported crimes which involved such an amount, neither was there a recent series which might have generated it.'

'It's a lot of cash for a thief to gain from a single raid,' Pemberton agreed. 'Especially one we don't know about.'

'There's also the fact he doesn't have a regular job. His bits of casual work would never earn him that much.'

'He was already on probation, was he? When he bought the car?'

'Yes, for that brick attack. He put the car on the road about ten days later, on the first of this month. Four weeks ago, that's all.'

'He could have won the money,' smiled Pemberton. 'Isn't that what they all say? A lottery or pools win, or a good day on the horses.'

'If he'd been quizzed, he might have put up that explanation. CI have checked with all the football pools firms, the lottery and bookies. No one with that name has had a big win in the past five years, although in many cases the real name of the punter is unknown, especially with bookies.'

'All right. So it appears we have a very successful young criminal – and one who's unusual because he's got brains. He's found a way of earning big money without anyone complaining about losing it, so it seems. If there's no complaints of such amounts being stolen or obtained by deception, where is he getting it from?'

'Blackmail, sir?' smiled Williams. 'Computer crime?'

'I'd wouldn't have thought computer crime would generate large amounts of ready cash, and he could be traced doing that, surely? But go on,' invited Pemberton.

'When the family was evicted to Dovedale, Greater Balderside Crime Intelligence Unit and our own agreed to keep tabs on them. Clearly, sir, with manpower shortages and budget restrictions, surveillance had to be limited and so Sidlesbrough's own CI unit decided to target Darren. That was chiefly because of his sudden wealth, and also because he was often seen on their patch.'

'Fair enough, I'd have done the same.'

'He's been under fairly close surveillance for the last nine or ten months but he's never led anyone to his fountain of cash. From observations we know he lives mainly at home – unlike his brothers – and that he drives into Greater Balderside most days in his new car. It takes about forty minutes to reach the outskirts and another twenty to gain the town centre, an hour or so each time give or take a few minutes for traffic problems. According to Probert, he's always smartly dressed, sometimes in a dark business suit, sometimes fairly casual in a blazer and slacks or even just a light shirt on a very hot day. He carries a black briefcase and sometimes a hold-all, and in his new car he looks like a business rep or even a young professional. There are photos of him in some situations – not easily obtained, I might add, but far better than a police mugshot, we've got them in the file.'

'So when he gets into Greater Balderside where's he go, Andy? What does he do?'

'That's the problem, sir. No one knows – apart from the fact he's been noticed regularly in both Sidlesbrough and Port Haverton. He seems to favour those parts of Greater Balderside rather than any other.'

'So surveillance teams must have followed him?'

'They've tried, but he soon loses them, sir. He's lost every tail that's been put on to him. He knows both Probert and Baxter and can spot them a mile off, wherever they're concealed. He seems able to smell a copper at a thousand paces, man or woman, old or young, in disguise or not. On one occasion, Sidlesbrough put a couple of detectives imported from Cleveland Police into a plumbers' van complete with overalls and bags of tools, but he spotted them and gave them the slip.'

'It's obvious he *is* up to no good, otherwise why make the effort of losing a tail? Unless he does it for a bit of fun – or unless he's leading us away from something his brothers are doing?'

'That thought hadn't escaped Sidlesbrough Police, sir. They are keeping tabs on all the brothers but they can't maintain it for twenty-four hours a day every day. There just isn't the personnel available, especially with five of them all doing different things. Everyone's confident Darren is operating on his own in some enterprise not even his family know about.'

'So, logically, if Darren has gone away and if he's found a lucrative new way of earning money, he might be extending his business empire beyond the boundaries of Greater Balderside?' Pemberton suggested.

'We thought that would explain his father's apparent lack of concern, sir,' chipped in Lorraine, using Pemberton's official designation as they were in company and on duty. 'Perhaps Jack Mallory knows what Darren's really up to?'

'That makes sense, but I can understand him not wanting anyone else muscling in on his lucrative new activities, not even his own flesh and blood.'

'There is something else to consider, sir,' added Williams. 'Darren's not the only person to have vanished from Sidlesbrough in recent times.'

'Really? Who else has done a runner?'

'A man called Joseph Campion, a high profile professional villain from that part of the world. He's heavily involved in the stolen car market, transporting high value vehicles to the Continent and the Middle East after they've been stolen to order. There was also a possibility he's operating a drug smuggling ring, using legitimate car trading as his cover. He's under regular surveillance by both Customs and police, and he has some business links with the Mallory brothers – they steal cars to order for him. He vanished about six months ago, Saturday 19th January to be precise. He just went out of the house, telling his wife he was popping down to the pub for a couple of pints, but he never came back. He never got to the pub either. The police have checked hospitals and accident records, but there's no record of him being a casualty. We must consider whether he could have double-crossed one of the local gangs – even the Mallorys – or informed on them, or something, and was bumped off for his trouble. The Mallorys don't do murder, though. Campion hasn't been found but there's also a strong chance he might have gone overseas on a false passport. He's done that before, quite often it seems, and according to Probert, the National Crime Squad favours that explanation. Bearing in mind his past tendency, they think it's more likely than him being murdered but they've an open mind.'

'Do they want us to ask about him as well?' asked Pemberton.

'No, Campion's their problem and he has no known links with anyone or anything within our force area, apart from sometimes working with one or other of the Mallorys. They don't see a connection between him and Darren in the case we're looking into.'

'Force and county boundaries can be a real pain when investigating crimes, but this is getting curiouser and curiouser,' said Pemberton. 'I guess a man like Campion would throw up a smokescreen if he was doing something secretive, so if it was down to me, I'd treat his absence with great caution, Andy. Two local villains vanished without explanation, eh? That's hardly a coincidence but Darren's our immediate concern. So, Andy, I'd like to know how he shakes off his tails, how does he manage to lose such experienced shadows as Greater Balderside's finest?'

'After he's driven into Sidlesbrough, or sometimes Port Haverton, the tail generally picks him up on the outskirts, and follows. He seems to realize he's being tailed, even if traffic is heavy, and he always leads the tail into a large busy car park. Big supermarket parks are one of his choices, and others where there are huge retail outlets all sharing the same free parking space. He parks his car then goes into one or more of the stores, deliberately trying to lose us – and he succeeds. He'll go out of another entrance, disappear into the staff quarters, put on a white coat or something similar and mingle with delivery men . . . you name it, he's done it. He carries a hold-all, we think it might contain a disguise of some sort, different coloured coat or sweater, white coat, brown smock, cap or hat, wig even, or umbrella, anything to make him look like a customer or member of staff employed by some big outfit. He always chooses a busy time and he can always lose the tails among the crowds, and when he comes out, we think he either hails a waiting taxi, gets on a bus or even has another car parked somewhere. In town, he does the same – picks a busy car park adjoining somewhere like Marks and Spencer or British Home Stores, walks in and straight out of another door into a different street. Most of the tails have only been a crew of two – they can't be everywhere, and he knows how to dodge them. You can't beat a supermarket aisle full of chattering shoppers and trolleys for causing a blockage.'

'If he can dodge the police, he can dodge anyone else who might be keeping tabs on him. So having dodged his shadows, what's he do then?'

'That's what we don't know, sir. That's when he earns his money. He's even been spotted hanging around outside various police stations, watching faces going in and out, learning to identify some of our teams. We think he's a cheeky sod, too. He'll even go into the bigger police stations around Greater Balderside to look at our noticeboards! They're there for the public, of course, and now most of the counter staff know him. If they ask if they can help, he'll come up with some crack that he's thinking of joining the force or the specials, or he might laugh and say he's checking to see whether or not he's on a "wanted" poster.'

'He's having fun at our expense, Andy. So what are your plans?'

'Various members of Sidlesbrough Police have been to all his known haunts in and around Greater Balderside, checking everywhere over the last few days – including the Blue Raven and his girlfriend – and always coming to a dead end. Now we know the full background, we can check things on our patch.'

'Dovedale, you mean?'

'Yes, dig deep around his home, but expand our enquiries further if necessary.'

'That means visiting his house? How does Crime Intelligence feel about that?'

'I've had words, sir, they don't mind, not on this occasion,' said Andy. 'In fact, they want us to do it, to make it look like an ordinary enquiry. We do have a positive reason, remember, Darren's been reported missing by his probation officer. That's the only official reason we've got. His home's our logical starting point, I'd like to see his room, to see if his belongings are there, or to see if he's been in touch with his family since he vanished. That's perfectly normal in this kind of enquiry.'

'This isn't a normal family, Andy, and it's not an ordinary enquiry. From what I hear, though, his old man will never let you in and won't even talk to you; apart from that, Darren might have left a false trail anyway. If his toothbrush and razor are still at home, it will mean nothing, he'll have got himself new ones.'

'Point taken, sir, but I think we must go and see old man Mallory. If we don't get anything out of him, word of our interest in Darren will spread among the villains.'

'OK, we want that to happen, so go ahead. You've got my blessing and I wish you all the best with him!' grinned Pemberton. 'But I bet you never get inside his house!'

'How much?' snapped Lorraine, mischievously.

'A fiver!'

'You're on, sir!'

Chapter Three

It was noon when Lorraine and Andy Williams arrived in Dovedale and they had no difficulty finding the Mallory household. It was called Hill Top House for no other reason than it occupied a stunning situation on the skyline to the east of the summit of Dovedale Hill. This boasted a notorious winding gradient of one in three for most of its climb, and the twisting hillside road was almost a mile in length. It was renowned because it was one of fourteen similar hills in the depths of the North York Moors, each with a similar gradient.

Some said the hill was steeper than the more famous Chimney Bank at nearby Rosedale while many experts claimed the gradient of Dovedale Hill was even more acute than its official sign suggested. Cyclists, including those competing in the Tour of Britain race, were among them. From time to time, the Tour had passed this way, usually taking in Chimney Bank too, but to ride a cycle up either of these hills was no mean achievement, even using modern multi-geared lightweight machines. To do so at racing speed must be sheer torture.

On the treeless summit there was a large flat area which served as a car park for tourists, along with a picnic area and viewing point, while the route of a long-gone iron-stone mine railway crossed the moor near the hilltop. In the form of a level cutting through the heathery, bleak and rock-strewn landscape, it came from the west, passed the northern tip of the car park, and continued across the wilderness towards Rosedale Chimney Bank Top in the east. In its heyday, it had carried train-loads of ore to the blast furnaces of Teesside.

The rails and sleepers of the former line had been removed many years ago and it now formed a cinder track popular with hikers, mountain bike enthusiasts and even four-wheel drive off-road motor vehicles. One could trek along this route for miles, following its former route into industrial Teesside and Greater Balderside along embankments, through cuttings and across immense heathery wastes rich with bogs, bracken and grazing sheep. The route was clearly visible from any elevated position even if it was now used almost entirely for leisure purposes.

Hill Top House lay almost a mile from the car park along that track. Lorraine suggested Andy drove as far as he could; she had occasionally walked this route with Pemberton and knew the cinder base was sound enough to bear the weight of their car. Having a car conveniently to hand was a wise idea when confronting people like the Mallory Mob, she reckoned, and so Andy took the unmarked police vehicle off the road and on to the surprisingly smooth path of old black cinders. Ahead, to the right of the track, stood the impressive dark grey granite-built bulk of Hill Top House. Two storeys high, it was solid and formidable with blue slate tiles and remarkably small windows along the front and rear. Small windows retained the interior heat. Two doors emerged from the rear on to the land adjoining the cinder track – when the track had been operative, those doors would have been some distance from the rails. Judging by the good state of the sheep-shorn grass in front of those doors, they were no longer used. The house faced south and there must be stunning views from all rooms, not that views were important to those who had built the house – or houses, as it had once been. Shelter from the elements was their prime consideration and the entire construction, including the size and position of doors and windows, was more for protection against the weather than for comfort and panoramic aspects. There were chimneys galore, a reminder that fireplaces had existed in all rooms, and there were lots of stone outbuildings, also with blue tiles. The general appearance was that of a stout fortress built in the dark grey, almost black granite of these moors. It was not a welcoming house, Lorraine felt; forbidding was the adjective in mind as their little car made its approach.

'What do we know about the house?' asked Lorraine as they approached. 'Probert gave you a plan, didn't he?'

Long before reaching the house, Williams eased the car to a halt and produced the plans from his briefcase which was on the rear seat.

'Courtesy of the county planning department, Probert acquired these the moment he knew the Mallorys were being installed here,' he said. 'Every room is shown, very handy if you've got to search the place or install listening devices. The plan is up to date, it was redrawn after the building had been converted from four little cottages to one large house, and it was amended again when the "change of use" from a domestic home to a communal retreat house came along. During that period, the parking area and sanitation had to be improved and it had to be fitted with fire escapes and so on.'

'Is it bugged now?' she asked.

'Nobody has said so, but it wouldn't surprise me if it was. There's plenty of detectives trying to keep tabs on this lot, even from a distance, and there was ample time to plant devices before the Mallorys actually moved in. In its early days, it was owned by the ironstone mining company and housed a few workers, then long after the boom ended those four little cottages were knocked into one big house, but without water, electricity or sanitation. Then, just after the war, an outfit called the Eremitical Word and Prayer Society bought it at a give-away price and converted it into a retreat house, with electricity, running water and septic tank sewage. It was just the sort of place to which the faithful could come for a spiritual uplift in conditions befitting a hermitage! It continued like that until the late 1970s. Then it fell into disuse – no one wanted to live in such a godforsaken place. It needed further modernization and a large amount of cash spending on it.

36

The religious group, which had by then dwindled to a handful of doubting followers, couldn't sell it or even rent it. No one was interested, so they kept it, they had no choice.'

'On my walking trips in this area, I've seen people coming and going from it,' Lorraine said. 'Earnest folks with rucksacks and sad expressions.'

'That's very likely. Before it was made fit to live in, I think some of their group continued to use it as a rough camping place. It was little more than a shelter from the elements – and then some wizard hit on the bright idea of installing the Mallorys. The council pays the society a rental, and the Mallorys are supposed to repay the council, but at a lesser rate than for their town house.'

'And they're all here? The entire Mob! That's amazing!' she smiled.

'No one knows why they agreed to this but Jack was keen and he's still the boss. So come along, let's meet the fearsome Jack Mallory. From what I hear, he played to the crowd in his former neighbourhood. After all, he had a certain hard-man image and tough reputation to maintain, but out here, he's got no neighbours to impress. I've never met him, but he can't be as bad as people say, can he?'

Folding his map, Andy Williams drove the car until he found a convenient place to pull off the track, used the radio to book off the air at Hill Top House – a form of security for himself and Lorraine if things went wrong (the office would know where they were) – and left the vehicle. A high wooden gate led through a lofty wall at the rear and he pushed it open, revealing a large open space littered with old vehicles and a range of junk, including settees, armchairs, old kitchen units, television sets, car parts and much else besides. To the left was a large stone shed with a grimy window and a closed door, behind which a light glowed and from which came the sounds of someone at work, drilling wood by the sound of it. The house was to their right, and the side door was closed. There was no sign of anyone in the house – they could see into the kitchen and a rear room.

Andy indicated the shed. He led the way, reached the door but did not knock – a well-tested police ploy which did help establish some kind of dominance. He simply pulled it open. Inside the light came from a single bulb hanging shadeless from the ceiling, and a large untidy man with a shock of unruly black hair was working with wood on a bench, engrossed in his task. He was using an electric drill to bore holes in a length of timber and due to the noise, he hadn't heard their arrival.

'Hello,' shouted Andy, hoping his voice would penetrate the whirring sound.

The man turned to face him; immediately, his momentary surprise changed to a look of hatred and signs of a powerful black mood began to register on the big man's dark and heavy features. Then, with studied ease, he switched off his drill, laid it on the bench, took a step in their direction, pointed to the door and said, 'Get the hell out of here, both of you.'

Andy stood his ground. Lorraine dithered.

'Is your Darren in?' was Andy's opening gambit.

'I said get the hell out of here.' The man came further forward, full of menace, and Lorraine noticed that his fists were clenched. Still Andy did not move. The man halted and so Lorraine remained where she was, sheltered by Andy.

'And I asked if Darren was here,' repeated Andy in a very soft but firm voice.

'No, and if he was he wouldn't speak to you.'

'Where is he?' persisted Andy.

'You're the filth. I can smell the filth on you. I don't talk to the filth. You should know that.'

'Darren's missing, his probation officer told us.'

'So what? He's a grown man, he can go where the hell he likes.'

'You're not worried then? About him being missing?'

'Didn't you hear me? I said I don't talk to the filth and he can go where he wants, when he wants and how he wants. What he does is nowt to do with me and nowt to do with you. Now clear off,' and the big man advanced on

Andy. 'Leave us alone, leave Darren alone. Out. Now! Before I chuck you out. This is private property. You're trespassing.'

And still Andy did not move. Lorraine was growing increasingly nervous for the big angry man looked extremely threatening with his fists opening and closing as he struggled to find a means of dealing with this unflappable and dapper detective. She had no idea what Andy Williams would do if Mallory resorted to violence but Andy seemed to be coping very well. He simply stood his ground and never raised his voice, neither did he display any fear or apprehension. Lorraine watched with surprise and admiration; Andy was showing real character here, courage even, and Jack Mallory's volcanic anger was evaporating with every passing moment. He stood rock-still, staring in disbelief at the man before him.

'Can I see his room?' Andy asked calmly after the passage of what seemed an eternity.

Mallory came alive again. 'You must be joking . . . are you dim or something? I said get out, I said I'm not talking and I've said Darren's affairs are nowt to do with you. Now, out. Or I'll chuck you out, filth or not, woman or not, warrant or not.'

'It's more than ten days since Darren was seen.' Andy Williams continued his stance in the doorway to the shed.

'So he's gone on holiday, he's gone away to work, he's got a business meeting somewhere. How the hell should I know? Why do men go away? Mebbe he's found a woman. He is grown up, you know. Some blokes are away all the time.' The man halted only inches before Andy. 'He never tells me what he's doing with himself and I never ask. It's his life.'

'We're worried that he might have come to some harm.' Lorraine decided to play her part, the gentle part.

'Harm? What sort of harm?' The big man frowned at them. 'Who says he might have come to some harm? What the hell are you talking about?'

'He's not kept in touch with his probation officer, he's

not been seen in his usual haunts in Sidlesbrough or Port Haverton, he's not here, you've not seen him, we've not seen him for ten days . . . We're not after him to arrest him, we're just concerned that he might have come to some harm, Mr Mallory,' smiled Lorraine, making full use of her charms.

'So what brought this on?' Mallory demanded. 'Why this sudden show of concern by the filth? For a son of mine.'

'Greater Balderside Police are worried as well, we've had words with them.'

'They've been here, snooping. Why is everybody worried about our Darren all of a sudden? I don't talk to the filth, like I said. And I don't believe all this crap about him being harmed. I can't believe the filth would ever show concern about my lads. Not that sort of concern, so pull the other one, missy. I wasn't born yesterday, you know.'

'Can you really ignore his absence?' she asked. 'I mean, if he really is missing, you'd want him found, wouldn't you? You're a family man, Mr Mallory.'

'That other lot said they was looking for him, they didn't say he might be harmed.'

'I know,' said Lorraine with sympathy. 'But if he had been, I'm sure you'd want him found. Which is why we're here, we want to trace him and we don't give up easily.'

There was an uneasy silence for a few moments, then Mallory, with his voice softened, asked, 'So what sort of harm do you think it is, then?'

'We don't know,' Lorraine admitted. 'We thought you might have a better idea than us. You know who he knocks about with, what he gets up to, who might have it in for him.'

'I don't know nothing about him these days, what he's doing, who he's knocking about with, what he's getting up to. He just comes here to sleep and eat sometimes, that's all. Late to bed, up early and away. He never talks about his work, not to me, not to the lads even, but I think he's doing well, he's got a new car, ready money and he's a snappy dresser. Works a lot on his own now, but you'll know that.'

40

'Has he taken his toothbrush and razor and things?' asked Williams. 'Clean clothes, the sort of thing he would take if he was going away for a while? That's why I wanted a look in his room.'

Mallory looked at Williams and said, 'You're a persistent bugger, aren't you? I could have felled you just now . . .'

'I'd have floored you first,' smiled Andy, swiftly adopting a karate pose. 'Or broken your arm. Or both of them.'

'Would you?' frowned Mallory.

'Like to try me?' challenged Williams, momentarily readopting the pose.

'No need, is there?' grinned Mallory, suddenly relaxed. 'So, his things. Did he take anything when he left?'

Mallory shook his head. 'No, I checked after your lot came before. His room's just as he left it, razor and things there. Clothes. He's taken nothing.'

'So it looks as though he hasn't gone on holiday or away on a business trip?' Lorraine said.

'I haven't a clue, honest,' sighed Jack.

'Has he contacted you since a week last Saturday?' was Andy's next question. 'He was seen in the Blue Raven, with a very nice girl, he got into his car, that new Vauxhall, and set off to come home, we think. No one's seen him since.'

'So your lot were keeping tabs on him?'

'They were,' admitted Andy, knowing better than to lie to this man. 'He's earning good money somehow, we were keen to find out where and how he was doing that. He knew were interested, he lost us every time we tried to tail him, but then he disappeared and that changed everything.'

'I don't understand you lot.' Mallory shook his head. 'One minute you're persecuting my lad, trying to fit him up for a job or two, then next minute you're worrying about his safety . . . it doesn't add up.'

'Our duty is to protect life and property. Everybody's,' smiled Lorraine. 'It's as simple as that.'

'It's not simple at all, missy! It's bloody complicated if

41

you ask me, the way you operate. So what happens next, if he is missing, I mean?'

'We have to find him, Mr Mallory, to convince ourselves he's not been harmed.'

'Well, I can't help and that's the God-honest truth. I've no idea where he is. What can I do? He's gone, he never told me where he was going. I don't know where he's gone or why or for how long. You can't get owt from me even if I wanted to help.'

'What about your lads?' asked Andy Williams. 'Would they know?'

'They're not here, none of them. They won't talk to you anyway, it's a rule of the house!' and Mallory grinned again. 'You should know that, an' all.'

'We do know that. So can you ask them? For us?' Lorraine put to him. 'Then let us know? I can leave my phone number.'

'Me grass on my own family? Now you are joking, missy!'

'It's not grassing, it's being co-operative, helping your own family. So you'll ask them? If they know where Darren is, if they've seen him or heard from him since he left the Blue Raven? A week last Saturday night.'

'They haven't seen him, I've already asked. After those other coppers came.' He sighed. 'I am bothered, missy, you know that, don't you? He is my son no matter what he's done.'

'And?' she smiled.

'They've not seen him, like I said, and they've not had word. Nothing. He's just upped and gone. I wasn't worried really, not until you lot came pestering.'

'He might be all right, Mr Mallory, we just want to be sure,' Lorraine said.

'I really am worried now, you know that? You've made me right worried, especially with him not getting in touch and not taking his things. My lads have been asking around town, they've good contacts as you'd expect, lots of 'em. Nobody knows nothing, or they're not saying. If he's all right, you'd think somebody would have told my lads. But they haven't. So who'd harm our Darren? He's such a gentle lad, not like the others, he could be a real gentleman if he tried. Mind you, we never kill and we never do drugs, that's another Mallory rule. But if somebody's killed him and I find out who it is, I might just break my own rules. Rules are there to be broken, eh? When it's necesssary,' and he laughed loudly.

'Have you reported him missing?' asked Williams.

'Reported him missing? You must be joking! I told my lads he seemed to have vanished and if they can't find him, nobody can. They'll find him even if your lot can't.'

'So they're out there now, are they? Looking for Darren?'

''Course they are! Blood's thicker than water, so whoever's done him an injury had better watch their backs . . .'

'Look, we need to know if he's safe, then we can call off our enquiries. So if they have discovered anything . . .'

'Well, if they have, they won't want you lot to know! That's for sure.'

'I hope you will see the sense of telling us if he's all right – that's all we ask, we don't want to know where he is or what he's up to. Just that he's safe,' said Lorraine.

'You can always ask,' he said, looking at the floor.

Lorraine realized they were rapidly coming to the end of their tolerated presence even though they had not searched the house to see whether Darren, or his body, was concealed anyhere. She felt that would be a most unwise thing to request – it could alienate Mallory after what she considered to be a remarkable piece of co-operation with the enemy. She wanted to build on this relationship, short and difficult though it was. This kind of co-operation might not last, it might not happen again and she felt that any further demands might halt the progress they'd made. 'We're going to keep asking and looking. Can we come back after a while to see what your lads have discovered?'

'If you do, make sure my lads are not here, they don't want the fuzz coming to the house, not for anything. If they knew I'd talked to you like this, they'd have my guts for garters, big as I am. I'd be out on my neck, make no mistake, boss or no boss, dad or no dad.'

'You like it here?' asked Lorraine. 'It's a mighty big change from that council estate.'

'I love it!' he said with a sudden show of happiness. 'Really, I do. It changed my world, missy, like I never thought would happen to me. If I'd lived in a place like this when I was young, well, I'd have not been the bloke I am now, I might have gone straight. I always wanted a big house in the country, you do, don't you? With land and space and lots of little sheds and outbuildings . . . I thought they was only for the nobs, not for the likes of me. Made me real bolshie, it did, think they had it all and I had nowt. Anyway, when the council said we could have this place, I jumped at the chance . . . lovely, isn't it? Those views, all the space . . . and I'm paying the rent on time because I want to stay here.'

'And there's no neighbours to harass you!' smiled Williams.

'No neighbours from hell, eh?' chortled Mallory. 'Just me . . . it's great, it really is.'

'I'm pleased for you,' was all Lorraine could think of saying.

'It's just me that likes it, though. My lads don't, they hate it, they're townies and only come home to sleep, and then not every night . . . they've got a place in town they can use . . . I told 'em to leave if they wanted but they've nowhere permanent, no place of their own, not yet, not like they used to have . . .' and his voice faded as he realized he might be saying too much.

'You're making something?' asked Lorraine, taking advantage of the moment as she indicated the timber on the workbench.

'A wardrobe. Pine. Old pine, redressed. I did the kitchen here, fitted it myself . . . do you want to see it?'

'I'd love to,' smiled Lorraine with total surprise.

'Not a word to any of my lads that I've let you in mind . . . not one bloody word . . .'

And with her eyebrows raised towards Andy in exaggerated surprise, she followed Jack Mallory to the door of the house. He opened it and said, 'Well, go on then, missy, get inside for a good look. And your mate.'

She stepped into the kitchen and Andy followed. It was a large airy room with a window overlooking the dale below and the entire place was fitted with pine cupboards, all new and all beautifully crafted. A handsome pine table stood against one wall. Although the breakfast things were still in the sink, the rest of the place was surprisingly tidy and clean.

'Nice, eh?' Mallory was actually smiling.

'You did this?' There was genuine surprise and appreciation on Williams' face.

'Yes, all my own work. I did woodwork at school, you know, years ago when I was a lad, and I liked it. I should have stuck at it but I just larked about, wasted my time. Mebbe I should have gone in for carpentry, but I never got the chance once I left school, not till I came here. I made a few false starts, got things wrong, made mistakes measuring up, messed up my joints and things, drilled holes in the wrong spot but I learned fast and I did all that, the whole kitchen.'

'Would you do work for someone else if they asked?' Williams put to him.

'Make summat for a customer, you mean? Me? I've never done that, mister, never.'

'Well, this is high quality work, Mr Mallory. You'd earn a good living doing this sort of thing, you know.'

'What if the tax man found out? Or the dole?'

'You'd have to tell them all, do it on the level, as a business, keeping books and things . . .'

'No, that's not for me. Mebbe I would knock up a piece of furniture for somebody as a favour, but I'm no business-man . . . not me. I was a docker, mister, a trouble-maker, I hated the self-employed, I hated successful folks, I wanted everybody to work for the state, to be equal and all that . . . I've changed my mind a bit now . . . at least, I think I have.'

'That was all a long time ago, Mr Mallory, things have

changed,' said Lorraine. 'But thanks for letting us see this. We won't keep you any longer, but we will be in touch about Darren.'

'Yes, well, right. I don't know what to say about it all. I think he might have a reason for going off without telling anybody but it is a bit funny, isn't it, all this time with not a word. So what can I say?'

'Then say nothing, Mr Mallory. Just try to do your best and think where he might be or what might have happened to him. He could have let something slip to you . . . dropped a hint somewhere.'

'Right,' he said following them to the door as they left. 'Yes, right, I'll try. But you did mean it, didn't you? That he might have come to some kind of harm? You're not having me on, trying to wheedle yourselves into the house or something, using that as a kind of sob story?'

'No, not on this occasion,' Andy assured him. 'We're on the level. This kind of thing is too serious to treat lightly, Mr Mallory.'

And they left with Mallory standing in the door of his kitchen to watch their departure.

'So what do you make of all that?' asked Williams as they drove away with Mallory still watching from the gate.

'I felt sorry for him,' said Lorraine. 'It looks as if a whole new world is waiting for him at Hill Top. And we got inside the house, so the boss owes me a fiver!'

'Do you believe him? About not knowing what Darren's up to?'

'Yes, I do. I think none of his lads, as he calls them, takes him into their confidence either. He's a bit of a loner now, but he's doing something worthwhile. He's making the best of this move into the countryside, he's got to be admired for that.'

'I wonder if those lads of his will find out where Darren's gone? Looking for him is the sort of thing brothers would do, even villains of this kind have some kind of family loyalty. It can be very strong in them. If they can't find him, what are our chances?'

46

'If Jack Mallory is genuinely worried about Darren – which I think he is – he'll recruit help from all his contacts and they could be our best eyes and ears, knowingly or unknowingly. But if the family does discover anything, do you think they'll tell us?' asked Lorraine.

'We've got to accept that those lads might not even tell their dad,' said Andy. 'I'm sure we'll never know if they do find him, whatever state he's in.'

'That's my feeling as well but I do think we made some progress there, Sergeant. Now what?'

'Down to the pub, I think. It's time for a bar snack and there's no better place to start asking a few local questions.'

'Drive on,' she smiled.

Lorraine knew of Andy Williams' renowned love of food. While engaged on enquiries, he had an uncanny knack of finding delightful pubs and cafés which offered good food and he always made a beeline for them when the pangs of hunger struck – which they often did! The Collared Dove was a traditional English pub set on the side of the road which led to the hilltop. A long and low stone building, it dated from the seventeenth century and had once been a farmhouse. Now it was a fine inn with a high reputation for good food, comfortable accommodation, a bar with a roaring log fire which burnt even in summer, and thick walls to keep out the harsh weather.

Andy parked outside the front door, took his briefcase and led the way inside. The scent of burning holly wood greeted them as they made their way to the bar. Each would buy their own lunch – they were paid a subsistence allowance to cover meals eaten while on duty away from their station. They both chose a prawn sandwich, Andy requesting chips and salad to accompany his, and then he ordered a pint of Yorkshire bitter in the knowledge that a single pint would not put him over the blood-alcohol limit for driving, and Lorraine settled for a dry white wine. They opted for bar stools rather than a table; it enabled them to talk to the barman, who in this case was also owner of the premises.

Apart from a middle-aged couple in hiking gear who had settled near the fire, the bar was empty upon their arrival and the plump landlord was happy to chat as he pulled Andy's pint.

'Visitors, are you?' was his opening gambit, one he had used countless times.

'In a way,' smiled the affable Andy. 'Lorraine's been here before, walking, but it's the first time for me. We're just looking around, finding our way about the place.'

'It's good walking country, we get lots in here, making a detour from the Cleveland Way or just exploring the moors and the old mines. Serious hikers and Sunday ramblers, we get the lot. You know the old railway on top?'

'I do,' smiled Lorraine.

'If you didn't, I was going to recommend it for you – you're not in hiking gear, I see, and it's a good base for a long easy and clean walk in ordinary clothes. And you get some great views from up there.'

He prattled on with his well-rehearsed tourist chatter as he organized the drinks, placed an order with the kitchen and pulled a further two drinks for the hikers – a pint for the man and a half for the lady. He told them about the sights not to be missed in the district, the best vantage points, the history of the village, current developments such as a pottery manufacturer in an old barn and an art gallery in another one. Then, by chance, he mentioned Jack Mallory.

'There's a chap moved into that big old spot on the hilltop,' he said. 'Quite a talent for woodwork, so the postman told me. He's done his kitchen out, all by himself, lovely fitted units, all pine. He's not been there long, but we're all wondering if he'll develop his carpentry into something, a craft shop maybe, selling things for the tourists or even doing jobs for customers. I hear he's rented the place from that outfit who own it. Some weird happy-clappy group. But there's room for another craftsman in this village, a lot of us depend on tourists and anything that brings 'em here must be good.'

'We've just come from there,' Andy explained. 'We went

48

along the old line and got chatting to that chap at the big house, then he showed us his kitchen.'

'He's shown it to all sorts of folks. Postman, milkman, vicar, the woman who delivers the parish magazine. He's proud of it, you can see that. Came here from the town, a few months back, with a big family of lads.'

'Five of them, he told us,' smiled Lorraine.

'There's no missus, but I don't know the story.'

'Does he come in here? And his family?'

'Darren's been in, he's one of the lads, he used to come on Sundays for his lunch and a couple of pints. A tall quiet lad, good-looking, dark hair like his dad. He would just sit in a corner reading the Sunday papers. I can't say I've seen the others in here, not that I'd know them anyway. The old man's been in a couple of times, he doesn't bother much with the village, but he came in one night, a couple of weeks back, and then again last Wednesday, just for a pint and a bar snack. By himself, he was, a bit on the shy side I thought. His family are away a lot, so he said. We haven't seen much of them in the village, though, they're not country folk. I think they came from Greater Balderside, townies with townie ways.'

'Darren's not been in for a while then?' pressed Williams.

'Not for a couple of weeks, no. He never said he was going away, but there again, he doesn't say much about himself. Like his dad. Plays his cards close to his chest.'

'Did Darren mix with the villagers? Get involved? Darts teams? Pub chatter, women?'

'You the police, are you? You don't look like tourists,' smiled the landlord as he realized the direction of the questions. 'We had some of your lads in from Sidlesbrough not long ago, asking similar questions. And the local bobby. Looking for Darren as well. He's wanted, is he? Done something wrong?'

'He's missing,' Andy said. 'We're looking into his disappearance now he's come to live on our patch. He's not been seen since a week last Saturday. We've just been to see his father, he's not seen him either, or heard from him.

No one knows where he is or what's happened to him, so there's a wee bit of concern.'

'That's what the other lot said. Well, apart from him coming in here like I said and being very quiet, I've not seen him around since then.'

'Maybe you'd keep an ear open? Bar gossip can often lead us in the right direction. As things are, he's vanished into thin air without a word to anyone. We just want to be sure he's not come to any harm.'

'Sure, if I hear anything, I'll give you a call. Where are you based?'

'Rainesbury CID, Detective Sergeant Williams is the name, or Detective Constable Cashmore.'

'Fair enough.' He made a note on a pad beside the till and obtained their telephone number. 'Ah, here's your sandwiches.'

A tall slender girl entered bearing a couple of plates, one of them piled high with chips. As she passed them over the counter, a group of half a dozen hikers walked into the bar and the landlord's attention was diverted as he launched into another of his touristy chats. Andy and Lorraine decided to claim a table near the fire; they'd achieved their purpose with ease. Their visit had been productive even if it had not produced much of overt value – at least it had established that Jack Mallory was not quite a hermit on the hilltop and that he would talk to them even if he didn't say a great deal.

There was the added factor that his new-found skills were already being recognized. And there'd been no mention of the criminal background of the newcomers. Clearly news of the family's true reputation had not filtered down to the pub. It seemed the Mallory Mob were following one old, respected but unwritten rule – you should never mess on your own doorstep. Perhaps the biggest slice of information was that the Mallory lads were also looking for Darren. That alone suggested his absence had not been planned or discussed with his family.

Lorraine and Andy carefully avoided any further discussion of their work as they enjoyed their meal. Andy told her about his recent holiday in Spain, paying particular attention to the delicious food, and Lorraine countered by explaining something of the joys of the moorland around them. When they had finished, Andy mimicked Mallory by saying, 'Well, missy, where now?'

'The postman?' suggested Lorraine. 'Or the milkman. Both have been in Hill Top, they might have seen or noticed something.'

'Good idea. Postman first.'

As they left the pub, they thanked the helpful landlord and Andy asked, 'Where will the postman be about now?'

The landlord glanced at his wristwatch. 'Ten past two. I'd say coming down from North Dovedale, he always calls at Mrs Stewart's for a cup of tea after leaving Throstle Nest. Try her, it's the last house in the village going out towards Haverdale. Dovedale End Cottage, it's called. If he's been, she'll know where he's gone from there; if he hasn't been, he'll be due at her spot before too long. You can't miss him, he's got a little red Postman Pat sort of van. Laurie Kipling's his name.'

Chapter Four

Andy and Lorraine found the distinctive red van outside Dovedale End Cottage. It was unattended but, rather than invade the postman's moment of private leisure, they waited in their own car. A few minutes later, a small man in postman's uniform emerged from the cottage. Andy hailed him as he strode towards his vehicle.

'Laurie Kipling?'

'Who wants to know?' Post Office delivery persons were almost as suspicious as police officers, especially when accosted by complete strangers.

'Police,' said Andy, showing his warrant card. 'Detective Sergeant Williams, and this is Detective Constable Cashmore. We're from Rainesbury.'

'OK. What's wrong?' Kipling blinked from behind thick spectacles, his grey eyes showing some concern. He was in his late thirties, estimated Williams, a slightly built man with thinning fair hair and a rounded, cheerful face. He wore a well-fitting navy-blue uniform, but no cap.

'Nothing's wrong,' smiled Williams. 'But can we talk? Have you time now?'

'Sure, I can spare a few minutes. Here?'

'It's as good as anywhere,' agreed Williams. 'You do this round regularly?'

'Most days, yes.'

'And you call at Hill Top House? The Mallorys' place.'

'Not often but yes, I deliver there. DSS stuff mainly, Benefits Directorate or whatever they're called now, circulars sometimes. They don't get much mail, they've not been there all that long.'

'Do you know them? Or any of them?'

'The old man talks to me sometimes. He likes a chat, he spends all day by himself up there. I think he gets lonely. He showed me his kitchen, he's done it all himself, he told me, fitted the whole place out in pine. He seems right proud of it.'

'And the others?'

'There's no Mrs Mallory, you know that?'

'Yes, she left home a few years ago, so we're told, before they came to live here, but there's five sons as well, all grown-up,' Williams went on.

'I've never set eyes on them.' Kipling shook his head. 'They've usually gone off to work by the time I get there. They're from Greater Balderside, the whole family I mean. A council relocation, so I was told. Trouble-makers. From a big estate. I think those lads go back there every day, for work I expect. Or just to see their mates. It's usually ten o'clock or so when I call at Hill Top, it's my last call before I come to the far outposts on this side of this dale so they've gone by then. As I said, I don't call every day and I don't live in the village, so I don't come across them much. Can I ask why you're asking all these questions?'

Williams pulled a photograph of Darren from his pocket. 'This is Darren Mallory,' he said. 'The second son. Good-looker in his mid-twenties. He's disappeared, we're trying to find him.'

'A wanted man, eh? I've a pal works in our sorting office at Sidlesbrough and he told me about the Mallorys when we heard they were moving out here. He said the lads were a bundle of trouble.'

'We've not heard of them causing trouble here,' smiled Lorraine.

'Me neither. I've had no hassle from them – not that I've encountered them yet – and so far as I know, there's been no complaints from the village. So what's this Darren done?'

'Nothing that we want to talk to him about,' Andy Williams explained. 'We're not looking for him to arrest him. He's disappeared, that's the problem, no one's heard from him in the last ten days. We've been to the house and talked to the old man. He knows nothing. It's a bit odd to say the least and to be honest, we're worried about him.'

'You're worried? Crikey! Is it a gangland thing, you mean? Some other bunch sorting him out? My mate said the Mallorys were vicious. Are you saying somebody's sorted out this Darren? Got their own back, that sort of thing?'

'That's what we're trying to find out. It might be nothing like that, he might have just gone away for a holiday,' Williams continued, Lorraine being content to let him *to d* the talking on this occasion. 'So what else did this pal of yours say about them?'

'They operate as a gang, terrifying others, working the clubs and bingo halls for protection money was one of their scams, and ladies' hairdressers, doing over anybody who stood in their way or refused to pay up. They've done some brutal beatings-up in town but the victims don't talk. They're scared.'

'I thought they don't do murder,' said Williams.

'Mebbe they don't, but they get pretty damned close to it. They lend money, then get their debtors to distribute drugs to pay them back – with interest – big interest. That sort of thing. But, as I said, I've never set eyes on them since they came here, they've done me no harm. The old man seems quite a decent chap, not a bit like I expected, all he wants to do is talk about his woodwork and show it off.'

'We heard they don't do drugs.' Williams wanted to stress that point.

'Then you've heard wrong. I heard they'll do drugs if it suits them.'

'I was told they never mess on their own doorstep, never do drugs and never do murder, they know better than that,' nodded Williams.

'That's not what I've heard,' said Kipling. 'Unless they've changed their tactics.'

'That might be the answer, and you might be better

informed than us. It's Darren who interests us though. I'm trying to establish if he's been seen around the village. If so, who with, and when. That sort of thing. He's got a nice car, a Vauxhall Omega, silver-grey. A new one.'

'He's not had it long. I've seen it at the house, one Saturday morning about a month ago, I'd say.'

'That suggests he does spend some time here, in Dovedale.'

'Could be, but I've never seen the lad himself. Mind you, I wouldn't know one from the other. Like I said, I've only met the old man.'

'OK, thanks, Mr Kipling. If you do hear anything about Darren, give us a call? We're at Rainesbury police station. Detectives Williams and Cashmore.'

'If he has come to harm, it wouldn't happen out here surely?' The postman frowned as he scribbled their details on a scrap of paper. 'There's one good thing – out on that hilltop, they can't upset many folks! You could play music as loud as you want and nobody would hear it, or work on your car repairs at night. My mate said they were the neighbours from hell, that's why they got booted out here, loud music, fights, you name it, it all happened in or around their house. Some jokers said the music was to drown the screams of their victims under torture. The lads were bastards, he said, totally evil and ruthless. Whatever's happened to Darren, though, if it was a gang battle of any kind, it would happen in Sidlesbrough, wouldn't it? Or Port Haverton? Their stamping ground on Greater Balderside. Not out here.'

'Greater Balderside Police have come up with nothing, that's why they've asked us to help at this end, it's because the Mallory clan live on our patch now.'

'Well, sorry I can't help more. I'll keep my ears to the ground, as they say, our people often see things others don't, being out and about at funny hours. I'll let you know – so long as they never find out I'm talking to the cops.'

'Thanks, and they won't,' smiled Williams.

'Thanks.' Lorraine honoured him with one of her lovely smiles too.

'Now I must get on, it's Bilberry Farm next. Now there's an isolated place . . .'

Kipling returned to his van, started his engine and pipped his horn as he departed.

'What do you make of that?' Andy asked as they returned to their car.

'I'm getting the feeling that Jack Mallory isn't as bad as people have made out.' She expressed her honest opinion. 'And it does seem his sons are trying to impose gangland rule on Sidlesbrough or Port Haverton while ignoring the family rules. Now that Jack's nicely out of the way, tucked away in the moors without a car, he's been made impotent, hasn't he? Side-tracked, shunted into a siding. Call it what you like. That could explain why those lads didn't object to being transferred out here. They spotted the potential of having dad out of the way, somewhere he couldn't keep his eyes on them. I'll bet they're expanding their empire without him – and getting into drugs. It's drugs that make the money.'

'I can see that makes sense, Lorraine, but would those lads murder the opposition? I reckon they would, I reckon they'll turn to both murder and drugs if it's necessary. It makes me wonder if Darren could have upset that other lot, the Clarksons? Have they got rid of him for some reason?'

'It's possible but that's out of our league, Andy, gangland wars beyond our boundaries aren't our problem, are they? That's been made pretty clear!'

'No, but even if they are operating off our pitch, we need to know what they're up to. In this case, their enterprise, whatever it is, might have spilt over into our area. And Kipling did state the obvious, didn't he?' Williams mused. 'If there is some kind of gang warfare going on, and if Darren is a gangland victim, he's probably met his fate in Sidlesbrough or Port Haverton. He could be in the dock, eh? Under several feet of water.'

'Or he could have been dumped on these moors,'

Lorraine suggested. 'All that open space where humans rarely set foot. Down a pit shaft or in a bog, or in a remote gulley. There's thousands of places a body would never be found.'

'You're suggesting he's dead, then?'

'We can't ignore that possibility.'

'If you're right, searching for his physical remains on these moors would be like looking for the proverbial needle in a haystack. Then there's the coastline, and all the rivers and dales and forests. We've absolutely no clues so where do we start? Or do we rely on a dog walker to come across him?'

'To decide that, we need to know even more about Darren, don't we? Or his pals.' Lorraine had reached the car now. 'And that won't be easy.'

'We're not getting very far, are we? I hope we've not come to a dead end. What we can do is talk to that girlfriend of his, but come along, let's see if we can find the milkman. If those villains leave here early for their drive to so-called "work", or if they come home in the early hours, the milkman might have seen something. Next question – where do we find him?'

'We can ask at the shop,' suggested Lorraine. 'It doubles as the post office.'

'Then lead on, Macduff!'

Dovedale's village store occupied a spacious site on the corner of a long terrace of stone houses, and what had once been two large rooms in a private house now served as the shop-cum-post office. Quite literally, it sold everything as most village stores do – groceries and vegetables, hardware, motor spares, children's clothes, tools and DIY materials, gardening equipment, flowers and seeds, wines and spirits, frozen foods, dairy products, kitchenware, herbs and spices, eggs and bacon . . . and more besides. There was also of course the entire range of post office goods such as stamps, postal orders and stationery. There were no customers in the shop as Williams and Lorraine entered, but a grey-haired woman with a friendly face peered around a pile of touristy books upon their arrival.

'Hello,' she called cheerily. 'Can I help?'

'Are you the postmistress here?' asked Lorraine.

'I am, Alice Fenby. Mrs Alice Fenby.'

'We're wondering where we can find the milkman.' Lorraine acted as spokesperson here.

'Oh, I can let you have some milk, miss, or is it a yoghurt you want? Cream perhaps?'

'No,' Lorraine smiled. 'We're police officers, we'd like a chat with the milkman . . .'

'Oh, he's not been misbehaving, has he? You know what milkmen are supposed to be like . . .'

Lorraine smiled. 'No, he's not in trouble, we just want to pick his brains.'

'Oh, he's got brains, has he?' She laughed. 'You could have fooled me! Well, you'll find him at home, I expect, he gets his morning round over by about ten thirty or so. He works at home after that, he repairs watches and clocks, mainly old ones like grandfathers and hunters and things.'

'Where does he live? And what's his name?'

'He's got a spread along Keldwell Lane, second right after leaving here. Roy Marshall's his name. You'll see his van outside.'

Andy Williams decided to quiz the postmistress before leaving.

'We're asking about Darren Mallory, from Hill Top, the new family up there,' he told her. 'He's vanished from home and there's some concern for his safety. With Mr Marshall being out and about in the early morning, we wondered if he might have seen anything that's of use to us. And we'd like to ask the same question around the village.'

'We had some other police in here, last week, asking the same thing. They were from Sidlesbrough and our local bobby's been in as well. All of a sudden, a lot of folks want to know where he's gone!'

'All police officers, I trust? We're from Rainesbury CID,

and Dovedale's on our patch. Were you able to help our colleagues?'

'They all said they were police but I can't say Darren's ever been in here. His father comes in looking for wood-working things, chisels, tools, stains and things, but he doesn't say much and there's some other brothers, isn't there? Four or five in all. I don't know them either. No women, though, mother or sisters, wives or girlfriends. They keep themselves very much to themselves on that hilltop.'

'So can you help in tracking Darren's routine move-ments? What time he goes to work, who his pals are, what time he comes home, that sort of thing.'

'Sorry, no, I just don't know. I'm not sure if Roy will be able to help, unless those Mallorys set off very early in the mornings.'

'That's what I'm hoping,' smiled Williams. 'Well, thanks anyway.'

And so they left. Roy Marshall's collection of old build-ings spread around a modern bungalow was a short drive from the centre of Dovedale and they found it without any trouble. His milk van was parked in the spacious yard and they found him in his workshop among a pile of pieces from a longcase clock. After they had explained who they were and why they had come to talk to him, he halted work.

'I do deliver to Hill Top,' he said. 'One pint a day, three or mebbe four at weekends. Those lads go off most days, even at weekends. All day. They leave the old chap all by himself, he always pays me when I call on Monday evenings.'

'You've no trouble getting money then?' asked Andy

Roy Marshall shrugged his shoulders. 'Not so far. I'd heard on the grapevine they were a problem family who'd been chucked out of their council house on Greater Balderside but so far, touch wood, I've had no problems. Always cash. I'll just stop delivering if they turn awkward, whoever they are.'

'Mr Marshall, if those young Mallorys want milk, they'll

get it from you whether or not their dad pays the bills. Don't cross them – that's my advice. But it seems old Jack is OK, he's even taken up woodwork.'

'He likes a chat, yes, and he showed me his kitchen so I said he could come and look at one of my renovations, it was a longcase clock I was repairing. I was fitting a new base to a two-hundred-year-old case. He said he'd like to see my work and in fact he did pop in one day, he was having a walk around the village. He loved looking around my workshop, said working with wood was something he'd always wanted to do but he'd never had the chance.'

'You know their reputation? The Mallory family?'

'Laurie told me, he's the postman. His mate from Sidlesbrough knows them but old Jack's been fine with me. Take as you find, that's what I say.'

'He seems to get on with most folks, he even invited us in to see his handiwork!' smiled Lorraine.

'That's him. I do think he wants to make a go of living out here.'

'Let's hope you're right,' continued Andy. 'Now, Mr Marshall – Darren. He's the one with the smart Vauxhall Omega, the silver-grey one. A tall good-looking lad in his mid-twenties, dark hair. Have you seen him knocking about during your early morning travels?'

'Yes, several times. Some days he leaves home early and I see his car going across the moor, heading for Greater Balderside.'

'Alone?'

'Yes, I've never seen anybody with him.'

'He was seen a week last Saturday night, in Sidlesbrough, that's one of the boroughs on Greater Balderside. It was about midnight, outside a night-club, he was saying goodbye to a girl. We know who she is; she's not seen or heard of him since and has no idea where he might be. She's a decent young woman. Have you seen him since then?'

'It's a while since I saw him – I couldn't say for certain

when it was but if you pressed me, I'd say it was a couple of weeks or thereabouts.'

'Did he ever talk to you?'

Marshall shook his head. 'No, he was just a commuter heading off to town like thousands of others leaving early to beat the rush hour, he never had the time or the inclination to stop for a chat with the milkman.'

'Rushing off to work? Is that how it looked?'

'Yes, it did. A commuter. He usually had a smart suit on, or some other smart clothes. He wasn't a scruff, and he's got that nice car now. He looked like some manager or businessman going to the office.'

'Did that surprise you?'

'Well, yes, it did, especially after what I'd heard about the Mallorys.'

'And the others? Did you see them heading off to Greater Balderside?'

'Sometimes, but they had bangers, different cars, sometimes they went all in one, sometimes separately, there was no pattern with them. And they'd be quite a bit later than that silver Vauxhall.'

'Was Darren always separate from his brothers? When they were travelling?'

'Hard to say, but yes, I'd guess he was. I'd see the silver Vauxhall with only the one chap inside, then the bangers and others later, sometimes full of blokes, sometimes with just one in, and sometimes three or four cars. But Darren was always alone, heading towards the smoke! The others aren't as regular as him, he goes off every day, mebbe not Sundays or Saturdays, but the others go only once in a while.'

'We think they have a base in town.'

'I reckon so, they only come home once in a while, they never spend much time here, they're townies through and through.'

'Did you ever see Darren with a girl?'

'No, never. Like I said, he was always alone. Smart and efficient, he looked.'

'OK,' smiled Williams. 'Thanks. If you do hear anything

about Darren, or come across anyone who's seen him in the last few days, give us a call. Rainesbury police station.'

'Sure, I'll do my best.'

And so they parted. Lorraine and Andy Williams spent the rest of the afternoon making enquiries around Dovedale, calling at those places open to tourists, visiting the garage, a private hotel and anywhere else which might receive members of the public or be privy to the news in the tiny village. It seemed they were following the tracks of a local constable who'd been asking the same questions but that served only to reinforce the importance of their task. They stopped several people in the street – dog walkers, mothers with children, pensioners out for exercise, tourists – but gleaned nothing about the family on the hilltop. No one had noticed the silver Vauxhall around the village at odd times, nor seen any suspicious characters – although it was difficult to be sure of that with all the tourists around, some dressed in peculiar outfits. The net result of their enquiries was nil. Darren's fate was not known – indeed, Darren was known only to the few they'd already quizzed, and then only as a commuter, not a trouble-maker.

They decided to return to their office, almost an hour's drive away. There, over a cup of tea with Pemberton, they related their negative results. He listened carefully, then said, 'If this is the result of just one day's full excursion into Mallory country, it seems a week's going to be a long time.'

'I reckon we've already exhausted enquiries in Dovedale, sir,' Williams told him. 'It's a very small place, we've talked to everyone and at every new place we visit, we come against a dead end. There's no way we can justify a week there.'

'So how do you fancy a visit to Greater Balderside force area, Sidlesbrough in particular?'

'If we're going to bottom this case, sir, we ought to go. We shouldn't rely on what we've been told by the local force, we need to make our own enquiries.'

'What sort of things would you be asking?'

Lorraine said, 'I'd like to find out where the mother went, sir. I know they said she never kept in touch but I can't imagine a mum not sending birthday cards or something to her children, the young one especially. Garry. He'd be only ten when she ran off.'

'There's more than a hint of gangland warfare too, sir,' Williams added. 'And there's talk of drugs now the old man's been shuffled aside. We need more words with Greater Balderside Crime Intelligence Unit, either at their headquarters or through their men in Sidlesbrough and Port Haverton, just to find out what really is going on.'

'Fair enough,' smiled Pemberton. 'You've convinced me.'

'We got the general drift from Probert and Baxter, but if we're going to get genuine answers, we need to dig deeper into Darren's life in that part of the world, not remotest Dovedale.'

'The local police might not tell you everything.' Pemberton sounded cautious. 'They won't want country coppers stealing their thunder – if they're targeting Darren for any reason, they'll want all the glory for themselves. You might have to ask elsewhere. But if you think it'll do any good, I'll agree to a visit to Greater Balderside. I'll pave the way for you right now.'

And with no more ado, he pressed his intercom switch. There was a moment before he responded. 'Ah, Roger. Pemberton here. Who's your oppo in charge at Greater Balderside?'

'Hansfield, sir. DI Hansfield. Patrick,' replied DI Roger Kirkman.

'We need to visit his patch to ask questions about Darren Mallory's disappearance. Is there something I should know before I talk to him?'

'Only that the Mallorys are under constant surveillance by his teams, sir, along with other major criminals in their area, but I'm sure you know that. If there's any kind of operation afoot, he'll not want your officers getting in the way. But yes, ring him. Give him my regards. Are you wanting to visit Greater Balderside?'

'Not me personally, but I need to send a team.'

'Then have words with him, don't send your team in unannounced.'

'Thanks, Roger.'

Pemberton rang Greater Balderside Police Headquarters and was soon speaking to DI Patrick Hansfield.

After identifying himself and explaining his purpose, Pemberton said, 'So I'd like to send two of my best officers into your patch, Mr Hansfield.'

'I need to talk to them first,' said Hansfield. 'But not at the police station.'

'I'll put DS Williams on the line,' said Pemberton. 'You can make arrangements direct with him.'

Hansfield suggested meeting Andy Williams and Lorraine in Row D of Tesco's car park in Sidlesbrough at ten o'clock tomorrow morning. He suggested the end nearest the shop's main entrance and Williams agreed; Hansfield then took the number of the vehicle Andy would be using.

'So that's fixed,' smiled Pemberton when the arrangements were complete. 'A nice task for tomorrow, but I do ask you both to be very careful.'

Chapter Five

At five minutes to ten the following morning, Wednesday, Andy Williams and Lorraine, dressed in casual gear and hoping to resemble a pair of shoppers, parked their unmarked Fiat near the end of Row D as instructed. At ten precisely, Andy emerged from the car with Lorraine at his side and he looked around, almost as if he was lost – which he was because he'd never been here before – when a dark-haired man, thirtyish and powerfully built, appeared from between two cars positioned nearby. He pointed towards the supermarket entrance with exaggerated hand gestures, but spoke quietly: 'See you in wines and spirits. Twenty minutes. Get yourselves a trolley and use it.' And then he walked away towards the entrance.

No one else was close by at that moment and no one seemed to be taking the slightest bit of notice of them, but the man's rapid strides took him away towards the building. Very quickly, he put a lot of space between himself and them, but they resisted the temptation to maintain his pace or to follow directly in his footsteps; they also resisted the temptation to look around to see if they were being followed or observed. Clearly, Hansfield had expected to be seen and had taken some action to divert the attention of potential observers; they realized his initial gesture was one of guiding strangers to the store. But that wouldn't fool a practised observer . . .

Lorraine and Andy walked as if they were live-in partners on a shopping trip, secured a large trolley from a covered park and pushed it through the revolving doorway. They would consider a selection of groceries whilst progressing through the store and would purchase some to maintain their cover.

As they ambled up and down the aisles, Lorraine selected a few oddments, choosing things she actually needed. They tried to ascertain whether or not they were being observed, and when they reached wines and spirits Hansfield was already there. He had a trolley half full of items and he was examining bottles of French red wine. He was not alone in the aisle, they noted; there were five other men, all apparently shopping alone and independently, and all with half-filled trolleys as they selected drinks; there were half a dozen couples doing likewise, one pair being pensioners and another with a child sitting on the kiddy seat. There was a young woman too, all alone with a trolley containing very few items. Watchers or not? None seemed to be taking any particular interest in Hansfield or Lorraine and Andy, but the scenario was enough to make Lorraine feel a sudden chill in her spine. There was no way she could be sure she was not under observation. But if she was, who, among these people, was it? Just one? Or all of them? Or none? And, she noted, internal security cameras were focused on this department – she knew that bottles of expensive spirits were constant targets for thieves and she realized that if Hansfield wished to check the shop for anyone watching his officers, he would be able to gain access to the shop's security tapes.

'Let Hansfield take the lead,' Williams whispered when he was sure of not being observed or overheard. 'We don't want to foul things up.' And then he added in a louder voice, 'Let's look at those French reds.'

As they studied the range of wines, Hansfield eased his trolley to a halt very close to them but did not speak; instead, he removed a bottle from the shelf, read the label and replaced it, doing likewise with several more. Then he addressed Lorraine and Williams as a stranger might do: 'The snag with this place is that they've too much choice. If there was just one wine, I'd take it . . . I hate having to make all these decisions. I know nothing about wine, other than it comes in bottles and is various shades of red . . . my wife's the expert, so she thinks . . .'

And he took another from the shelf and studied the label. He chatted to them as any stranger might having struck up a conversation in a supermarket, stressing his ignorance of French wine while saying his wife was particular about what she drank.

Then he asked, 'If you were choosing, which would you take?'

Andy Williams beamed and responded in his finest accent, 'Well, in my view, it's hard to beat a good Merlot . . .'

'Merlot? Ah, down here . . .' Hansfield selected one from the bottom shelf, read the label and said, 'I'll give it a try, I can always blame you if she doesn't like it! Thanks. Now I must dash. Thanks for your help,' and he offered his hand for Williams to shake. Andy took it and realized it contained a piece of paper which was pressed firmly into his palm; Andy reacted swiftly enough not to look at it but clutched it in his fist as he said, 'Cheers, I hope she likes it.'

And then Hansfield said, 'Well, must dash. Thanks for helping.' He pushed his trolley away, leaving Andy with a piece of paper in the palm of his hand. He concealed it temporarily simply by gripping the handle of his trolley and wheeling it further along the shelves, now ostensibly examining bottles of white wine. Five minutes later they were leaving the store with their trolley half full of groceries and heading for their car, the slip of paper now safely in Andy's pocket.

'That didn't take long,' Lorraine smiled, but she did not comment further on their experience inside the supermarket, having the sense to wait until they were in their car and heading from the car park; no one appeared to be watching them as they unloaded their goods into the boot, returned the trolley to the covered area and drove away.

'So where to now?' Lorraine puzzled as Andy accelerated out of the car park.

'Room 117 at the Mayflower Hotel, we're to ask for Mr

Fellowes,' smiled Andy. 'And let's make sure we're not followed.'

'How do you know that?' she asked with evident surprise.

'Hansfield slipped me a piece of paper in the supermarket,' he told her. 'With directions. He must have good reason for taking that kind of precaution.'

'I thought this sort of thing happened only in films!'

'Where do you think scriptwriters find their ideas? Anyway, it's a good way of letting us know we're not dealing with amateurs,' and Williams was serious when he said that. 'That short experience has sharpened my senses more than a little!'

'Perhaps it was designed to do that?' she acknowledged. 'It's put me on edge as well. Do you know your way to the Mayflower?'

'It's on my bit of paper!' he smiled. 'It also says the room's booked in the name of Fellowes.'

They found the small private hotel without any difficulty, did a circuit of the streets to shake off any likely followers although they'd noticed none, parked on the street a hundred yards away and emerged from their car. Andy remained confident they were not being observed or followed, but performed a rapid scan of the street before entering the building. None of the shoppers who'd been in the drinks aisle appeared to have followed them and none of the parked cars contained people reading newspapers! At reception, he said, 'I'm to meet a Mr Fellowes here, Room 117.'

'Our small conference suite, sir. Yes, first floor, second room on the left at the top of the stairs. He and his colleague are there now.'

With Lorraine at his side, Andy knocked on the door and waited, then a balding middle-aged man looking like some kind of sales rep in a smart dark grey suit opened it.

'We're here to meet Mr Fellowes,' announced Andy.

'Come in,' and, with no one in the nearby corridor, they were admitted to a small foyer and the door closed immediately. The man then asked to see their warrant cards and added, 'Glad you could make it. I'm Detective Inspector Hansfield. So you weren't followed here?' As he spoke, he showed them his own warrant card.

'No, I checked,' said Andy.

'So did we,' smiled Hansfield.

'So it wasn't you at the supermarket!' Andy used his finest voice.

'No, just one of our officers doing his stuff. But you trusted him?'

'I thought it was you.'

'Well, there are you, mistake number one, Sergeant!'

'But I couldn't ask to see his ID in that situation and all the other factors fitted the circumstances . . .'

'I'm not criticizing you, just stating facts. But that's in the past. Come in.'

He led them into the small conference room in which a table was standing with four place settings, each with a small pad of notepaper, pencil and glass of water. A decanter of water stood on a table mat in the centre, and as they walked in, a second man appeared, younger than the first. He had been waiting near the window, looking out. There was a good view of the street below.

'This is Detective Inspector Cartland, John Cartland, he's from F Division of the local force,' and Hansfield made the necessary introductions. 'Coffee will be here in a few minutes, we'll start the meeting once it has arrived. I might add that this room is secure, it's been swept for devices.'

Hansfield chatted about nothing in particular during that short waiting period – the weather, the latest state of Middlesbrough's football team, a strike at a local factory, traffic delays due to roadworks in the town centre – and then, following a tentative knock on the door, a young waitress entered with a tray of coffee complete with cups, chocolate biscuits and hot milk. She placed it on the table as Hansfield said they would serve themselves, then she left.

Hansfield watched her leave, turned the key in the lock of the outer door and invited them all to take a seat.

'I apologize for the cloak and dagger stuff.' Dark-suited and with his balding head of dark hair, Hansfield looked like a senior business executive, but he had an infectious smile which revealed a set of strong very white teeth. Lorraine thought his face was friendly, but that it revealed an inner toughness. His career as a detective would have produced that. 'We think it's necessary at this point in time. So, DS Williams and DC Cashmore, our target Darren Mallory. We know his background, you can skip that. You wanted this meeting, or your boss did. Tell us why. There are such things as telephones, you could have rung me.'

Williams, being the sergeant, acted as spokesman. 'I prefer personal contact, sir, especially in matters of this kind. We've turned up absolutely nothing about Mallory on our patch and we know that most of his activities, crime, work, socializing, are in your force area. We feel that if we are to find him, or any trace of him, we need to ask questions on your patch, to get under his skin as it were, find out who his pals and enemies are. In addition, I'm concerned there might be some kind of undercover operation afoot in your area, this morning's cloak-and-dagger stuff has just strengthened that belief, and we don't want to get in the way of that.'

He paused to see what effect that comment produced, but the expressions on the faces of Hansfield and Cartland did not alter. They remained impassive and neither made any comment for a while, then Hansfield said, 'Go on, Sergeant.'

Andy continued his positive approach. 'We would like to talk to his girlfriend, the one he met at the Blue Raven, and that probation officer, Dent; we also need to know more about his brothers and their activities, especially with other criminals, and we need to know the state of any possible gang warfare he might have been involved in. So far as we know, none of his activities, or those of his brothers, have happened, or are likely to happen, in our very rural area. Theirs is essentially urban crime. In short, we've nothing to go on, sir, nothing at all and thought a chat would be worth countless phone calls. And, with all due respect to you and your efforts, it boils down to the fact that if we are to find Darren we need to know as much as possible about him and his contacts.'

'Clearly, your force is taking this very seriously. It's only a missing person you're looking for, Sergeant, a Missing From Home, that's all, not a serial killer.'

'We take our work seriously, sir,' smiled Andy.

'You can't be criticized for that! All right. I'll be quite frank, Sergeant. We don't know much about Darren either. That's the problem. Young Darren has become very good at keeping most of his activities out of our sight. He lets us see what he wants us to see, he's a very devious young man.'

'But you must know more than us? He comes here every day, to work as he might put it, he's got convictions in your area, he operates on your patch, socializes here. You've tried to shadow him whenever you can, you were watching him when he left the Blue Raven. I realize this could be more than a normal missing person enquiry, so can I ask the real reason we've been asked to look for him?'

'Because his home address is on your patch, Sergeant. That's perfectly normal. Let's just say we want enquiries to find this man. Your brief is to make those enquiries on your own patch, not to dig into what are essentially matters for my own force. Leave our problems alone, Sergeant, and concentrate on yours. Your job is very simple – find Darren Mallory and in that, we'll help all we can.'

'I appreciate that, but with all due respect, if we are to find him we need to know more about him and you must know more than you're revealing – what I'm trying to say is that there must be some very important or unusual reason for there to be such interest in this man. The fact we are in this hotel room confirms it. If we are to pick up a trail which might lead to him, we must be told more, we must know what to avoid as well as what to look for.'

Hansfield turned to Cartland. 'Well spoken, Sergeant. Over to you, John.'

'I'm in charge of Sidlesbrough Crime Intelligence Unit,'

Cartland told them. 'Mr Hansfield has overall responsibility for Criminal Intelligence force-wide, and so Mallory came to my notice through the diligence of my teams, both covert and overt. As you know, we tend to target criminals nowadays, we gather evidence through intelligence-led operations.'

'I know how it works,' agreed Williams.

'While we were targeting Darren, we realized he wasn't actually committing crime – he'd given up stealing cars, raiding bookies, burgling and conning old folks. He never announced he'd changed his lifestyle, we noticed it for ourselves.'

'Has he genuinely reformed, do you think?' asked Williams.

'I don't think reform's the right word, changed direction perhaps. Leopards never change their spots. He's still a criminal. Even though he's given up the appearance of committing active crime, he has a good lifestyle. There's no sign of a proper job though, and, as I said, no sign of committing crime. But he has nice clothes, plenty of money, a good car . . . all visible evidence of success. Naturally, that made us take a greater interest in him.'

'And he dodged you?' smiled Williams.

'He did. He seemed to know all our operatives – we knew he'd been watching comings and goings at various police stations – and he managed to avoid our teams, dodging them or losing them. Playing cat-and-mouse in fact. Apart from that family house in Dovedale, we've no idea where he spends most of his leisure time. We know he goes to one or two local clubs or pubs and perhaps a betting shop or two, but we don't know which is his base. We don't know where he keeps his money or how he earns it. That's the crucial bit, Sergeant, how does he come to have so much money on such a regular basis? He has been spotted carrying a hold-all in recent months, we think he carries a spare set of clothes, a different coat or jacket, sweater, hat, anything to disguise himself. He goes into a supermarket, say, wearing a dark suit and emerges dressed in a cagoule and woolly hat or something different, so our operatives can easily miss him. He's very skilled at that, I might add.'

'You must have some suspicions, about the source of his money?'

'He goes to the bookies, he's been seen popping into various betting shops in town, but his income, if that's the right word, is too consistent – and plentiful – to come from betting on horses or dogs alone. Besides, we've checked as well as we can, there's no record of him having a substantial win anywhere – lottery, horses or whatever – or even being moderately successful. We're sure his money doesn't come from a big win somewhere, or a legacy. We've checked that too.'

'Do you think he's stopped committing crime altogether?' asked Lorraine.

'I doubt it, we've no hint of blackmail, no sign of a one-man protection racket and no sign of a regular job. Having said that, he doesn't mix with his brothers like he used to – that's one clue, and he operates entirely alone now, no partner, male or female,' said Cartland. 'We've checked with the National Insurance and Inland Revenue and elsewhere, there's no record of him being employed, not even being self-employed. He's a cash-only man, Sergeant, he doesn't even use credit cards. If he did, we could trace his movements. He's very successful at what he does, and he's not a pimp or a window cleaner either!' And suddenly Cartland smiled.

'I can understand why you were interested in him. So what about those other agencies? Inland Revenue, National Insurance and the like. Have they been targeting him?'

'Not to our knowledge, but they don't always level with us. His probation officer has no idea how he earns his living, I might add. It's clear he's found a way of earning good money and it could be something innocent and quite lawful, but we do suspect that it's somehow linked to crime, big crime.'

'Drugs?' That was an obvious theory.

'We've no evidence of his involvement in drugs,

although I wouldn't say the same about his brothers, not now,' said Cartland. 'He's not a user and there's no sign of him dealing. We kept him in our sights for months, trying to get something positive on him, but he could always dodge us. He knows when we are keeping tabs on him and that's what makes him so successful in dodging us. We know he went home most nights, to Dovedale, but he didn't get up to any tricks there. Then he vanished. Without a trace. We've circulated his description nationwide, and details of his car. Result? Nothing. Our own enquiries have produced absolutely no information at all, except that brief meeting with a girl at the Blue Raven. So we're going right back to basics. We're treating him as an ordinary missing person with uniform cops keeping their eyes open for him. They might come up with something we've missed. But because his family don't co-operate with the police, we had to ask his senior probation officer to do the honours for us, to give us the necessary lever. Happily, he did.'

'I still don't think you've told us everything!' said Williams. 'I'm convinced there's more to this than you're prepared to tell us.'

Hansfield spread his hands in a gesture of openness. 'If there is, then it's up to you to find out, Sergeant. But don't interfere with our force procedures, leave our crime enquiries to us, we can deal with them without any help from the rustics. After all, this is just a missing person enquiry, ideal for plods from rural England!'

'I understand that.' Lorraine now said her piece and deliberately ignored the country bumpkin slurs. 'I'm not a high-ranking police officer and I'm from a force you think concerns itself only with sheep rustling, but it does seem peculiar to me that you've gone to all this trouble to keep this meeting secret. It seems to me that Darren has got himself mixed up in something quite big and quite dangerous. I agree with my sergeant, we should know what it is if our enquiries are to be effective.'

'I'll admit we don't know what he's up to.' Cartland produced a rueful smile.

74

'Maybe we can find out for you, sir?' grinned Williams with more than a hint of cheek.

'Don't count your chickens, Sergeant,' Hansfield laughed. 'Stick to your moors and your sheep, leave the real policing to us. I very much doubt whether your enquiries will reveal anything, but if they do, give us a call. As I said, you're welcome to make enquiries in our area so long as you restrict yourselves to Darren, and even if it means going over ground we've already covered. To show our goodwill, we don't mind you seeing the file we've accumulated to date. John?'

Cartland lifted his briefcase on to the table and took out a buff-coloured file which he passed to Andy Williams. It was marked 'Confidential' and bore the name of Darren Mallory.

'That's a copy of our original, Sergeant, you can keep it. Read it at your leisure, I think you'll find it contains little more than we've already discussed.'

Williams accepted it, flipped it open and scanned the first few pages, then kept it on the table before him. 'Thanks, sir, I'm sure it will be useful.'

'Can we talk to that girlfriend he met at the Blue Raven?' asked Lorraine.

'We can't stop you from talking to anyone, nor would we wish to.' Hansfield smiled thinly. 'But in that file, you'll see we did speak to the girl, not as police officers I might add, but merely as one woman talking to another about a lad they both fancied. Our detective did a good job but the girl knew nothing of him and he never gave her any hint of himself leaving the area.'

'I'd like to talk to Darren's mother,' Lorraine said. 'I know she left the area a long time ago, but I can't really believe she'd never get in touch with her family, especially her youngest son . . .'

'She lives in the Midlands, Miss Cashmore,' Hansfield told her. 'We cannot reveal her address, we promised we'd never do that in any circumstances. She is fit and well, with a nice job, and she has no idea where Darren is. He's not with her, I can assure you of that. We've asked her.'

'I thought he might have found her and gone to see her.'

'No, he hasn't. Now, I'm not sure what other enquiries you want to make in our area but I would ask that if you do come up with any new evidence or suggestions of any kind, please let us know. I trust you will respect our wishes that you don't involve yourselves with investigations inside our own boundaries! Stick to Darren, that's your brief.'

'Of course, sir, we understand fully.' Andy Williams, by this stage growing increasingly aware that he was unlikely to learn any more from this visit, was now anxious to close the discussion. He guessed the file would not help either – it would contain only what he already knew.

'Is there a link between Darren and Joseph Campion?' asked Lorraine, determined to mention that name before leaving.

'You know about him?' Hansfield showed some surprise. 'He's a local villain, from our patch, but he's a very big name in the wider criminal world. We've a thick dossier on him but so far as his disappearance goes, no clues have been found. No body either. He could be overseas under a false name or he could be the victim of another gang. We favour the former and we're working on Campion, you can leave him to us.'

'Fair enough. So what can you tell us about gang warfare, sir? In your force area? It might be relevant to our enquiries.'

'It goes on,' admitted Hansfield. 'Clearly, neither side is going to complain to the police, so if one lot's illicit warehouse full of porn videos gets torched or a member of the other lot gets a thrashing with an iron bar after leaving a club, no one is going to make an official complaint to us. It's sorted out between themselves, they have their own territories and a code of behaviour quite beyond us. We let them do what they want to each other, provided the general public is not harmed. If that happens, we step in. The Clarksons' territory is north of the Balder and the Mallorys run the south. Trouble comes periodically, it flares up from time to time. Small gangs try to muscle in, but the Mallorys and the Clarksons soon see off the small boys, the minnows. And, as you'll understand, the river's a wonderful boundary.'

'And Campion, is he part of a gang?'

'No, but he's not averse to using either the Clarksons or the Mallorys if they can produce what he wants. At the moment, there's an uneasy truce between the Mallorys and Clarksons, each knows how far the other will go. I don't think Darren is involved in that kind of thing, that's down to their respective heavies to sort out, Darren's brothers in other words.'

'Is there any suggestion Darren might have done something to deeply antagonize the Clarksons?' asked Lorraine. 'Something bad enough for them to eliminate him?'

'With this lot, nothing's impossible, Miss Cashmore. All I can say is that we've had no hint of it.'

'But suppose the Clarksons – or even Campion – had dealt with Darren for some transgression, how would the Mallorys respond?'

'With all guns blazing, I suspect. They'd seek revenge, with all the force they can muster. That's the last thing we need, but thank God we've no hint of that kind of warfare brewing. But those are our problems too – leave them to us.'

It was clear that the meeting was drawing to a close and when Andy and Lorraine realized the Greater Balderside officers were not going to provide them with any more information, they decided to leave. They bade farewell, left the room with their file and made their way to the car, with Andy once more checking for observers. They regained their car without noticing anyone; the two detectives did not appear either.

Lorraine now wanted to speak to the girl who'd met Darren at the Blue Raven and Williams agreed. The file said her name was Julie Carver, she was twenty-three and worked for the Sidlesbrough Building Society at their Benton Street branch. They drove to the address, parked in front of the office and after pressing a security button to announce their names, walked into reception, having now abandoned much of their previous caution. A lone girl was sitting before a VDU and she left her screenwork to attend to them, coming to the counter at which they now stood.

'Yes?' She was very pretty with shoulder-length brown hair, brown eyes and a healthy pink complexion.

Lorraine opened the questions.

'I'm Detective Constable Lorraine Cashmore.' She introduced herself and Andy Williams. 'We're trying to trace the whereabouts of a young man who has vanished, it would be some ten days ago, or more, and we know he talked to you at the Blue Raven on the Saturday night before he disappeared.'

'Oh dear, that's sounds dreadful . . .'

'Darren Mallory is his name, he lives in the countryside, in Dovedale.'

'Yes, we did get chatting,' she told them quite openly. 'Darren seemed a real nice man. He said he might see me the next Saturday, but didn't turn up. I never thought much about it . . . actually, a friend of his was asking as well, but I said I'd never seen him since that Saturday. He's not in trouble, is he?'

'Not to our knowledge,' smiled Lorraine. 'It's just that he's not been seen for several days and there's some concern for him. What time did he leave you?'

'I can't be absolutely sure, but it would be about midnight, maybe a minute or two either side.'

'Can you remember him saying anything about going away, for a holiday perhaps, or to do with work, to see his mother, she lives away from the area.'

Julie shook her head. 'Sorry, no. I didn't know him well, there wasn't a relationship or anything like that, we just chatted that night and I think he bought me a drink, it was nothing more than that. He told me his name and I told him mine. I explained where I worked and said if he wanted to contact me during the day, it wouldn't cause problems. That was it, really.'

'Did he tell you how to contact him?'

'No, he said he was on the road all day, working, doing deals, he said, he rarely knew where he'd be from one day to the next, he travels all over the country but he said he got most Saturday nights off and would see me in the Blue Raven the following Saturday, after nine, he said. But he never turned up. That's life, there's plenty of other pebbles on the beach!'

'Did he ask about your work?'

'No more than anybody else,' said Julie. 'I'm just a receptionist, not the manager or anything important like that. I told him about that raid we'd had, a year ago it would be, when two gunmen burst in one afternoon before cashing-up time and got away with nearly £3000, but it was in all the newspapers and on telly, so I wasn't giving secrets away. He didn't seem very interested, we've tightened up our security anyway.'

'You didn't get the impression he was trying to get information out of you?'

'Oh, no, we get that all the time, people chatting us up to see how much cash we carry during the day and how we get it into the premises, but he wasn't like that. That's why I liked him. Besides, we openly talked about the raid. We got all our money back anyway, we put a reward in the local paper and someone told the police where the thief was hiding the money. We got it all back – Darren knew about the raid, and said he'd read about the reward.'

Julie was a very affable and chatty young woman, but as they talked it became clear to Andy and Lorraine that she could offer no further information about Darren Mallory; her contact with him had been little more than a brief encounter.

'While we're in Sidlesbrough, I think we should talk to that probation officer, Dent. James Dent,' suggested Andy as they returned to their car. 'If the police won't talk to us, he might.'

Andy, a regular visitor to the town, knew the location of the offices of the Sidlesbrough Area Headquarters of the probation service. They parked in the visitors' section of their car park and went to reception. Fortunately, James

Dent was in his office and agreed to see them; they were guided to the second floor and moments later were seated before him. He was a small man in his early forties with thin fair hair, a very pale skin, blue eyes and almost invisible eyebrows; he wore a multicoloured sweater, jeans and trainer shoes. The dress for modern probation officers who were not supposed to look superior to their 'customers'?

'So how can I help you?' he asked after inviting them to be seated before his desk. 'You are police officers, so reception said? But not from our local force?'

After the introductions, Andy said, 'We're here about Darren Mallory.'

'Ah!'

'We have been charged with the task of finding him, he lives on our patch. I believe you reported him missing?' began Andy.

'Sidlesbrough Police asked me to make the report,' he said. 'Darren hadn't fulfilled the conditions of his probation, he hadn't reported to my staff at the appointed times and when we tried to trace him, he was nowhere in the locality and not at home. I notified the police – that's standard practice – and at first they said they would make a note of it and we would put into action our usual procedures to trace him, but later I was asked to make an official report to the police, to formally report him as an MFH – Missing From Home.'

'Is that unusual?' asked Lorraine.

'I am sure it's been done before by the probation service, many times I would imagine, but I felt it odd that I was specially asked to do so, by Sidlesbrough CID.'

'What would have been the normal procedure, if he'd apparently left the area?'

Dent explained that enquiries would be made, initially by the probation service, to try and ascertain where the subject had gone, and why. His friends, family and contacts would all be approached and if there was some deep personal reason for breaching the conditions of the probation order, he would be treated sympathetically.

Dent continued, 'Darren kept all his appointments and fulfilled his conditions prior to his disappearance so the occasional breach doesn't cause too much concern. I know Darren should have told us if he was going away, for a holiday, to do with his work, visiting friends or whatever, and he didn't. But, to be honest, I saw no reason at that early stage to mount a police search for him.'

'But you agreed to make that report?'

'I did, the police said it was important and after all, his probation order had been breached. Going by the letter of the law, we were right in making a report.'

'So who asked you to do this?' asked Andy.

'Detective Inspector Hansfield, you know him?'

'We've just come from a meeting with him,' smiled Andy. 'So you have no idea why you were asked to do this? Or where Darren has got to?'

'No, I thought it must be important, I knew his family would not report him absent and so I did as asked. It seemed the sensible thing to do if they thought he'd come to some harm.'

Lorraine then asked, 'The incident which led to the probation order. When did it occur?'

'It was in May this year, I forget the precise date, but he was at court in June, 21st June.'

'Thanks. We were told there were mitigating circumstances which led to the rather lenient penalty. Do you know what they were?'

'I'm sorry, I have no idea. The snag with talking to Darren is that you never know when he's telling the truth or not, he's a very smooth operator, he can tell a very convincing lie. I wasn't in court, one of my colleagues was there, so I didn't hear the actual case. From what I understand he attacked another man with a heavy stone or a brick, fractured his cheeks and nose and knocked some teeth out. The chap's face was a real mess. The stone just happened to be conveniently nearby. When I talked to Darren about it, he said the man had tried to snatch his wallet while he was walking over some waste ground late one night. He claimed he acted in self-defence, his victim

81

said it was an unprovoked attack. What's the truth? The court accepted Darren's version.'

'And the victim? Do you know who it was?'

'It's in the file. I'll see if my secretary can put her hands on his file.' Dent pressed an intercom button and made the request.

During the wait, Dent said that in the short time he had known Darren, he had been impressed by his intelligence and his desire to rid himself of the criminal tendencies with which he had been reared since a child. The probation officer assigned to him had been impressed by him, even bearing in mind Darren's propensity for smooth talking. He was not sure how Darren earned his living, except that Darren had said, 'By wheeling and dealing, I'm a self-employed dealer.' But he would not elaborate. Then the secretary arrived with a buff file, handed it to Dent and departed. He flicked through it.

'Here we are. The victim was Dylan Welch, twenty-seven years old. His occupation was given as unemployed steelworker and his address at the time was 19, Shotley Terrace, Sidlesbrough, a lodging house. He's not there now, I checked after I reported Darren missing. His landlady has no idea where he went – he left before the case was heard but funnily enough turned up on the day to give his evidence.'

'Welch could have left a forwarding address with the Post Office,' said Andy.

'We'll do our best to find him as well,' Lorraine told him. 'We'd like a chat with him – he might know what's happened to Darren.'

'Revenge, you mean?' asked Dent. 'For that attack?'

'It's as likely an explanation as any other,' said Lorraine.

Chapter Six

Unable to glean anything further from James Dent, they went immediately to Shotley Terrace which lay in the Port Haverton area of Greater Balderside. To the south of the River Balder, it was a dockland street of back-to-back houses dominated by the outlines of rows of cranes which rose above the townscape. Their tall slender towers with arms outstretched looked like metal sculptures of giant stork-like birds, almost top-heavy as they overlooked the waterside end of this row of houses. In fact, the cranes and docks were some distance away but it seemed they were only yards from the end of the street. This illusion was furthered because, between the buildings, portions of the bulk of huge ocean-going tankers and cargo ships could be glimpsed too, with container ships being either loaded or unloaded as smaller craft dodged among them, going about their own lesser business routine. There were signs showing the way to each wharf and more signs indicating the route to the ferry terminal. Two identical ferries plied daily across the North Sea to Holland. One left here at 8 p.m. while the other left Rotterdam at the same time; they passed each other midway and each docked at 7 a.m., day in, day out. A new terminal was under construction for the modern high-speed ferries, soon to be brought into service. The activity of this busy riverside was carried on day and night amid the noise of hooters, bells and engines, and heavy vehicles constantly moving out of vision. These docks seemed to be part of the town; in some places, the distinction between town and dock was marked only by tall mesh fences topped with barbed wire, most of which bore prohibitory notices.

Shotley Terrace was a dingy place with paint peeling from the woodwork of doors and windows, vandalized cars parked in the gutters, a cast-off fridge standing on the footpath, graffiti on the house walls and a sea of plastic and paper litter permanently shifting about in the wind. That wind never stopped, it blew persistently from the sea to find its erratic way into this and other nearby streets, ideal when the Monday washing lines hung across the road. Several women were standing in doorways, chatting or merely standing motionless, and they watched as the police car, not bearing any insignia, cruised along in search of number 19.

Infants played among the rubbish, the older children would be at school – or should be at school – but Lorraine noticed there were no men in the street. Those not at work would be at the bookie's or the dole office or even in the pub. Number 19 had a battered grey door, and one pane of glass was missing from its window, its replacement being a piece of cardboard. Andy eased to a halt outside.

'You ask at the house,' he said. 'I'd better stay with the car.'

Lorraine rattled the heavy knocker and eventually it produced a response from a middle-aged woman with curlers in her dirty blonde hair. She wore plimsolls and a long denim dress which reached down to her ankles; Lorraine felt that once long ago, in her teens perhaps, she would have been quite beautiful. Now, in her late forties, she looked as if she was in her fifties or even sixties. Fate, or life, had not been kind.

'I'm looking for Dylan Welch.' Lorraine did not say she was a police officer.

'He left weeks ago.' The woman shrugged her shoulders as if to say she had no cause to think about him.

'He was your lodger?'

'He was – and that's all he was. Lodger in the back room, nothing else. You're not his missus, are you?'

'No, I'm not. Where is he now?'

'How should I know? He paid up and left.'

'Does mail come for him?'

'Mail? You mean letters? No.'

'People then? Callers?'

'No.'

'What do you know about Dylan?'

She shrugged her shoulders. 'Nothing. Why should I? His business is nowt to do with me. Keep yourself to yourself, that's what I say.'

'When did you last see him?'

'He got put in hospital with that chap hitting him, he came out, paid up and went. Home I expect, wherever home is. I can't remember when it was but it wasn't all that long since.'

'Did he come to see you when the case was being heard?'

'No, why should he?'

'Was he looking for work while he was here?'

'He tried, I'll say that for him. He wasn't in work. Steelworker, he said, at Scunthorpe. Laid off. There's no work in our steelworks though. He thought he might find summat on the docks, but he never did. They're laying blokes off. You don't need as many stevedores now they've got container ships and the ferry has its own crew, Dutch most of 'em. He spent ages down there, day in and day out, looking for work, talking to bosses, standing in queues waiting to be seen, going to the Job Centre. Stuck it a while, paid me on the dot and cleared off. Pity really, he was a nice lad, dead straight. Not many of them about these days. Lads like him.'

'Had he a car?'

'If he had, I never saw it, he never parked it on this street. I don't think he had one, he was hard up.'

'Did he mention his family? A wife? His background? Where he'd worked before? What he'd done with himself in recent months?'

'Just Scunthorpe, like I said. No talk of a family or a missus, and he never said what he'd done before coming here. Apart from the steelworker bit. You ask a lot of questions, miss. You the police?' She glanced at Andy, waiting outside. They could be from anywhere, this man and woman – the dole office, tax people, probation service, council offices. Such representatives of authority and officialdom would be regular visitors and so Lorraine avoided the question.

'One of his friends is missing,' she told the woman. 'We're trying to find him – the friend that is – and we wondered if Dylan might be able to help. He's not in trouble, not him or the friend, but we wonder if something's happened to his friend.'

'He never had any friends while he was here, I can tell you that, spent all his time alone in his room, he had one of those little computer things you carry in a case . . . I reckon he was logging into them porn channels to pass the time . . . like the kids around here. Them with computers, most likely nicked them from schools and places.'

'Is the room let now?'

'No, who's going to come down here to lodge? I only charged him fifteen quid a week, that's all he could afford, he reckoned. He found his own meals, he just wanted somewhere to get his head down. A chap at the docks put him on to me. I'm not really a boarding house, but sometimes I take people in, it gives me a bit extra.'

'Can I see his room?'

'It's not the Ritz, you know, so why do you want to see his room? I can't imagine you wanting to rent it.'

'He might have left something behind, papers maybe, something we can use to trace him.'

'He left nothing, very tidy he was, not a scrap of anything, except a tip for me. A fiver. Decent of him. Like I said, he was a decent chap. But if you want to look around, you can, I shan't stand in your way. It's no skin off my nose.'

The small back bedroom, with the house's only toilet and bathroom next to it, was surprisingly clean and tidy. A single bed, with a purple and green coverlet in place, stood against one wall; there was a set of cheap drawers, an MFI-type wardrobe and a tiny table with a chair before it. A couple of coloured prints were hanging on the wall in cheap frames – cheery and colourful garden scenes, she noted. Skilled at searching, Lorraine pulled out the drawers, opened the wardrobe, looked under the bed and under the mattress, all the time with the householder standing in the doorway with her arms folded, watching.

'Can you remember the dates he was here?' Lorraine asked.

'He arrived just after New Year, then left when he came out of hospital. I can't remember the dates. Was he into drugs, then?'

'Not to my knowledge,' Lorraine admitted. 'So far as I know, he wasn't in trouble and never had been, we just wonder if he knows where Darren's got to. That's his friend. That's why we want to find Dylan. People some-times leave things behind, things they don't want.'

'Well, you'll find nothing here. I cleaned up after he went, there was nothing then. Like I said, he was a tidy lad, was Dylan, the sort any mum would be proud of. He was just a lad looking for work, not a thief. Not Dylan.'

'Did he ever mention anybody called Darren? Or did Darren ever visit him?'

'No, not a word, I never saw nobody come and see him.'

'And the attack with the brick? What did he say about that?'

She shrugged her shoulders. 'Nowt. Not a word. He never talked to me about it, but he was a right mess I can tell you, his face I mean, black and blue . . .'

'Did he say anything about the court case then?'

'Not him. I knew they got somebody for it but Dylan never talked about it even though he got put in hospital. I went to see him, you know, in hospital, 'cos he had nobody. The hospital told me he was in, he gave this address. He was only in overnight, though, he said he wanted to leave. His face was a mess, mind, that bloke should have been sent down for it. Dylan left here straight after that, next morning it was.'

'You know who it was then? Who hit Dylan?'

'Some local tearaway, they said. I've no idea who. And he never said.'

Lorraine quizzed the chatty woman a little further, but had to conclude her enquiries without discovering anything else about the mysterious Dylan or Darren Mallory.

'Another enquiry that's come to a dead end, eh?' sighed Andy Williams when she returned to the car and explained. 'Maybe we can't find anything because there's nothing for us to find? Maybe Darren has just gone off for a holiday, nothing more than that.'

'Sergeant,' Lorraine said, 'we have learned something, we've discovered that three men are now missing, whereabouts unknown. Dylan's the latest. How can anyone simply vanish without trace?'

'It's been done before, lots of times,' he smiled. 'Think of Lord Lucan – and he's just one among many who've vanished off the face of the earth.'

'Darren's hardly in his league!'

'Absolutely right! It means we can include Darren in our Missing From Home circulars in the usual way. His name can go on the computer too, some police officer somewhere might decide to check him for something. I suppose Campion's name is listed as well? Mind you, I can't see how we can regard Dylan Welch as missing, he'll have moved on to find work.'

'I haven't checked the lists for Campion,' Lorraine admitted.

'Me neither. That's another job for us. And we haven't talked to Darren's brothers but I can't see the point in that.'

'I'm hoping we'll get some feedback from the old man about their enquiries,' Lorraine smiled. 'It'll be worth having another chat with him in due course.'

'I'll let you do that, you've already charmed him into breaking his own rules,' laughed Andy. 'Now, I'm starving, so let's have some lunch, that's if we can find a decent eating place near this godforsaken spot.'

A twenty-minute drive took them to the outskirts where Andy said he knew a nice pub which produced good bar snacks with lots of chips, and soon they were sitting down to a pleasing meal with an artificial log fire producing a warm glow at the end of the room. The file received from Hansfield was safely in Andy's briefcase, which he kept within sight at his side. Lorraine restricted herself to a sandwich and coffee because she'd be eating her main meal tonight; with considerable gusto, Andy tucked into a deliciously-smelling mountain of haddock and chips. As they ate, a crowd of office workers, young men and women, came in and suddenly the place was filled with noise and laughter. Drinks were bought, meals ordered, jokes told and shop-talk endured. The eruption of sound enabled Andy and Lorraine, the only other customers, to talk without being overheard because the jolly party was concentrated around the bar counter. It was Andy who broached the topic.

'Is there any justification in spending more time on this one? We've come to a dead end every time so what's the point of chasing round and worrying about Darren Mallory?'

Lorraine sighed. 'I'm becoming increasingly convinced there's more to this than we think, Andy. To be honest, in my opinion that business about the attack on Welch just does not ring true. On wasteland, it was said, with a brick. So who called the ambulance for Welch, and how did Darren get arrested for it? Who were the arresting officers? Maybe we should talk to them. Then there's the question of Campion's disappearance which may or may not be related – Hansfield doesn't want us to dig into that one either – and the oddity about Welch using those awful digs and having a laptop. It makes me wonder if he was hiding from somebody and now he's gone too. So where is he? Where did Dylan Welch come from – and who was he, Andy? Is that his real name – it sound like a fictitious one to me, all those Welsh sounds – and what was he really doing on the docks?'

'Welch was probably a nobody, Lorraine, a minor villain

who got his come-uppance from one of his own kind! Hard-up and out of work. Perhaps he stole that laptop? Maybe he lives on what he can steal as he moves around the country under a false name but when he tackled Darren, he met his match.'

'That's a reasonable theory, but think about this. Why were the police called? If Dylan was a villain who was trying to mug Darren, he wouldn't have called the police if his victim retaliated, would he?'

'With his injuries, he'd have been taken to hospital, the hospital authorities would call the police.'

'All right, so who called the ambulance? Who got him to hospital? Was it Darren? That still doesn't explain how Darren got arrested for that assault – if he'd called the ambulance, would he have given his real name? No chance! Who identified Darren as the attacker, Andy? I'd like to know a lot more about that incident, it might be very relevant to our enquiries.'

'You are digging deep, aren't you? You could be creating mysteries where there are none.'

'What bothers me is that there might be something we haven't found – and should have! I'd really like to get to the bottom of all this. And we still don't know how Darren was earning his money, do we?'

'You mustn't forget Darren's a criminal, Lorraine, a clever one, and very enterprising with it. He's a villain, plain and simple, and I think he's gone away for reasons best known to himself. If we can't find him, does it matter? Is it really necessary to spend any more of our time on this?'

'I'd like to keep asking,' she sighed. 'Really, I would. We've got the rest of the day if we want to use it. Are you suggesting we pack up and go home now?'

'If we continue for this afternoon, we need to do something useful, not just wander the streets and finish up in more blind alleys.'

'All right,' she said. 'We could check in the library, they'll have newspaper cuttings of the case, and we could pop into the local Crown Prosecution Service office to look at their file on the Welch attack. And the hospital, we can check to see if Welch really was admitted. Another thing is to see if the name Welch is on the council lists as an occupier of premises anywhere in Great Balderside, we can look at the register of electors for the same reason . . . we can check with the Police National Computer to see if Welch's name is recorded for any reason . . . and Campion . . .'

'You're concentrating on Welch now, are you? Instead of Darren? I don't think that's in our brief, we mustn't let ourselves be sidetracked. Besides, that attack wasn't in our area, remember.'

'Andy, Dylan could have got revenge on Darren so we must find out what happened between them, wherever it was. It could give us the lead we want. Is Dylan known to the police and is he living locally? And were there any witnesses to the attack? Whoever found the injured Welch that night might have seen more than we realize, more than is recorded in the court file.'

'You don't give up, do you!' he smiled. 'All right, Lorraine, I'll go along with you. We've got the whole afternoon to complete those enquiries, so let's split, each with specific tasks to undertake. That'll cut down the time involved, then we'll meet up. Say at four thirty?'

'Right,' she agreed. 'That makes sense.'

'You go to the CPS first,' he said. 'See if you can get access to their court file, check with the hospital – or hospitals – and then go to the central library to see if they've anything in their cuttings collection.'

'Right.'

'I'll go to the council offices to see what kind of records they keep, they'll have a copy of the electoral register too and I'll see if the name Welch is on record. I'll also call in a sectional police station I know in the eastern suburbs – the sergeant-in-charge is a pal of mine from training school days. I'll ask him to check his own records for Welch – and Mallory – and Campion. He might even let me ring Scunthorpe Police as well, to see if they know Welch. And

I'll ask him to check the PNC for all those names while I'm here.'

'So where shall we meet?'

'Inside the library? It's the ideal place to meet up. Four thirty as I said. Does that give you enough time?'

'That's fine,' agreed Lorraine. 'You know where to find the library?'

'I do. And if either of us is late and the staff want to shut for the night, there's a café right opposite. Baker Street Tea Rooms. They do wonderful scones . . . see you there maybe?'

'Fine.' She smiled at yet another display of his knowledge of eating places.

'And keep your eyes open for shadowy figures watching your movements!' Andy chuckled. 'I'll need the car, by the way, to get out to that suburban police station, it's about three miles from the town centre.'

'No problem so long as you don't let my shopping get nicked. I'm better without a car in town.'

'Keep your mobile switched on.'

'And you.'

And so they parted.

Lorraine knew the whereabouts of the Crown Prosecution Service offices; they were in what had once been part of the Town Hall. When she presented herself at reception and explained her purpose, she was told to sit down and wait. She did so as the girl scurried into the depths of the building to find someone of higher authority. After quarter of an hour, there appeared through a door at the end of the corridor a severe-looking man with half-rimmed spectacles perched on the end of his nose. In his fifties, he wore a baggy grey suit, grey pullover beneath it and a dull red tie with the tiniest of knots.

'Blenkinsopp,' he introduced himself. 'Duty solicitor. How can we be of help?'

Lorraine identified herself and presented her warrant card, then explained how she was endeavouring to locate Darren Mallory. She provided the name of Detective Inspector Hansfield as a contact should this fellow want to check the authenticity of her enquiries. She referred to the Welch case and said she'd like to examine the file in the hope it would help her to track Mallory.

'Every avenue we've checked so far has led to a dead end,' she said. 'Mr Hansfield has given us a copy of his file but it offers practically no help with this incident.'

'I doubt if our file will contain much of value to your enquiries.' Blenkinsopp produced a thin smile.

'There may be something which is not contained in the police file. I'm interested in the court case because it occurred to me that Mallory's confrontation with Welch might have some bearing on his disappearance. If possible we'd like to trace Welch because I'd like to get his side of the story.'

'I remember the case,' Blenkinsopp told her with the tiniest hint of another thin smile. 'Welch is not a local man, I'm sure you know that, and he disappeared before the case reached court. He left no forwarding address. There was concern he would not appear to give his evidence, but he rang us to ask for the date of the hearing and turned up as large as life on the day – Friday, 21st June, gave his evidence and then left. We were most relieved, I can assure you. But yes, Miss Cashmore, I will allow you to examine our file. Come with me.'

He led her into an open plan office where a mass of people seemed to be poring over files and staring at VDUs, then found a vacant desk in one corner and invited her to sit down before it. He went off to find the file and even asked if she'd like a cup of tea. She accepted and he said Laura would bring it to her. He vanished through another door, and some three or four minutes later a young woman with long hair and horn-rimmed spectacles appeared. She was carrying a tray bearing a cup of tea, milk, sugar and a plate of digestive biscuits, and had a green file tucked under her arm.

'Miss Cashmore?'

'That's me,' said Lorraine.

'With the compliments of Mr Blenkinsopp. When you

have finished with the file, come and see me. I'm at that desk under the clock. Laura is my name.'

And so Lorraine settled down to read the file which formed the basis of the prosecution's case against Darren Mallory. The style of presentation was familiar to her – Mallory's personal details, his antecedents, his responses when interviewed were shown. There were also details of his response when later charged with causing actual bodily harm rather than the more serious grievous bodily harm, the record of his detention in the cells, along with visits and supervision, and the conditions of his bail. He had been bailed out under section 38 of the Magistrates' Courts Act 1952 to return to the police station pending the charges which in fact were made, and he'd also been later bailed to appear at court. In all cases, he had responded to the conditions. And, she noted, the arresting officer was Detective Sergeant Page who was based at C Division of Greater Balderside Police, based at Sidlesbrough.

Lorraine was interested in his responses to the charge. There was no written statement from Darren – such characters know never to commit themselves to writing – but when he was interviewed, he said, 'The maniac attacked me, he was after my money. I just picked up the brick and hit him, I had to, it was me or him,' and when charged, he had said, 'I was defending myself, that's all. What else could I do?'

When it came to Welch's particulars, he was listed as 'the injured person' (injured meaning victim of crime rather than any physical hurt). His personal details read 'Dylan WELCH', the surname printed in capitals to ensure it was not misspelt as, say, Welsh. Then followed his date and place of birth – 14th January 1976 at Scunthorpe, his occupation – unemployed steelworker, and his then current address which was 19, Shotley Terrace, Sidlesbrough. There was a very brief witness statement:

'I can't say a lot about what happened. I was just walking over that bit of waste ground on my way back to my digs. It was Thursday, 23rd May, about 11 p.m. and it was dark. I was aware of a man in front of me. Without warning, he suddenly turned on me, I saw he had a stone or a brick or something heavy in his hand and he hit me with it over the head. I ducked and tripped as I tried to get away from him but he hit me again and again all around my head and face and mouth . . . I didn't know anything else until I woke up in hospital. I do not know the man, I have never seen him before and did not do anything to provoke him.'

Attached to Welch's papers were details of his injuries and a statement from the doctor who had attended him in Sidlesbrough General Hospital. His cheekbone had been broken and that, along with some missing teeth and other injuries, all to the head, was sufficient to justify a charge of assault occasioning actual bodily harm. Any discrepancy between the two versions of the incident, it was felt, could be resolved only by a court – and Mallory *had* admitted hitting the man, if only in self-defence. Lorraine could now see why Darren had been placed on probation: even though the court – and it was the local magistrates' court – had found him guilty, they had come down slightly in his favour. He had wounded the man, he'd admitted that even if he'd claimed self-defence, but the question of whether the defence was reasonable in the circumstances had led to the court's decision. The verdict was contained in the file, along with details of the penalty and the fact that Mallory had been placed on probation for two years.

The file, she felt, was brief in the extreme, nothing more than the merest of outlines of the case, but when she turned over the pages there was nothing else. She realized, of course, that this was not the police dossier of the incident, it was a file used by the CPS and concerned itself only with the constituents of the offence. It did not explain who had found the injured man, who had called the ambulance or when the police had become involved. In Lorraine's mind, it raised even more questions – for example, how had Mallory been identified in the darkness as the attacker and where had he been caught? And who had caught him? Detective Sergeant Page of C Division was listed as the arresting officer – and so she must talk to him. This file threw up more questions than answers. She thanked Laura for the tea, handed the file back to her and was shown out after asking that her appreciation be conveyed to Mr Blenkinsopp.

In spite of her desire to talk to DS Page as soon as possible, Lorraine decided to visit the library to see how much of the case had been reported. She needed more than the sparse notes of the CPS version of the incident. The library was just around the corner. She decided she need not visit the hospital: the CPS file had confirmed that Dylan was admitted due to that injury and a doctor had confirmed his injuries – that's all the proof she needed.

She entered the library and found an assistant to whom she explained her purpose – looking for a court case in the local paper – and was told that all local newspapers, and a selection of the nationals, were now recorded on microfiche and could be accessed by computer. All she needed was the date of the trial, the venue of the hearing and the name of the accused. Locating the report, which was in the Friday edition of the *Balderside Evening Gazette* under the heading of 'Magistrates' Court Today', Lorraine found that it was very brief.

It said, 'Darren Mallory, aged 24, a self-employed businessman from Dovedale in North Yorkshire, was this morning found guilty of causing actual bodily harm to Dylan Welch, 27, of Shotley Terrace, Sidlesbrough. The court was told how Welch was walking across wasteland at the rear of Shawcross Road, Port Haverton at 11 p.m. on Thursday, May 23rd, when he was struck by Mallory. Mallory had used a stone or brick as a weapon and Welch suffered a broken cheekbone and other facial injuries. Mallory claimed he had acted in self-defence although no weapon was found on Welch. The two men claimed not to know each other and no motive was alleged. The court found Mallory guilty and he was placed on probation for two years.'

And that was all. No mention of any police officer giving evidence, nor details of how the attack had become known to the police. Lorraine made a photocopy of the item, thanked the assistant and left. It had not taken anywhere as long as she had anticipated and she had about an hour and half to while away before reuniting with Andy Williams.

That was enough time to see if Detective Sergeant Page was on duty in C Division.

Chapter Seven

Not knowing the location of Greater Balderside's C Division offices, Lorraine decided to visit force headquarters in Perthland Lane, close to Sidlesbrough town centre. There was a distinct likelihood that the C Division building would be nearby, C probably referring to Central. Her anticipation was correct. The receptionist referred her to a block of modern offices in the adjoining street and soon she found herself approaching yet another reception desk.

As she entered the spacious foyer, she saw that a woman was standing at the reception desk, which was staffed by a uniformed constable. As Lorraine approached, she heard the woman begin to describe her handbag, alleging it had been stolen while she was sitting on a park bench eating her sandwiches; while the desk constable dealt with her, Lorraine wandered across to a huge noticeboard to while away a few minutes. It occupied a large part of the wall on the left of the main doorway and, as she studied the posters, she realized one section was set aside for rewards. On the right of the noticeboard were posters about force whist drives, Colorado beetle, recruiting requirements, foot and mouth disease restrictions in the rural areas, rules governing headlights on cars, braking regulations and the rubber depths on car tyres, and one or two descriptions of persons wanted for local crimes.

The other section, on the left half of the board, comprised announcements of rewards for information leading either to the arrest of criminals or the recovery of stolen property.

There was a £50 reward for the recovery of a lost kitten, a £500 reward for information leading to the arrest of a man who had grabbed jewellery from a shop in the centre of Sidlesbrough, a £20 reward for the recovery of a statue stolen from a suburban garden and a whopping £50,000 reward from a millionaire whose wife had been raped in Newcastle-on-Tyne. He would pay for information leading to the arrest and conviction of the suspect. But the most amazing was a reward, offered by a consortium of art dealers throughout Europe, of £200,000 for the recovery of a *Madonna and Child*, a painting by Giovanni Bellini, which had been stolen during a raid on the car carrying it to an exhibition in Rome. There was no condition that the thief or thieves should be convicted – recovery of the painting was the major concern. That was the most impressive of the adverts, and an international one, while the others were all very localized.

Then the woman thanked the constable and left and so Lorraine approached the reception desk. The constable responded, coming towards her with a welcoming smile – it wasn't often such a stunning young woman graced the enquiry counter.

'Yes miss?' He was a senior constable, somewhere in his fifties with a mop of grey hair growing rather too long and more than a hint of five o'clock shadow around his jowls. With no headgear and a uniform that needed cleaning, he looked crumpled enough to have experienced the entire range of incidents that might beset a town-patrolling bobby during a thirty-year career. Now his experience and detailed local knowledge were being put to good use at the enquiry counter.

He said, 'I trust you're not hoping to win one of those rewards. That's the most popular noticeboard in Sidlesbrough, we get all the villains coming to look at it. Pensioners too, hoping to find stray cats, people thinking it's easier than winning the lottery. The villains come to see if they're on the wanted list, or mebbe they hope to win one of those rewards. Anyway, what can I do for you?'

'I can't claim any of them,' she said ruefully. 'I'm a police officer.'

She approached the counter, produced her warrant card and said, 'Detective Constable Cashmore, from North Yorkshire. I'd like to talk to Detective Sergeant Page if he's in.'

'Ah! Is he expecting you?'

'No,' she said, adding for effect, 'But I've just come from Detective Inspectors Hansfield and Cartland.'

'I'll see what I can do.'

He ambled across to his tiny office and switchboard, pressed an intercom and said, 'There's a Detective Constable Cashmore in reception, asking for Keith Page.' There was a pause and he said, 'Sorry, no, I've no idea what it's about, but she's just come from DIs Hansfield and Cartland.' Another pause, then 'Right,' and he replaced the handset. He returned to the counter and said, 'They're sending someone down to take you up to his office. Third floor.'

She turned away from the counter to avoid small talk and once more studied the array of notices placed for the edification of the public, wondering how many rewards were eventually claimed. Then a woman's voice said, 'DC Cashmore?'

'Yes.' Lorraine turned to find a sturdy twenty-something redhead before her.

'DC Grieves. Judy,' said the other. 'DS Page can see you, he's in his office, tidying his desk. Lucky you caught him. He's on leave from tomorrow, he's going to the Algarve for ten days.'

'I'm Lorraine,' and she followed her guide. They took the lift to the third floor where Judy escorted her along a maze of corridors and into the Divisional CID's general office. It was a huge room full of rows of paper-filled desks, one or two bearing flickering VDUs but most lacking occupants as the detectives were either out in the town or not working this shift. Judy led the way between them and tapped on a partially open door. A voice called 'Come' and then she was inside. A well-built tough-looking detective in jeans and a T-shirt rose to greet her; in his mid-thirties he looked like a rugger player or even a wrestler, an appearance supported by his shaven head and battered nose.

His desk was piled high with papers, most of which seemed to be in his out-tray. He extended his hand. 'DC Cashmore? Nice to meet you. So what brings the county constabulary into our mean and tough city streets?' He indicated a chair and she settled upon it as he called after the departing girl, 'Wouldn't say no to a cuppa and a biscuit, Judy. For two.'

Lorraine noticed he did not ask if she wanted tea or coffee, but tea would be very acceptable. Clearly, he was desperately trying to shift a mountain of paperwork before leaving for his holiday but he did not react antagonistically, so she said, 'I don't want to take up too much of your time, it's good of you to see me.'

'You wouldn't be here if it wasn't necessary.' He flashed a warm smile.

'It's about Darren Mallory,' she said. 'And Dylan Welch.' She spoke their names first so that his memory of events might be revived. 'Darren Mallory lives on our patch, at Dovedale, I'm sure you know all about him. He's been reported missing and we've been asked to look for him. It's a joint operation with your force. I've talked to your DIs Hansfield and Cartland about it.'

'Right,' he said, 'I'm aware of the concern for him, blokes like him don't just vanish without reason. So why come to me and what's all this about Welch? So far as we're concerned, that incident is closed. It finished in court.'

Lorraine told him of her enquiries to date – and her lack of results – then broached the incident with Welch.

'I'm concerned that Welch might, in some obscure way, be responsible for Darren's disappearance.'

'I doubt it,' he said. 'They were just a couple of toe-rags sorting out some personal dispute, that's how we saw it.'

'I understand they didn't know each other.'

'That's what they said. Can we believe them? Mallory doesn't know the meaning of truth. Can we believe anything either of them say? Mallory claimed it was self-defence, but Welch wasn't carrying any kind of weapon, not even a pocket knife. Neither would explain things so we presented what little evidence we had and let the CPS decide whether to test it in court. Which, as it happens, they did. Welch got quite a hammering from Mallory, I suspect you know that.'

'I know he was knocked about a bit. It occurred on wasteland, behind Shawcross Road,' she said. 'In darkness. Where is that?'

'Down near the docks in Port Haverton,' he said, 'a couple of streets away from where Welch was living in digs. The council knocked down two derelict streets, for redevelopment, they said. That was years ago, but nothing's happened to the site. It's a big open space full of junk and burnt-out cars, prostitutes use it. And druggies. If you go there, look out for needles lying about, always wear thick-soled shoes!'

'I'll remember that!' she smiled.

'It's not exactly a tourist attraction,' he laughed. 'I think Welch was heading for his digs after a pub or club or something, and Mallory happened to be there. I've no idea why he should be there, he never said. We've got to wonder whether Welch was short of cash and decided to rob Mallory . . . or it could be the other way round. Mallory might have had the same idea . . . who knows? It's one villain's word against another. Mallory was lucky to get probation.'

'I think it's a very odd sort of incident, Sergeant . . .'

'I agree, but we're not bothered about the motive or the reason, we got a conviction – and better still, we got one of the Mallorys convicted. That's not a very common event around here, I can tell you.'

'You were the arresting officer.' She now came to her point.

'I signed the charge sheet, yes,' and this time he frowned.

'I just wondered how you managed to catch him.'

'I don't follow?' He frowned again, now studying this persistent young woman.

'Well . . .' She took a deep breath, wondering if perhaps she was being silly, or if she'd missed some valid point in her researches, or even whether she should not be asking such a question, a question that might be interpreted as a criticism. 'It was 11 p.m., it would be dark, it was a patch of wasteland and neither of the two men reckoned they knew one another. If Welch had attacked or insulted Mallory for any reason, Mallory would have responded – as he did in fact – but I think the police would not have been aware of that.'

She paused a moment to allow the significance of her observation to register, then continued, 'On the other hand, if Mallory had decided to rob Welch and thrash him with a brick – with neither of them knowing the other – then surely Mallory would have made good his escape. He'd never have been identified as the attacker, would he? Welch did not know him. So, you see, I am wondering how you managed to catch Mallory. Who identified him as the assailant? Who rang for the ambulance, who got Welch taken to hospital? How did the incident come to the notice of the police?'

'We were there, at the scene,' said Page in a matter-of-fact manner.

'We?' queried Lorraine.

'Detective Inspector Cartland and myself, we were keeping observations, we were established in a plain white van on that waste ground, watching. It was another operation, quite unconnected with Mallory or Welch. We didn't see the actual attack due to the darkness, but we heard a commotion, put up our headlights and saw Mallory making off. Welch was lying on the ground.'

'You recognized him? Mallory, I mean.'

'I did. I know him well enough to identify him even in those conditions, and we radioed for the ambulance. One of our support units, on the same job, picked up Mallory, only yards away. He didn't get far, not with a full-scale police operation going on! Welch was unconscious, he needed treatment. That's it, Miss Cashmore. It was one of those coincidences – unlucky for Mallory, lucky for us.'

'You just happened to be in the right place at the right time?'

'We did. It happens from time to time. We took full advantage of it.'

'And the other operation? Was it successful?'

'No, we had to abort it.'

'Because of Mallory?'

'I don't know, the activity might have persuaded our other targets not to come on to that piece of land. I can tell you about it, there's nothing secret now it's been abandoned. We'd heard there might be a drugs exchange or big delivery on that site, something coming off a ship, so we set up a reception party for the villains. Mallory and Welch unknowingly brought it to a premature conclusion, though. We couldn't ignore the injuries to Welch – we thought he was in a very bad way, there was a lot of blood about and after all, our job is to protect life and property. Another factor was that Welch wasn't known to us, he's got no convictions, no form of any kind. He's no part of our criminal set-up, although I must admit we did think he was a villain in disguise. He wouldn't say anything to us, we tried after he came out of hospital, but got nowhere.'

'He was hiding his true identity, you think?'

'I'm convinced he was up to no good, otherwise why get digs in Shotley Terrace of all places? I reckon he was using a false name for whatever reason he was on our patch, but the name he used isn't in any criminal records or on the wanted or suspected index.'

'There was no hint of a reason for their battle?'

'Nothing. We thought they were sorting out some personal dispute. Maybe we were wrong, although if our original information was correct, either of them might have been there to pick up the drugs . . . we don't know. There is just a suggestion they had spotted us waiting and staged the fight to make it look as if they were not our targets. That's always an option, savage though it was. All

I can say is that once we took them away, nobody else came along – we did leave an observer behind, nicely concealed.'

'I understand the Mallory Mob don't do drugs?'

'That's the order from the old man, but he's been shunted into a siding deep in your moorland paradise, hasn't he? Safely away from it all. And while the cat's away . . .'

'You're saying the Mallorys might be into drugs now?'

'It's something we're keeping an eye on, that's all I can say at this point.'

'Thanks. So, Welch might not be as innocent as we think. You didn't get his fingerprints or a DNA sample?'

'He wasn't under arrest, there are rules about such things.'

'And there are ways around the rules,' she smiled.

He laughed. 'We did get a sample of Welch's DNA from the residue left on the brick, bits of his face in fact. There's no match in our data bank. I know that doesn't mean a lot, but it does mean he has not passed through police hands since DNA become part of our crime-fighting armoury – the late eighties or thereabouts. And it's not led us to a positive identification of him.'

'And you're certain Welch has nothing to do with Darren's disappearance?'

'Not a hundred per cent certain, I must be honest with you. Can anyone be one hundred per cent certain? My gut feeling is that I don't think he's got anything at all to do with Darren Mallory. They didn't know each other, so they said, and I think that's true. We've been keeping tabs on Darren for some time and he's never been seen with Welch. I'm sure they're not involved in any kind of joint enterprise. So far as we are concerned, Miss Cashmore, the case is now closed.'

'There was no evidence at the scene?'

'We didn't find any drugs they might have dropped, or anything else except the bloodstained brick. Darren dropped it when he ran, he got rid of the evidence, or so he thought. That kind of thing happens all the time, the

Mallorys are noted for sorting out those who cross them, remember, and most of the time we never know why or when. This time we did – and I repeat it was by sheer chance.'

'Do you know what action your force is taking to trace Darren?'

'I'm not fully informed but I understand it is the usual Missing From Home routine. It's fairly low key, except we've got DS Probert and DC Baxter looking into it, asking around town, just as you are looking into it in your force area. And our uniform branch has him listed. We are putting on a bit of show, just in case he's found dumped somewhere with his head blown off.'

'There's no big search going on then? Turning houses and flats over? Digging up gardens, that sort of thing.'

'No, nothing like that. We've no reason to think he's been eliminated, his family won't talk, we've asked them, all of them. Nothing. If they thought he'd been killed, I reckon they might co-operate, just a little. As things are, they say it's nothing to do with the police; if Darren wants to go off somewhere then it's down to him, that's their attitude. It would be a waste of time talking to them. And we've not found his car. He could have gone on tour or something, we have circulated details of him and his car, nationwide on the PNC.'

Lorraine, not wishing to delay Page in his desk-clearing operation, nonetheless could not miss this opportunity to ask about the Mallorys' criminal activities. She hoped Page might know more than she'd been told. Keeping it brief, he told her of their protection rackets, raids on building societies and attacks on places which continued to have cash on the premises, but he did say that with modern surveillance techniques many of their activities had been curtailed. Most of their protection rackets involved shops and business premises which were themselves crooked or operating illegally and so the police tended not to involve themselves with those.

'Let dog eat dog,' said Page. He confirmed that Darren was not currently involved with his brothers in their operations, and also confirmed that he was now operating alone, apparently making good money but from sources unknown to the police. He added that it was a money-making system which appeared to have attracted the interest of the local informants. They seemed more than a little interested.

'There is a lot of minor crime in the town and its environs,' agreed Page. 'Usual stuff – burglaries, car crime, kids snatching mobile phones or vandalizing property, confidence tricksters preying on old folks and so on. There's a good living to be made from crime. The docks generate a lot of stuff too – ourselves and Customs and Excise are always alert to smuggling operations, ranging from refugees hiding in lorries to stolen art works being ferried through, not to mention drugs, stolen cars and even exotic animals and birds. We tend to leave much of that aspect to Customs officers, they're very efficient, although we are involved from time to time. Special operations, undercover work and so on. I must admit our detection rate has dropped – our paid informants aren't as good as they used to be and we need more detectives at the so-called sharp end, that's for sure – but I must stress that neither Darren working alone nor the Mallory Mob working as a team are of major concern to us at this moment.'

'Are you sure the Mallorys won't talk about Darren?' Lorraine asked.

'Not a chance, it would be a complete waste of time. They don't talk to us, we rely on mutual contacts, informants and so on, to discover what they're up to.'

'And Joseph Campion? He's one of your local criminals, I'm told, and he's vanished as well.'

'Don't worry your head about Campion, he's never at home for long. He's too fond of spending his money abroad – and he's got plenty, all the proceeds of crime. He's into high living, fast cars and expensive boats . . . We've a general alert out for him which operates all the time, chiefly to find out what he's up to at any given moment. He took off in something of a rush in January, probably a cover plan of some kind because he knows we're interested in him. I think he's overseas, living the life of Riley! He's got access to false passports and his money will buy whatever he wants. He's posted as missing because we like to know where he is and what he's up to, routine and low-key enquiries can sometimes produce worthwhile results.'

And so, having gleaned a little further information about Darren and Welch, and Campion too, Lorraine thanked Detective Sergeant Page for his help and left. But even before she had left the building, Page pressed his intercom and called Detective Inspector Cartland.

The library was closing as Lorraine made her way towards its front door, so she crossed the street and went into the café opposite; Andy Williams had not arrived and she ordered herself a pot of tea, a scone and strawberry jam, and a slice of fruit cake, then settled at a corner table to await him. To occupy herself, she began to make up her official pocket note, writing down details of the meetings and events which had recently transpired. Williams arrived half an hour later.

'Sorry about that,' he said. 'Traffic's heavy, it's rush hour and I wanted to get my business finished anyway. Have I time for a cuppa? I'm hungry and I'm parched!'

He ordered himself a pot along with a ham sandwich, and Lorraine opted for a fruit juice to accompany him. They were tucked neatly into a far corner of the café. Music played through loudspeakers and the coffee machine seemed to be constantly hissing, humming and whining, so they could speak to each other without being overheard.

'How did it go?' Lorraine asked as he settled at the table and arranged his food trophies to gain maximum enjoyment from them.

'Fine.' He sighed heavily. 'Fine but unproductive. The council offices have hundreds of families called Welch on their books, it's a local surname. Council tax records and so on. And Welsh too, with an "s"; dozens of them. The staff were able to access their computer, but there is no adult called Dylan Welch or Welsh on their records.'

'At least we've established that!' she smiled.

'We ran a check on the electoral register too – same result. Welch and Welsh by the truckload.'

'But no Dylan?'

'Right. So if our friend was a relation of any of those locals, you'd think he would try to get digs with them, especially if he was from Scunthorpe, broke and looking for work. He wouldn't pay to doss down in one of our grottiest areas.'

'But if he wasn't a relation, and if he's using a false name, it's a good name to use. If you give a name which is local to the area, people think you've local links.'

'Point taken. He could have been using a false name – there's nothing to show he was, though, and nothing to show he wasn't. The outcome of all this is that my visit to the council office and my search of local records suggest he does not live in this area. Like the man said, he was here looking for work – a perfectly acceptable reason.'

'Another dead end though?' sighed Lorraine.

'We seem to be good at this, getting stuck in dead ends. Anyway, off I went to see my pal in his out-station in the leafy suburbs but he couldn't help a lot, except to confirm what we knew about the Mallory Mob. It seems the local Crime Intelligence Unit circulates the occasional bumph about their activities but the general attitude is that local CID and uniform branch leave the Mallorys well alone. The Mallory Mob is under constant surveillance on a force-wide basis. The local Crime Intelligence Unit and the National Crime Squad have been showing interest recently too, they tend to act when they've got enough evidence to nail their suspects – not that anyone's very good at nailing the Mallorys.'

'Except accidentally!'

'Eh?'

'I'll explain in a minute.'

'Right. But their attention to the Mallorys does have a spin-off – sometimes, they recover stolen goods. Tip-offs, often prompted by rewards, have led the police to stolen property which has been hidden in lock-up garages and old warehouses. He did wonder if the Mallorys themselves were stealing the goods and providing the tip-offs to claim the rewards for recovery of the property. Or it might have been the Clarksons doing the same thing. Some of their warehouses have been found and raided too. But whatever the background, somebody with inside information has been tipping off the authorities and claiming the rewards.'

'Did you access the PNC while you were with your pal?'

'We did. Darren's picture is on the Missing From Home file, along with a good physical description. They've used that photo we've got. His name's on various other lists too, like Suspected and Wanted just in case he gets arrested, and he's also on the motoring files. If any plod anywhere in the UK stops and interrogates Darren, we'll know about it.'

'I wish you wouldn't call uniformed officers plods!' she chided him.

'They love it!' he laughed. 'The image of PC Plod . . . wonderful stuff!'

'And Campion? Did you check him?'

'He's on the Suspected and Wanted lists, the local police are always interested in what he's up to, but he's not been seen for six months or so. The general consensus is that he's overseas on a false passport, probably on some kind of stolen car deal. His name doesn't occur on any flight lists or seaports.'

'So what else did you learn about the criminals of Sidlesbrough and district?' she asked.

'My pal keeps his ear to the ground, as they say, he knows what going on, he can smell corruption and graft, even among his own kind . . . and he reckons there's some kind of big operation afoot in Sidlesbrough and Port Haverton. A detective superintendent has been suspended from duty, the press hasn't picked that up yet, and she's

currently under investigation, both by the Police Com-
paints Authority and the CID.'

'She?'

'That's what I was told.'

'Is it something we should know about? For our
enquiries?'

'I don't know enough about it to answer that, but
officers from a Midlands force have been drafted in to
make the enquiries. It's all very hush-hush, Lorraine . . .
but the dirt is being stirred up and I don't know what the
suspended officer is supposed to have done. Personally,
I can't see how a petty villain like Darren can be linked to
a police disciplinary investigation, but nothing would surprise me.'

'I wonder if our boss knows about that?' She was speaking her thoughts. 'If it had been linked, you'd think Mark
would have warned us before sending us here.'

'There are times when a need-to-know policy is necessary, Lorraine, and officers at the bottom of the ladder, like
us, aren't often included in that. You mustn't expect Mark
Pemberton to tell you everything just because you live
together.'

'I don't, I respect his judgement,' she assured him. 'Now,
another thing. The Scunthorpe connection. Did you manage to contact anyone there about Welch?'

'I did. They ran a check of all their computer records –
driving offences, criminal records, suspected and wanted
lists, missing persons. Nothing. Dylan Welch has never
come to the notice of Scunthorpe Police, and his name
isn't on their electoral register either. It makes me even
more certain that he was using a false name. And that makes
me wonder why he spent a lot of time hanging around the
docks. What on earth was he up to, Lorraine?'

'I wish I knew,' she sighed, and then told him about her
day, especially her talk with DS Keith Page.

'I'm beginning to think you're right about something
going on behind the scenes, Lorraine,' he said after listening
intently to her account. 'It's all adding up to something
peculiar. I think we might be part of it, unwittingly and

unknowingly, a small cog in a very big wheel of some kind. Our task could be to bring Darren's name to the fore in our locality for reasons we don't know. So what do we do next? Everywhere we turn, we meet a dead end, so do we pack it all in by saying we've exhausted our enquiries, or do we dig deeper? I wonder what's really expected of us?'

'If we start digging too deep, especially in Greater Balderside, surely someone – like my Mark Pemberton – will order us to stop. On the other hand, he did tell us to give this job our best shot, if only until Saturday!'

'As we always do!' he grinned.

'I think we must continue to dig,' she stressed. 'Tomorrow, I think we should analyse everything we've learned so far – which isn't much – and then decide where we should concentrate our next enquiries. Now, though, it's home time.'

'Mark, I need to talk about Darren Mallory.'

'Not at home, darling!' He smiled as he poured a large sherry for Lorraine. 'You know the rules of the house!'

'I know, but we do make exceptions sometimes, and this is one occasion I'd like to break the rules.' She accepted the glass and settled on the settee, curled up her feet and tucked them beneath her, then relaxed with an audible sigh.

'All right, I'm as curious as you about your day. The meal will be another twenty minutes or so. I'll allow you those twenty minutes to state your case, then we close the shop! Do I detect you've had a hard day?' he asked, settling in an easy chair with a glass of malt whisky.

'Not hard. Frustrating. Lots of questions with no answers, lots of dead ends . . .'

'So you've learned nothing about Darren, and haven't found him?'

'No one knows anything, he's vanished like a puff of smoke. Andy and I have spent all day in Sidlesbrough and Port Haverton, we've even spoken to the CID, local Crime Intelligence and local coppers – I went to the CPS as well and saw the file about his assault case . . . and the result? Nothing.'

'So why do you want to talk to me about nothing?' he chuckled.

'It's difficult to know where to start – I get the impression something's going on behind the scenes, Mark, some kind of big enquiry or major operation. I think the local police aren't telling us everything, I think there's something not straight about that assault case . . . but I've no evidence to support my feelings, just my intuition . . . along with the fact that two other men are also missing.'

'Surely, though, if every avenue you try comes to a dead end, then you should accept it? If Greater Balderside has a big operation afoot, it's nothing to do with us and they won't want us poking our noses in. Maybe Darren has simply moved on, gone away for a while, changed his domestic routine or something, maybe that's all they want confirmed?'

'But two other men are missing as well, Mark. I think the whole thing stinks!'

'All right, tell me about them.'

She tried to condense her day's findings and concerns into a short but cohesive account and he listened carefully, sipping at his malt and not interrupting. Then she said, 'I've gone over this time and time again, always with no solution, no answers. I want to know where he got his money from, where Dylan Welch came from and who he really was – and why he really came to Port Haverton to lodge. Then there's Joseph Campion who vanished before Darren and who's known as a serious rogue, a professional criminal who's almost certainly overseas on a false passport – if he's not dead. He seems blessed with pots of money – and on top of everything else, Mark, I heard that a detective superintendent has been suspended on Greater Balderside, a disciplinary enquiry or worse, with an outside force carrying out an investigation.'

'You have been busy! So why are you bending my ear? Are you saying there's no point in carrying on that enquiry, or are you asking for more time to dig deeper?'

113

'At first, Andy was all for bringing it to a close, but now he's keen to continue. We would like to dig deeper, Mark, and I do wonder if Darren's been disposed of . . . murdered, by Welch even, that's my real concern. Or even Campion, he could be dead as well. People don't just disappear.'

'All right, I gave you until Saturday, didn't I? It's only Wednesday, you've a few days left. So keep going, Lorraine, keep going and keep digging – but don't get too involved with events in Greater Balderside. Campion's not our concern and they won't want you prying too closely into their responsibilities – so keep your distance, concentrate on our side of the border!'

'Mark, I appreciate there are things you must know about, and which you can't mention to me, but do you know what's happening on Greater Balderside? When they asked you to treat Darren as Missing From Home, did they tell you everything?'

'You know as much as me,' he told her seriously. 'More now, I'd say. All I can advise you is to keep asking your questions.'

'I think you do know something . . .'

'Just keep asking questions, Lorraine – with a view to tracing Darren.'

'You can be sure I'll do that!' she promised.

She chattered on a little more, going over and over the day's frustrations and then a timer sounded in the kitchen.

'Quiz time over!' he said, getting to his feet. 'I'll just go and check the oven . . .'

Before following him, she asked, 'Mark, you would never deceive me, would you?'

'Deceive you?' He halted in his tracks. 'Good God, no! Why do you ask?'

'I just wondered . . .'

Puzzled by her question, he disappeared into the kitchen as Lorraine realized that the future of her enquiries into Darren's disappearance now rested firmly on her own slender shoulders.

Chapter Eight

Lorraine did not sleep that night. In spite of the delicious meal and the lovingly relaxed evening with Mark, she found herself going over and over events of the last three days, asking herself questions, wondering what small facet she'd missed or overlooked, worrying whether Darren Mallory was in dreadful trouble of some kind and whether or how Campion and Welch were really linked to him. There was also the question of how drugs might be connected and whether the suspension of a senior police officer had any bearing on all this. Were all those facts associated or had she unnecessarily tried to link them through her own enquiries? Certainly, it was her dogged pursuit of answers which had highlighted those disparate strands but that did not prove the strands were connected. Perhaps only some were linked? If so, which? Or was she just being silly and taking all this too seriously? After all, as Mark had stated right from the outset, an adult man who leaves home voluntarily is of no official concern to the police . . .

The relentless activity deep inside her brain made her toss and turn in bed and even though she tried to relax and remain still for fear of waking Mark, she knew she must be disturbing him even if he appeared to be slumbering so peacefully at her side. The dim light from numerals on the bedside clock recorded the slow passing of the dark night hours; she watched it register one o'clock, then two, and when it was approaching three she crept out of bed, hoping she had not disturbed him, put on her slippers and dressing grown, then padded downstairs to make a cup of hot milk.

Soon she was sitting at the kitchen table with her dressing gown drawn tight around her slender body and the mug of steaming milk before her. She'd found a paperback and tried to read as she sipped at the hot drink, hoping it might distract her brain from its continuing reminders of Darren Mallory and all those strands she was unable to bring together satisfactorily. It was never easy, she knew, having any kind of enquiry which spanned force boundaries, let alone a minor one. In minor cases, no one was really interested and inevitably there were procedural difficulties and internal force politics to consider – not to mention the sensitivities and ambitions of members of the other force. Is that was she was facing on this occasion? Was her lack of success due to something as basic as local prejudice, or was it something more sinister and infinitely more complicated?

She realized she was not concentrating upon her book and she'd even let the milk grow cold as she was trying to unravel matters which always seemed to result in a dead end or a less-than-satisfactory conclusion. Suddenly Mark's voice said, 'That's where you are! Are you all right?'

In his dressing gown, he entered the kitchen and put an arm around her shoulders.

'I couldn't sleep.' She wanted to make it all sound so unimportant and ordinary. 'I thought I'd read a bit. I'm sorry if I disturbed you.'

'Is something bothering you?' She guessed he would be referring to her cancer scare. 'You've been down here ages!'

Her brush with cancer bothered him, she knew that, and there were times he could be excessively protective.

'It's not what you think. It just that I can't switch my brain off!' She tried to make light of it. 'It's a bit like a record that's stuck . . . going over and over the same thing, on and on with no way of stopping it.'

'Work, you mean?' He settled on a chair at the other side

of the table, with a look of horror on his face. 'I've never known you worry about the job before!'

'I'm not worrying, Mark, I'm thinking . . . I've been going over and over the Darren Mallory thing and can't find answers . . .'

'Damn it all, Lorraine, there's no need to lose sleep over it, it's just a Missing From Home, we're not looking for a serial murderer or a terrorist. Neither our bosses nor the press are hassling us for results, so there's no need to let it get to you, it's not worth it. All we have to do is make a few local enquiries and hopefully conclude that Mallory left the district for reasons best known to himself, then we can let it rest there. That's what Greater Balderside Police expect from us, they're the ones tying up the loose ends.'

'I can't leave it at that, Mark. I *know* something's not right, that business with the brick just doesn't ring true, more so when the police were watching that very location. They just happened to be there at the right time, on the spot and able to call an ambulance and arrest Darren. On top of that, his victim doesn't seem known to anyone, so who was he – really, I mean? And why did Darren attack him? It stinks, Mark, all of it, it really does.'

'It's not our concern, Lorraine, that attack wasn't in our area. Our brief was to make routine enquiries into a report that Darren was missing from home – nothing more. The only reason we're involved is because his home address is on our patch. We can't let ourselves be drawn into matters involving another force.'

'I can't help wondering –'

'Lorraine, don't! Now, speaking as your boss, I can't let you get involved in matters beyond our boundaries, it would be wrong of me to let you do that.'

'Sorry,' she said. 'Maybe I've let this develop into something bigger than I wanted, maybe Andy was right, maybe there is nothing for us to discover . . . all those dead ends . . .'

'Let's not worry about it now. Come back to bed, you'll get cold down here.'

117

'I'm sorry if I woke you . . .' She rose from the chair and he kept his arm around her shoulders as he led her back to the bedroom. Only when she was lying next to Mark beneath the covers did she realize how cold she had become and so she turned towards him, extended her arms and wrapped them around his body. He responded with his powerful arms about her until they were curled together like two harvest mice sleeping in a love nest, and then he began to gently caress her, from the back of her neck down the full length of her slender body . . .

'You slept well?' he asked at breakfast. 'After your early morning potter?'

She nodded. 'It was lovely, short but sweet. I never heard a thing till you got out of bed.'

'Well, try not to let this investigation worry you – but no more about that now, it's out of bounds. Come and see me in my office for coffee, and bring Andy Williams.'

During her solo drive to work, Lorraine found herself pondering once again. Without some new initiative, it seemed their lines of enquiry would dry up entirely and they'd learn nothing more about Darren Mallory. Switching off the chattering radio, she mentally examined what they'd done to date, going over and over it all yet again. And then she wondered if the press might help? Suppose she engineered a news release to the effect that Darren had vanished? They might publish his photograph and create an interest in him and his fate. That was something to discuss with Mark over coffee – a splash of publicity in the local papers might draw a response either from him or someone else. And she hadn't discussed the case at length with Paul Larkin. In his initial chat with Greater Balderside Crime Intelligence Unit he might have been provided with snippets he'd not passed on, trivia perhaps but maybe containing some gem of information having an importance of its own – and, she realized, she'd not really examined the knowledge possessed by Detective Sergeant Probert and Detective Constable Baxter. And she hadn't seen that patch of waste ground where Darren had attacked Dylan Welch either, nor had she covered the route supposedly taken by Darren upon heading home after leaving the Blue Raven. So there *were* new pastures to examine . . . and by the time she arrived at work, she was smiling.

She was still smiling when she arrived at her desk, at which Andy Williams remarked, 'You look happy! Won the lottery or something?'

'No, I'm just optimistic about work.' She eased her chair from the desk and settled down. 'How about you, Sergeant?' She addressed him formally when in the office.

'So so,' and he shrugged his shoulders. 'I've been thinking about this case and I've come to the conclusion we needn't consider further excursions into Greater Balderside, they get us nowhere. We should concentrate on our end of things. Dovedale and district. After all, that was our brief.'

'My thoughts too,' she smiled. 'We've today and tomorrow, then Saturday if necessary. Now, what do you think about publicity? Should we get the newspapers to highlight Darren's absence?'

'Oh no.' He shook his head vigorously. 'He might have just gone on holiday, we'd look right Charlies if we made it seem he was on the run from something. The press wouldn't like it either, we can't dress this incident up as something it isn't. No, Lorraine, I'm all for making use of the media, but this isn't one of those occasions.'

She accepted that decision, then mentioned DS Probert and DC Baxter from Sidlesbrough, saying she thought it might be a good idea to talk to them once more.

'I know you think it's pointless spending more time and energy in Greater Balderside, but I do think we need to dig a bit deeper into their knowledge of Darren, especially as we've learned a little extra. We know which avenues to explore and I wondered if we might meet them somewhere, say half-way like we did earlier?'

Lorraine was thinking of the attack on Welch as Andy said, 'Well, I suppose we could do that if they're agreeable. They won't want us taking up too much of their time

119

though, and I don't want everyone to think we're spending too much time out of our own patch.'

'I was thinking of that attack, Sergeant, on the waste ground in Port Haverton. I'd like to have a look at that patch of land, and I also think we should cover the whole route Darren would have taken on his way home from the Blue Raven.'

She found a map in the desk drawers and took it across to her sergeant, showing how there was only one direct route from the western outskirts of Sidlesbrough into Dovedale. It was a B class road for the first twelve miles, and where it crossed the National Park boundary it forked, the left-hand fork leading all the way into Dovedale.

'Fair enough, that makes sense,' he capitulated. 'We can drive that route, preferably in daylight, and while we're doing that, we can also have a look at that patch of waste ground, I can't see that will create inter-force problems. We'll present these ideas to the boss then set sail!'

Over coffee and with Paul Larkin in attendance, Pemberton listened and agreed with their decisions. They then took the opportunity to quiz Larkin in front of Pemberton, wanting to know if he was in possession of any facts unknown to them. But he had nothing extra to offer – he assured them he'd presented all his knowledge at the outset.

They left Pemberton's office with a promise to keep him informed, but before embarking on their enquiries, Andy rang Greater Balderside to try and arrange a rendezvous with Probert and Baxter. He knew that if he wished to catch them, he should ring now – in another half-hour they'd have completed their own morning conferences and would then leave to become lost in their work, somewhere in the vast industrial complex which was the modern Greater Balderside. He managed to catch Probert and explain the situation, and fixed a meeting for twelve noon on the waste ground behind Shawcross Road.

Lorraine found herself nominated as driver and opted for the coastal route between Rainesbury and Greater Balderside. An hour later they were driving through the docklands of Port Haverton; after searching the gloomy run-down streets, Lorraine soon found Shawcross Road and the gap which led from it into the area of wasteland near Shotley Terrace. This had once contained streets of back-to-back houses, a community of homes, but was now a huge expanse of undulating earth and rubbish, dotted with burnt-out cars, old refrigerators, parts of bikes, old mattresses, beds and wardrobes, bricks by the tonne and discarded syringe needles glinting in the morning sunshine. There were condoms too, lots of them. Used. Urban dereliction at its worst, a no-go area for decent people, she felt, as she remembered the advice about wearing shoes with thick soles. At night, this would be the haunt of sad people, the underclass of the area, but at this time of day, it was deserted.

Lorraine parked on a piece of tarmac which had once been a road into this area and they emerged from their vehicle to gaze in dismay at the miserable scene. Minutes later, they spotted another anonymous car come to a halt at the far side of the wasteland; two men emerged, one of them waved and they recognized Probert. He then drove around the edge of the wasteland through occupied streets and eventually came to rest beside Lorraine's car.

'Not as pretty as the moors in your part of the world,' greeted Ted Probert as he approached with Baxter not far behind. Baxter, the silent one of the pair, had lingered to lock the car doors. 'But this is all some people have, this is their only bit of open space, their recreation ground. Sad, eh?'

'Dreadful,' snapped Andy. 'Unbelievably dreadful, give me the countryside any day. Anyway, Ted, it was good of you to meet us again. And Dave.'

'It makes a break from our daily grind!' laughed Probert. 'So, it might seem a daft question, but why do you want to come all this way just to look at this patch of hell?'

Andy let Lorraine explain. She told them about all the dead ends they'd encountered in their attempt to trace Darren Mallory and referred to the observations which had been under way here on the night of Darren's attack. As she explained her reservations about the incident, Probert listened intently.

'I'll be honest with you,' he said. 'I don't know any of the details or background to that attack on Welch. I must say we've never had cause to link it to Darren's disappearance. If that possibility had occurred to me, I'd have dug a little deeper. I'll do that the minute I get back.'

'I'm happy to provide you with everything we've learned,' and she told him of her own visit to Sergeant Page, the CPS and the library, adding, 'If you decide to delve into this, you might see whether there's any link with Darren's disappearance.' She produced one of her most endearing smiles. 'And I would really like to know more about the victim, Dylan Welch. He's emerging as a real mystery man.'

'I'll do my best to come up with something, I'll call you at your office. That's a promise.'

'Now, this patch of ground . . .' Andy Williams waved his hand expansively. 'There's enough space to hold a premier division football stadium or a few streets of houses or a massive car park or even a supermarket . . . but now it's a wasteland, a dumping ground for rubbish and the haunt of the offal of our society. Darren came here for some reason, Ted, and whatever it was, he finished up hitting Dylan with a brick. So why were they here? Or why was either of them here? We know it's used by drug dealers, pushers and users among other criminal types, but according to Sergeant Page there was a police operation of some kind under way on the night Dylan was attacked.'

'That's very likely. It's very close to the docks, as you can see, and it's regularly used for hand-overs of stolen goods, drug dealing, prostitution, all sorts. Police observations and exercises are fairly common, not every night of course, but regularly enough to be a feature of the local night life! The trouble is we rarely catch anyone – that's why the villains come and use the place.'

'I can see there's plenty of escape routes!' laughed Williams.

'It's tailor-made for escapes. If you look around, you'll

see there are at least ten exit routes – all can be used by people on foot or on bikes or motor bikes, and about seven of them can take a car or a van. You can imagine how many police officers are needed to block ten exits, not to mention other escape routes that are used in emergencies, through surrounding houses and streets, for example, in the front door and out the back before the residents realize what's going on, and into back gardens and away . . . that sort of thing. And, if you look around, you'll see there are not many places to conceal a police presence – if we park a vehicle here, it'll always attract attention. But we keep trying, we have to show the flag, as they say!'

'Your men caught Darren here,' commented Lorraine.

'A bit of luck, I would imagine,' smiled Probert. 'Maybe he and Dylan didn't keep their eyes open for signs of a police presence . . . I should tell you that the place has such a reputation that the people living nearby never venture here at night, and rarely in the daytime. Those houses overlooking it will contain people who are watching us right now and wondering what we're doing here, but none will come to find out. If things happen at night – cars coming and going, people shouting, covert meetings, that sort of thing – we rarely get to know. Many is the time our routine patrols have entered this place at night, in vehicles, only to see people vanish into the darkness like rats bolting down holes. We've tried undercover tactics – that's how we know what goes on – but it only works for a time because they soon suss out a copper.'

'So the fact that Darren and Dylan were here might not be all that unusual, that's if both were criminals. We don't know about Dylan's past, do we?'

'I don't know anything about him. There were police watching, so you told me. That would scare away any experienced villains thinking of using that site, they'd soon spot the observations vehicles or whatever system was being used. Clearly, neither Darren nor Dylan did so, or if they did, they failed to appreciate they were police observers.'

'We need to know more about Dylan, Sergeant,' Lorraine

reminded him. 'He might not be a crook – he might not have realized he was being watched, or was likely to be watched. And Darren might not have been here for any unlawful purpose either, maybe he had no cause to worry about being watched.'

'I doubt if the observations were designed to catch him, he's well known to most of us. I think the police would be after bigger fish.'

'Dylan then? Were they trying to catch Dylan? Was Dylan Welch planning some kind of scheme, with Darren getting in the way? Darren might have gone there to meet someone or to do a deal of some kind and unwittingly scuppered Dylan's plans. Might that be the scenario?' put in Andy.

'It's all guesswork,' said Probert. 'Look, I'm sorry if I can't be more helpful, but there's not a lot I can add to what I told you when we first met.'

'That's when you mentioned Campion, Joseph Campion.' Andy decided to change the subject. 'You felt the fact he'd vanished was another coincidence, even if it was six months ago.'

'I've no cause to link his disappearance with Darren although he does use other people for his business dealings; he's used the Mallory brothers as you know, Darren included. And they get paid for their work too. Campion's not a gang member, he's a lone operator, but a successful criminal nonetheless. Wealthy, hard, cunning, enterprising – even if he'd been honest, he'd have been successful in business. We think he enjoys being a criminal for the excitement it provides – and the fact it provides a tax-free income. We've had him under observations for some time, on and off, but he's too cunning to be caught.'

'So he's a big-time villain?'

'He is, Andy, very much so. He's into drugs, car stealing, international crime too, we believe. We know he travels a lot, but we can never trace him when he does, he uses false passports, false identities and good cover stories. He never flies, though, he's terrified of being airborne, and we think he uses ports well away from his home area. He's been absent before, for several months at a time. This absence isn't all that unusual.'

'His wife must be used to it? I thought he'd gone for a pint and not come home.'

'He did, that's how he does it. Local enquiries will suggest he's had a row and left his wife – that's just one aspect of his cover story. His wife always claims she has no idea where he's gone. We tend to believe her – I don't think she ever knows what he really gets up to but she's pretty good at sustaining a believable "run away from home" story. A good cover story, to be honest.'

'Fair enough,' said Andy. 'Can I ask about the night Darren vanished? You said your men had had him under observations and had seen him at the Blue Raven with a girl – whom we've interviewed.'

'True.'

'If my memory is correct, you didn't follow him by car, yours was a foot observer.'

'Yes, Darren wasn't suspected of any crime, it was a collating exercise, intelligence gathering, recording his movements for future reference, should we need them.'

'I understand. What I'm lacking, Ted,' said Andy Williams, 'is proof that he actually took the road home to Dovedale. Everyone assumes that's what he did when he left the club, but if your tails lost him in town, who knows where he went?'

'I can't argue with that. All I can say is that whenever we've tailed him like that on previous occasions, he's gone home, driven out to Dovedale. It's one of his regular trips, he always spends Saturday night in town.'

'You know that?'

'We do.'

'You mean the Dovedale house was bugged?'

'We were interested in the activity of the whole gang, Andy, so before they moved into that house, we prepared it. It's not illegal.'

'So why don't you know whether Darren got home that night?'

'Because the old man refitted the kitchen and managed

to dislodge the bug we'd fitted! It was in the kitchen, where they do most of their talking and planning. Jack never knew he was being bugged, we think he threw it out with the other rubbish he generated when he began to knock the place to pieces and fit new stuff. Whatever happened, it's gone. And so we've lost our contact with the Mallorys in their domestic bliss. If Darren was behaving true to form that night, he would leave Sidlesbrough to drive home. The trouble was he never got there.'

'Have you searched the route?' Lorraine asked.

'No, although we did a routine check in our patch, that's in the town and the suburbs, car parks, side streets and so on, looking for his car. Nothing. Once he crossed our boundary, of course, he's yours, we didn't attempt to follow him out into the wilds of your dark moorland!'

'We're going to do that run when we leave here,' Lorraine said. 'I'd like to see what's along the route – old barns, farmhouses, derelict mine shafts, not to mention people who might have seen him, or seen something odd.'

'It needs doing, although I wouldn't know where to start,' said Probert. 'So, anything else I can help with?'

'You said when we last met that Darren went into bookmakers' shops. Was he alone? Meeting anyone?' asked Lorraine.

'Alone. Sometimes we got a man inside as well, but he was doing nothing more than making selections with his head into the racing papers. He went into the library too, we followed him once or twice, but all he did there was read the papers. I think he was leading us up the garden path, setting up simple trails for us to follow, like he does when he goes into police stations.'

'That *is* cocking a snook at authority!'

'If he was a child, we'd say he was downright cheeky! He likes to show us we can't touch him. He told one of the desk constables he was checking to see if his name was on the wanted list! He does it to wind us up, he goes for a look at the public noticeboard, reads the notices, grins at whoever's on the desk and goes out laughing.'

'You've noticeboards inside now? I saw one at your headquarters, in the foyer.'

'Most of those we erect outside get vandalized, and we've found that if we place them in our foyers and entrances people will come to look at them. We get a lot of people calling in for various reasons, sometimes having to wait if there's a queue, and so our notices do get read. I'm told that reward notices have gained a following, local folks trying to earn a bit of extra cash by doing a spot of detective work. There's one old chap who tries to recover all the cats that have gone missing and a Miss Marple type who tries to find out who's been raiding building societies.'

'And they attract villains as well as ordinary citizens?' laughed Andy.

'Sure, it's one of the few times villains will voluntarily enter our portals!'

'So these observations on Darren – are they collated anywhere?' Lorraine put to Probert. 'Do you have records of where he's been, who he's met, what he did when he went, say, into the library or police station and so on?'

'Oh, yes, we've a thick dossier on him, going back a few years. I wouldn't say we've got records of all his contacts and places visited but we've a very good selection in spite of the fact he manages to dodge us most of the time. It's a follow-on from the old Collator's filing system, when we targeted criminals, but now of course it's all on computer – intelligence led, as we say – so when we do nail him for something, we can check his whereabouts and contacts if he comes up with an alibi.'

'Now you tell me!' Lorraine gasped. 'So if it's all on computer, can I have a copy?'

'I could email it to you, yes,' he said. 'The minute I get back to my office.'

'Thanks,' and Lorraine passed him her card, complete with her personal email address. 'You won't forget?'

'Scout's honour!' he laughed. 'And if that material raises any queries, you know where to find me.'

'That's the best bit of news I've had all week!' said

Lorraine. 'It means I can make some sort of time-chart of his recent activities, to see if I can link them with anything that's happened in our part of the world.'

Andy Williams thanked Probert too, and when it was clear there was little more they could ask about Mallory, he changed the subject.

'We've heard on the proverbial grapevine that one of your top brass has been suspended, a disciplinary offence of some kind. It's no real concern of ours, and it's not featured in the newspapers, but because we uncovered the tale during our enquiries into Darren's absence, I am wondering if there's a connection.'

'You have been busy!' smiled Probert. 'Yes, I know about it, it's a detective superintendent. She's been suspended and there's an investigation by an outside force.'

'So what's she done?' asked Andy.

'Other than members of the Complaints and Discipline Department, nobody knows for sure. I did hear, though, through internal bush telegraph, that it's something to do with irregularities in the payment of informants. Dodgy stuff at any time . . .'

'Darren's not an informant, is he?'

'Not him! It's against his religion to grass on other villains, just like his dad, but I can't see she's got anything to do with Darren's disappearance. My contact reckoned it's nothing more than a bit of sloppy bookkeeping, always tricky when you're dealing with cash and people who don't want receipts or won't give names. But these days, heads roll for all kinds of minor things. All you need is a complaint from a bolshie member of the public and bang goes your career.'

'So you don't think we need concern ourselves with it?' asked Andy.

'I can't see how that could be linked to Darren,' said Probert. 'But I'll keep my ear to the ground, as they say, and if anything comes up which I think is relevant, I'll get in touch.'

Lorraine thanked him, adding, 'You've been very helpful. In fact, you've been more helpful than any of your seniors we've spoken to.'

'That's because they know nothing!' laughed Probert. 'They sit in their offices and shuffle a few papers and think they know everything that's going on. They can't know, not without getting rain down their necks and plodding up and down the streets talking to people. Dave and me – he's the noisy one as you'll have discovered – well, we get out and about, do observations, ask questions, poke our noses in, get under the skin of the townspeople . . . and we get results.'

'For which the bosses get all the praise,' said Dave, the first words he'd spoken.

They realized they had reached the end of this discussion, but before leaving Lorraine said, 'Would you mind if we went back to your headquarters? I was there yesterday afternoon but in view of what you've said, I'd like to ask the desk constable there if he recalls anything about Darren's visits – that's if he knows Darren. I didn't ask him that.'

'Feel free,' said Probert. 'We're both in this together, I know I can ask you for anything you might uncover. We can't watch our targets twenty-four hours a day, so anything extra is welcome.'

And so they parted. As the Greater Balderside detectives moved away to go about their daily routine, Lorraine, mindful of Andy's desire not to spend too much time away from their own area, asked, 'Would you mind, Andy, if I just pop into their headquarters again?'

'If you think it'll do any good, by all means go along. Seems sensible, now that we're in the area.'

It took them twenty minutes to fight their way through the town's heavy traffic and after parking in the visitors' car park, Lorraine led Andy to the main door of police headquarters in Perthland Lane. She was pleased to see the same crumpled constable behind the counter. He recognized her and registered his pleasure in a broad smile.

'Hello, back again so soon?' he smiled, glancing at Andy

Williams. 'You manage to chat to Detective Sergeant Page before he left, did you?'

'I did,' she said, 'Thanks. But something else has cropped up. This is Detective Sergeant Williams, by the way, from Rainesbury, we're working together on the Darren Mallory case.'

'Ah, so that's it.'

'Do you know Darren?'

'We all know Darren!' he laughed. 'Chip off the old block but much more charming than his old man. A rogue, mind, but a cheerful one. If he was eight years old, we'd all say we was a cheeky little devil, but now he's grown up and nearly twenty-five we know he's a cunning villain . . .'

'I'm told he goes into police stations to look at notice-boards?'

'Oh yes, quite regular, he is. He comes in here, goes straight over to our notices and reads them. There's no reason why he shouldn't, they're there to be read by the public. I have asked if I can help with his enquiries, but he just laughs and says he's thinking of joining the force, or going to one of our charity whist drives, or checking to see if he's on our wanted posters. To be honest, I've no idea why he comes in like this, the only excuse he gave once was that, because we're keeping tabs on him, he's keeping tabs on us. And then he just laughs at us.'

'Is it a regular visit?' asked Lorraine.

'Once a week maybe,' responded the constable. 'Some-times longer.'

'And does he visit other police stations like this, to read noticeboards?'

'Oh, yes. We've several police stations in town, divi-sional headquarters they are, five in all, both sides of the river. He goes to all of them, on and off, I did a check after he'd been here once or twice. Some might think he's got a strong nerve, doing this sort of thing, but that's Darren. And our notices are there for the public, as I said, but you try and follow him once he leaves – he can vanish like a genie . . . amazing man, really.'

'So when did he start this practice?' asked Andy.

'It's hard to say,' the constable said. 'A year maybe. Probably not much before then.'

'So what's on the board now?' Lorraine walked across to it. Some two metres long by a metre and a half high, it was a well-used pinboard on the wall directly opposite the counter at the other side of the foyer, and on the left as one entered through the main door. Below it, a wooden bench-seat was secured to the wall and there were half a dozen leather-covered chairs around a table – a waiting area for visitors.

Andy followed Lorraine. There were police recruiting posters, warnings about Colorado beetles and Warble Fly (all police stations posted such notices, even those in towns), details of foot and mouth restrictions still in force, notices about motoring law such as the breathalyser, tyre legislation and the need to ensure that all vehicle lights were in working order.

In addition to the posters she saw yesterday, there were new ones from Crimestopper detailing rewards for the recovery of stolen property, another where a firm of engineers offered a reward for information leading to the arrest of the murderer of one of their nightwatchmen, a coloured poster sponsored by the *Daily Mail* asking for sightings of a pensioner missing from Newcastle-on-Tyne, one about a missing tabby cat and one announcing a whist drive to raise money for police charities.

'There aren't any magazines or daily newspapers?' commented Lorraine.

'No, they get nicked!'

'So somebody wanting a cert for the two thirty at Redcar will have to go elsewhere?' laughed Andy.

'To the bookies, I suppose, if they can't afford to buy their own paper,' responded the constable. 'Or the library. I know lots of characters who spend most of their days in the library, reading all the papers. Funny you should mention that, Darren used to go there, one of our detectives has seen him there, quite often, ploughing through the dailies.

Getting tips for the horses, I reckon. You don't get many villains doing that, going into libraries, I mean.'

'And I bet you don't get many paying social calls at police headquarters,' laughed Andy.

'He's the only one to my knowledge,' the constable told them. 'Makes you wonder what he's up to.'

'It does indeed,' said Lorraine. 'Well, thanks for that.'

As she turned to leave, the constable smiled his farewell. 'Two days running, Miss Cashmore. Another visit tomorrow? Maybe I should get the kettle on?'

'I might return!' and she delivered one of her smiles. 'Thanks again.'

'Well,' said Andy as they returned to their car, 'what do we make of that?'

'I might have an idea,' she teased him. 'But first, I'd like to see that log of observations on Darren. Now, though, I think it's time for a drive across the moors.'

'You know the moors better than I,' said Andy. 'I'll drive, you be observer.'

Chapter Nine

'Have we a map in the car?' asked Lorraine.

'No need, I know the road,' responded Andy.

'I don't need it for that,' she retorted. 'I want to check things along the way, villages, hamlets, isolated farms, garages or pubs, any other old buildings, pit shafts and so on, especially those some distance off the carriageway. Places where Darren might be hiding, or even where he could be hidden.'

'Dead or alive, you mean?'

'We've got to think like that, and that means we should divert off the main road where we feel it necessary,' she suggested. 'Explore the villages, checking for sightings of him, or seeing if his car is parked up somewhere near a dangerous place, we've never done this yet, in this enquiry. We should have done it before now.'

They began at the county boundary, relying on Greater Balderside Police to have properly searched their area; fortunately, the boundary lay some distance out of suburbia, and for the first few miles afterwards there was nothing but enclosed fields. As they extended their run, the road began to climb towards the moors. The fields were left behind as acres of open heather-clad moorland replaced the meadowlands of the lower ground and soon they could see scattered and isolated farmsteads tucked into folds within the moors. Some were a mile or more from the road. With the map spread open upon her knees, Lorraine was identifying the farms as they passed and listing them in a notebook; in some cases, there were isolated stone barns, well away from the farmsteads.

There was insufficient time to visit every distant farm or building today – either the occupants could be traced through the electoral register and interviewed, or they could be telephoned. In many cases, Andy would make sure that local constables visited selected premises; they were already aware of Darren's absence and would be reminded to ask for sightings of him or his car, or indications of any incident which might have led to his disappearance. Some of those farms had converted barns which were now holiday cottages, invariably let on the short term to strangers. He could be in one of those. They could spend a few minutes in the villages along the route, showing Darren's photograph in the street, shop, post office or pub and asking for sightings of him or his car.

'There are seven villages,' Lorraine told Andy. 'Fremingthorpe, Dinnsby, Howekeld, Lammergate, Huttondale, Hangdale and Mireholm. All small places. Huttondale is the biggest and it straddles this road.'

'We'll just get there in time for a bar snack!' grinned Andy.

During their run, they managed to call at several inns and farms beside the road, as well as a couple of filling stations, but none of the people interviewed had seen Darren or his car. Their enquiries in the first four villages were equally fruitless. Huttondale, being the largest, had two pubs, the Crown and the Lamb, and three shops – a butcher, a general store, and small bakery with a café attached. There was also a post office adjoining the garage and an infants' school along the back lane.

Here, they had some luck. Upon seeing Darren's photograph, the lady in the bakery said she'd seen him on several occasions.

He would sometimes pop in to buy a sandwich or a loaf of bread and a cake or two. His visits might be in the morning, on his way to work, or later in the evening when he was going home. And, she told them, he would often fill his car up at the garage just across the road. She had no idea who he was, nor did she know his name; furthermore, he was always alone, but she was unsure of the date he had last called – certainly it was more than a week ago, probably two. Lorraine said they would ask at the garage, they might keep records of his petrol purchases. It was a small and typical country garage with a couple of petrol pumps standing on a concrete base outside a workshop which would accommodate only one vehicle at a time. The owner, a stout and oil-stained man in overalls and a flap cap, left his task of trying to fit an exhaust to a van. He thought they'd called for petrol.

'Sorry, no, we don't want a fill-up,' smiled Andy, showing the photograph of Darren. 'We're police officers, we're trying to trace this man. He lives at Dovedale, name of Darren Mallory.'

'Oh, we've had the local bobby asking as well. That man in your photo comes here for his petrol and oil.' The man did not hestitate in his recognition. 'Or he has done for the past six months or so. Decent lad, always pays cash. Nice car he's got, that new Vauxhall. What's he done, then, that makes you want to find him?'

'He's not in trouble,' said Andy. 'He's vanished from his usual haunts, he's been missing since a week last Saturday night. We're working with Greater Balderside Police to try and find him. He seems to have disappeared into thin air.'

'Well, he comes in here as large as life, or at least he did. Now, when was the last time he called?'

'That's what I was hoping you'd tell us!' laughed Lorraine.

'If you've got his car number, I might just do that,' said the man, heading for a tiny office beside his workshop. 'I allus keep car numbers handy for a week or two, just in case I get a dud cheque or a stolen credit card – or a fake £20 note or summat. We get a few fake notes here. You can't trust anybody these days . . . Now, where's my petrol book.'

Andy provided the registration number of Darren's Vauxhall and after rummaging among the clutter on his desk, the man found a grease-stained red-backed book and flicked through it.

Eventually, he said, 'Here we are. A week last Saturday, the twentieth. Morning it was. He topped his tank up and paid cash. £27.50.'

'Was he alone?'

'Aye, so far as I recollect. I can't say I've ever seen him with anybody on board. He was going to work, he said, even if it was a Saturday. He works in Sidlesbrough, he once told me, he has his own business but he never said what it was, and he expected to be late home that night, so that's why he got filled up. He liked to have a full tank for the weekend, for running about. I close at six, you see, so I'd be shut if he came past here later than that.'

'Has he ever said what his business was?' asked Andy.

'No, and I never ask, it doesn't do to be too curious about folks. So long as they pay their way, they'll do for me. And he does. Pay his way, I mean. Mind you, between you and me, I wonder why a businessman would pay cash, most of 'em pay by cheque or credit card and want VAT receipts and bits of paper for their accounts. He never does. Cash on the nail and off he goes. Suits me, though. Less paperwork.'

'Did he say anything about going away? Holiday? Business trip? Seeing relatives? Anything?' asked Lorraine.

'Not a sausage, miss. He just got topped up, paid me and off he went.'

'Do his brothers call in?'

'I didn't know he had brothers.'

Lorraine explained how the family lived on the hilltop in Dovedale, but the garage proprietor shook his head. 'Can't say I've seen any of them,' he said. 'But unless they said who they were, I'd not know they were his brothers, would I?'

They continued to ask him further questions but failed to glean anything more about Darren; likewise, further enquiries in Huttondale, including questioning the land-lords of the Lamb Inn and Crown Hotel where they had a bar snack, did not produce any information, neither did visits to Howekeld and Dinnsby.

In Fremingthorpe, however, they had more luck. They popped into the village store and were asking the storekeeper about Darren, showing him his photograph, when a customer entered. The shopkeeper shook his head and said he'd never seen the man.

Andy went on, 'We know he works in Sidlesbrough, and we know he left to come home that night. We don't think he got home, we're asking if anyone might have seen him or his car. Maybe you'd keep your ears open for us?'

'It'll be a pleasure,' he said.

The customer had overheard their conversation and joined in by saying, 'He might have been stopped at that road block.'

'Road block?' asked Andy.

'Aye, they were breath-testing drivers, at least I think that's what they were doing. They never pulled me in though, they just waved me through.'

'The police, you mean?' asked Lorraine.

'Aye, two policemen and a car, and a breakdown truck in a lay-by.'

'So where was this?' Lorraine asked.

'Between here and Greater Balderside, near Hangdale lane end.'

'What time? Can you remember?'

'Just after midnight, it would be, I'd been to a birthday party for my old mother . . .'

'And it was the night we're talking about, was it? The twentieth?'

'Oh, aye, that's right enough.'

'We'll check our own records, it's in our area so we should have details. Thanks – and your name?'

'Seddon, Joe Seddon. I've a smallholding just along the road.'

'Thanks, we'll look into this, Mr Seddon.'

As they left Fremingthorpe both Andy and Lorraine felt elated about this snippet of information – if Seddon was correct, Darren might have passed through the road check and, if so, his presence would have been recorded.

The final part of their trek contained more farms, cottages, pubs and filling stations both along the roadside and deep in the moors; they called at those which were conveniently placed but none of their occupants had noticed Darren or his car. And then they were in Dovedale.

'I'd like another chat with Jack Mallory while we're here,' Lorraine told Andy. 'He's had time to talk to his sons, or maybe Darren's been in touch.'

'No time like the present,' and so they drove up the steep gradient of Dovedale Hill and along the track to Hill Top House. It was just after four o'clock, Lorraine noted, when they parked outside the entrance they'd previously used. No other vehicles were parked outside and there was no sign of anyone being on the premises as they went through the gate. There was no sound of drilling or hammering either and the whole place seemed eerily silent. The kitchen door was closed and there was no internal light showing as a brisk moorland breeze sighed around the isolated house, blowing around dust and small pieces of debris. There were slivers of wood shavings which had probably escaped from the workshop, some dead leaves which had somehow been wafted up here from the dale below, a crisp packet and a chocolate wrapper, dry heather blown in from the moors.

'We'll try his shed first,' said Andy. 'The light's on.'

The shed door was closed and through the window they could see his bench with an unshaded bulb glowing above it, but no sign of Jack Mallory.

'He's probably walked down to the village,' said Lorraine as they approached. 'Maybe gone to get something for his tea or visiting that chap who fixes grandfather clocks.'

Andy knocked, a gesture of politeness which flowed from the co-operation they'd received during their previous visit, but when there was no response he did as before – he opened the door. Inside, they found Jack. He was lying on the floor; he looked lifeless, his head and face were smashed and bloody, and the wardrobe he'd been building was smashed into pieces with some of the bits lying across his inert form. The shed had been

138

wrecked too, jam jars full of nails and screws had been broken, shelves pulled down, a tin of paint spewed across one wall . . .

'Oh my God!' In a trice, Andy was on his knees beside Jack, listening for signs of breathing, testing for a heartbeat on his blood-saturated temples and the pulse on his wrists. His arms and face were warm to the touch. He shouted Jack's name but there was not a flicker from his closed eyes. 'He's alive . . . but only just . . . God, he's had a beating . . . look at the mess on his head . . . get an ambulance, Lorraine. Touch as little as possible, preserve the scene, all of it . . .'

Rather than return to the car, Lorraine used her mobile telephone to summon the ambulance, stressing the urgency and emphasizing the remoteness of the location. She was told one should arrive in twelve to fifteen minutes.

'Can we do anything for him?' she asked Andy.

'Best to leave him, we've no idea how long he's been here, not long, I think, that blood's hardly congealed – just congealing . . . he's got a terrible head wound and we might do more harm if we move him. He's unconscious, cover him with something to keep him warm. So what do you think has happened, Lorraine? Where's the weapon they used? What was it? This doesn't look like a burglary that's gone wrong, does it?'

'Somebody with a grudge by the look of it, attacked him and smashed his handiwork.'

'You stay with him,' Andy said. 'Don't touch anything. Call Scenes of Crime while I check the house and grounds, chummy might still be here.'

The kitchen door was not locked and so Andy let himself in, wondering whether to shout his presence in case the family were at home, or move silently in case the villain was inside. He chose the latter. The kitchen had not been damaged and as he passed quickly into the ill-furnished lounges, two rooms with chairs and settees, plus smaller ground-floor rooms like a toilet, storeroom and scullery, he realized the intruder had not ransacked the

139

house. Upstairs, he quickly checked all six bedrooms, all untidy save for what was clearly the one used by Jack – his bed was made, the room was tidy and clean and some of his clothes were over a chair – and he looked into wardrobes, under beds and in all other likely hiding places. Nothing. Although he was tempted to search for evidence of the activities of the Mallory Mob, there was no time. He returned to Lorraine. Jack was still unconscious on the floor, now with an old coat covering him.

'Whoever it was,' he told her, 'he's not ransacked the house, and he's not hiding there. It looks to me as if he came here fully intending to attack Jack. Smashing his handiwork looks like a lesson of some kind for him – or his family. This was no burglary.'

'Gang warfare?' asked Lorraine.

'Or something to do with Darren?' suggested Andy. 'I thought the Clarksons and Mallorys were having an uneasy truce right now.'

'But if it's something to do with Darren, or the others, why attack Jack?'

'He's the boss, father of the clan, he's still a force to be reckoned with. Put him out of action to teach the others a lesson. I would think that most of the villains in the north-east of England will know he's living alone on this remote hilltop, word will have spread. Poor old Jack's all alone up here and ripe for picking, as they say – especially if they don't know where to find Darren. What better way is there to stop Darren in his tracks than to half-kill his father?'

'So Darren must still be a problem, is that what you're saying, Andy?' She stooped to feel Jack's pulse. His heart was still pumping, but she thought it was very weak. Where was the ambulance? She wished she could do something . . .

'It's one explanation,' he shrugged.

'But you do think this could be linked to Darren?' She stood up. 'If it is, then it's important to us.'

'I must say it's speculation on my part, but it is a coincidence, isn't it? Suppose Darren's stumbled across something big, suppose he's trying to muscle in on some other villain's territory or gangland enterprise and his plans have been discovered . . . and suppose someone wants him stopped? They don't know where to find him, no one does. So they've used these tactics. It's one way of getting a message across. Ah, do I hear sirens?'

An ambulance was making its noisy way along the cinder track towards Hill Top House; moments after the sirens faded, two paramedics arrived at the door. Andy rapidly briefed them and one of them said that, thanks to Lorraine's earlier call, a doctor had already been alerted in the casualty department of Rainesbury District Hospital. With remarkable speed and gentleness, the unconscious Jack was placed on a stretcher, put into the rear compartment with one of the medics at his side and the ambulance began its journey to hospital with its siren sounding once more.

As it was departing, Andy phoned his own office in Rainesbury. 'Alan? It's Andy Williams. We've just put a local villain in the ambulance, he's on his way to A and E at Rainesbury Hospital. Name of Jack Mallory, currently living at Dovedale, a big name among the Greater Balderside villains, father of the Mallory Mob. Somebody's smashed his head in, with a hammer by the look of things, he's unconscious but I don't know the extent of his injuries. Have words with Uniform, get the duty inspector to detail somebody to sit by his bedside, first to protect him against all comers, and second to jot down anything he might say, either before or after he regains consciousness. If he ever does.'

That deed completed, Andy said, 'Jack won't talk if he knows we're at his bedside . . . not even if he knows who did this.'

'You know,' said Lorraine, 'if Jack's assailant is from Greater Balderside, we could have passed him as we were coming here . . . he'd be on his return trip . . .'

'I can't say I noticed anyone behaving oddly, racing home or whatever, but let's have words with Greater Balderside Police,' he said. 'They can always check the films in their speed cameras. I'll bet he was making his run home while we were checking those farms and pubs . . . but who was it? That's the question. Who would do this? And why? A member of the family? Teaching Jack a lesson for talking to us?'

'Surely not, you'd never get this sort of thing happening within a family, not even one like the Mallorys. Besides, none of them would know Jack had talked to us, he'd never reveal that, not to his own family. He said so.'

'You can get this sort of thing in some families, Lorraine, believe me. We can't ignore that possibility. Now, SOCO should be here soon, and we'd better try to inform some of his family. Where can we find them, I wonder? Apart from leaving a note on the door of this place.'

'They don't often come home, Jack told us that, so we'd better ask our friends at Sidlesbrough to try and trace one of them!'

'We can get Probert or Hansfield or one of their officers to put the word around Greater Balderside, they'll know someone who knows how to reach one of the Mallorys. They must have a base somewhere. And I'll want you to pop into the hospital to see how Jack's getting on, to talk to him about who did this.'

'Even if he does know, he'll not say anything, Andy, you know that!'

'True enough, but we've got to try.'

The Scenes of Crime Officers, a detective sergeant and detective constable in their unmarked and anonymous white van, arrived within half an hour and, after hearing Andy Williams' account, began their examination of the scene and its surrounds. Andy decided to wait until it was over, on the faint chance that the perpetrator or perpetrators had left behind a weapon or some other piece of evidence. They performed a very detailed search along with the routine dusting for fingerprints and other material evidence, gathering tiny items of debris and popping them into samples bags, just in case they were useful. They took extra care, fully aware that this could become a murder scene.

After about an hour, they concluded their work and

their leader, Detective Sergeant Jim Bailey, said, 'Not a lot, I'm afraid, Andy. I'd say one man was involved, a man who's careful enough not to leave any evidence. He's taken the weapon, whatever it was. Obviously we'll examine the prints we've found – probably all Jack's – and we'll check for DNA but if this was a professional villain, which I think it is, he'll have made sure he hasn't left any. I doubt if he'll have left anything that'll lead us to him, although if we do come across him there might be blood on his clothes or shoes. Just a chance. And I suspect he knew just how hard, and where, to hit Mallory without killing him. The fact Jack's alive, plus the smashed wardrobe and damage to the workshop, suggests a severe warning message. Somebody's telling Jack – or his lads – to lay off.'

'A warning to lay off what, I wonder?'

'Have words with Greater Balderside, Andy. They've had a few attacks like this, with a hammer. The Stonemason, they call him, the attacker. He uses one of those small, heavy hammers a stonemason uses, heavy enough to cope with a stone chisel but small enough to hide with the head in your hand and the handle up your sleeve. Call the studio tomorrow when we've had a chance to look at our findings more carefully. You might need a pathologist to look at Mallory's head wound, even if he survives. Ask him to try and make a match with the Stonemason's handiwork.'

And so the SOCO team did a rapid tour of the house and grounds, concluding that the assailant had not ventured elsewhere, then departed.

'We ought to search this house very carefully,' said Andy. 'Cupboards, drawers, hiding places. For letters, telephone numbers, diaries, notebooks, that sort of thing. Stolen property perhaps. Anything at all that might help in a criminal investigation – murder investigation even. We'll never get another chance like this, and we can show justification because of the attack. We can say we're looking for evidence of Jack's assailant. If we happen to find anything else, then that's a bonus. And it might help us find Darren.'

Lorraine had mixed feelings about this. On the one hand she felt she was abusing the trust placed in her by Jack Mallory, and invading his private territory without good cause and probably without any kind of legal justification. On the other hand, a serious crime had been committed and she agreed with Williams' reasoning because that meant a search could be justified. Their actions could ⱶ backed by Common Law because they were seeking Jac assailant, or evidence of the identification of that assail; – who might soon find himself classed as a murder. Lorraine agreed, but their long and careful search produced nothing of value.

They sought drawers with false bottoms, cabinets with hidden storage spaces, safes in the walls or boxes of treasure in the attics. They looked for letters and telephone numbers, names of contacts and places frequented by the lads, but they found absolutely nothing. They searched the grounds too, and the outbuildings, but failed to find anything of value in a criminal investigation – except the damage and bloodstains in Jack's workshop. Crime had indeed come to Hill Top House. Finally, Andy locked the house with the key hanging behind the kitchen door, and secured the shed with the key already in the lock. Then, in the best traditions of country life, he placed both keys beneath a large stone on the edge of the grassy patch, some distance from the house.

'The hallmark of professionals,' commented Andy as they concluded. 'The Mallorys will make sure they never leave any evidence at home.'

'They've not been here long,' Lorraine added. 'Certainly not long enough to establish this as a centre of operations.'

'I'm sure they'd never be foolish enough to do that, Lorraine, but we've done our duty. We've searched – and I must tell the boss we've been in Mallory's house again! Now, before we leave, let's see if we can raise anyone in Sidlesbrough who'll try and find one of those sons for us.'

Detective Constable Dave Baxter, the silent partner of DS Ted Probert, responded to their mobile phone call and listened as Andy explained. 'All I need, Dave, is for a message to reach one of the Mallory brothers. Jack has been attacked and he's in Rainesbury Hospital, A and E Department. I've no idea of his condition at this stage – he was in a bad way and unconscious when he left Dovedale but he was alive. We've a constable at his bedside. His ꙮmily must be told about this, one way or another. The ꙮꙮe is locked, by the way, and if one of the Mallory ꙮthers cares to contact me, with proof of his identity, I'll ꙮt him where to find the keys.'

Baxter assured Andy that a message would reach the Mallory brothers – but whether they would respond remained to be seen. They might even suspect some kind of trap – but Andy said, 'Dave, just make sure they're told. That's our job done.'

Although it was past their normal finishing time, when Lorraine and Andy left the lofty house and drove down the hill, they decided to remain in the village for as long as necessary, asking whether anyone had noticed any activity at Hill Top House. It was hardly likely visitors would have been spotted at such a distance although people did sometimes walk past, and hikers might have passed comment in the shop. But again they gleaned nothing. It was a sobering thought that someone could visit Hill Top House, murder the occupant or occupants, and leave totally unseen by anyone. But that was the nature of the place.

After exhausting their enquiries around the village, Andy said, 'Come on, Lorraine. Home. It's been a busy day.'

'Do you think our enquiries prompted that attack on Jack?' asked Lorraine as they were driving home. 'Have we stirred something up?'

'I didn't think we'd got ourselves deeply involved in whatever's going on,' he admitted. 'We're just country cousins on the very outer edge of all this so I doubt if we've even caused a ripple. After all, what do we know? What have we discovered? Not a lot. We can't even find Darren, all we can find is dead end after dead end with nothing beyond it.'

'I find that so frustrating, not getting answers . . .' she sighed.

'Didn't you have some idea about what might be behind all this? You never told me what it was, did you?'

'I'd like to think it through a bit more, if you don't mind. Or even talk it over with Mark.'

'I thought he won't let you talk shop out of hours?'

'He won't, he calls it our rule of the house – but sometimes I can persuade him to break his own rules,' she smiled.

'Tonight, perhaps?'

'I'll try,' she said. 'I expect he'll have left his office by the time we get back to Rainesbury, he's not on call this week and likes the early finishes.'

'Tomorrow's Friday,' he reminded her. 'We need to have one final onslaught. I'd have thought we'd have come up with something by now.'

'We have, Jack's been attacked. We found him, maybe we've saved his life.'

'I'll ring the hospital before we leave the office,' he said, pressing the accelerator.

Having garaged the official car and completed its log book, they climbed upstairs to the CID general office where Andy first rang A and E. He had some difficulty persuading the hospital operator that it was a bona fide enquiry, especially as he was not a relative, but eventually she relented and transferred his call to the relevant ward. A sister answered. He explained it all over again, asked if a uniformed constable was beside the bed, and was then told that Mr Mallory was still unconscious but his condition was stable. She said nothing about any treatment he might be receiving and then asked about relatives. Andy explained the difficulties in tracing them, but said every effort was being made; he did not refer to their criminality, although he did ask if he could speak to the bedside constable. This was agreed and the sister asked the PC to take the call.

'PC Johnson,' said the stolid voice.

'Detective Sergeant Williams here,' Andy said. 'This is

for your ears only, and for whoever takes over from you. Not for the ears of the hospital staff. Understood?'

'Yes, Sergeant.'

'The man you're looking after is called Jack Mallory. He's a known villain with a long history of operating on Greater Balderside, and his sons – all five of them – are villains, together known as the Mallory Mob. A violent bunch. We're trying to find the sons, or one of them, so we can break the news about dad, and if we do manage to trace any of them, they might visit him. I want you to listen to anything that dad might say, either in his sleep or otherwise, and I don't want you to leave that bedside, even if the Mallory brothers try to make you. And, PC Johnson, remember that somebody's had a serious go at old man Mallory – if they find out he's still alive, they might try again, with more determination. So be on your guard.'

'Yes, yes, I understand, Sergeant. Thank you for telling me.'

And the call ended.

Andy then went downstairs for a talk with the duty inspector and suggested Lorraine went with him. Inspector Reg Dawson was in charge of the uniform branch and was aware of Darren's disappearance; his men were keeping their ears and eyes open for signs of him. Andy provided a résumé of the attack on Mallory, asking that any constables on patrol in the Dovedale district be ordered to make enquiries in an attempt to trace anyone who might have visited Hill Top House that day or who may have been seen acting oddly in the village – even doing something as simple as asking for directions. He also supplied the inspector with Lorraine's list of the isolated farms, hamlets, pubs, garages and cottages between Greater Balderside and Dovedale, asking that the respective village constables make a point of visiting each of the places to ask about sightings of Darren and his car.

Then he asked Dawson. 'You had a breathalyser check a week last Saturday, on the road to Greater Balderside. Near Hangdale lane end.'

'Not us!' Dawson shook his head.

147

'It's in our division, though?'

'Oh, yes, well inside, Andy, but we didn't stage a road check. If there had been one, I'd have known. Who told you this?'

'A chap we met in one of the villages along that road. He reckons he drove home that way and saw the checkpoint. He wasn't stopped, he told us.'

'It could have been some kind of Greater Balderside operation,' suggested Dawson. 'I know that lane end's in our area, but sometimes very urgent and important matters ignore the niceties of things like force boundaries.'

'OK, thanks, I'll check with Greater Balderside.'

Back in their own office, Williams then smiled at Lorraine. 'Well, we've achieved something today. It means we can go home, things are moving. Jack's not regained consciousness but his condition is stable, and we've a guardian angel in size twelves at his bedside with lots of rural bobbies finding something useful to occupy them on their present shift. See you tomorrow, then? We'll check with Greater Balderside about that road block, and I hope the boss will talk to you tonight . . .'

And he left the office with Lorraine following, having confirmed that Mark had gone home. It was a short drive home but Lorraine found herself very tired – it had been a busy day with a lot of driving and all she wanted now was to soak in a hot scented bath, to have a nice large glass of sherry and then a delicious meal. She didn't really want to spoil things by talking about work, but Mark had to be told about Jack Mallory – although he might have been told already by someone in the office. She guessed he'd probably left for home before the news had filtered through, but whatever happened, she wanted to bounce her ideas off him.

She eased her car into the drive and Mark, busy in the kitchen, spotted her and waved.

She returned his cheery gesture and headed for the door.

Chapter Ten

'So how was your day?' The delicious smell of peppered pork under preparation assailed her as she entered the kitchen. Mark was stirring something in a pan on the hob.

'Mmm.' She breathed in the heady smell and it made her feel hungry. 'We've been very busy, I'll tell you about it later.' She went across and kissed him. 'Smells lovely . . .'

'It'll be another forty minutes or so,' he said. 'Time for you to sink into a hot bath or have a sherry or both.'

'Do you want any help?'

'No, I've been making the most of my rare nine-to-five routine, you're the working half of this partnership at this minute! So have your bath and I'll pour a drink ready for you when you come down.'

Ten minutes later she was soaking in the deep and scented bathwater with her eyes closed and the warmth making her feel almost sleepy, but she savoured those moments as the effort of coping with the activities of the day was replaced with an effort to keep her eyes open. Last night's broken sleep was catching up with her and she didn't struggle against it; she allowed her eyes to close as the lovely water caressed her and she swished it all over her slender body, washing away the workaday grime. But as she lay in the luxury of those moments, she could not help thinking about Jack Mallory – she must tell Mark, whether or not he liked her to talk about work, and she must present him with her theory about Darren.

He'd listened on other occasions, during those relaxed

minutes before eating . . . perhaps he'd break his rule again, in a similar way? She decided to wallow no longer and hauled herself upright before stepping out and drying herself. Minutes later she was descending the stairs in a comfortable pair of leggings and a cosy T-shirt. She entered the lounge to find a sherry already poured and standing on a side table near her chair. Mark heard her and called from the kitchen, 'That was quick, I didn't expect you to be down just yet. I'll be with you in a couple of minutes.'

'Shall I lay the table?' she called.

'No, just sit down and put your feet up,' came the response. 'I'm coping.'

She occupied herself by reading the *Rainesbury Evening News*. It contained a report about a burglary when a wealthy man had had jewellery and antiques stolen. He was offering a £5000 reward for the recovery of his belongings – one of the stolen brooches had belonged to his grandmother, and a photograph of it accompanied the article. Then Mark was at her side bearing a glass of his favourite malt whisky. He plonked himself on the settee and said, 'You smell good, even from this distance!'

'It was nice, the bath.' She put down the paper and smiled at him. 'Nice and relaxing.'

'You've had a busy day, you said? It shows – or showed when you came in,' he told her. 'You look better now.'

'I need to tell you about it, Mark.'

'Need to?'

'Yes, need to. Not just want to. Can I? Before we eat?'

He realized it was important to her and smiled. 'Of course, rules are made to be broken when necessary. So what's happened?'

She decided to tell him about her day in chronological order – that was the police way of recording things – and so she began with her meeting with the Greater Balderside detectives and the visit to the wasteland where Welch had been attacked. She explained how she was unhappy about the lack of results, the constant dead ends she was encountering, the peculiarities of the assault on Welch, and then she told Mark about Darren's visits to bookmakers' shops, the library and the police station, one positive piece of information which had been revealed by today's enquiries. She told him about the enquiries she'd instigated at the farms and isolated places, the sightings of Darren in Huttondale and the road block through which he might have passed.

'And out of all that, what have you learned about Darren?' he asked. 'Was he being deliberately devious, setting up false trails for the local police? Letting himself be seen when it suited him?'

'On occasions, he did seem to want to make himself noticed by the police, and yet he could vanish completely when he wished,' she agreed. 'So yes, there is an element of cheekiness there, boldness even, but I don't think he intended to leave home, Mark. From what he told the girl and that garage, it seems he intended being around all that weekend, and the next weekend. I don't think he vanished deliberately, Mark, but that's not all.'

'Go on.'

'You might not agree with me over this, but I think I know why he was in the library, and the police stations . . .'

'Go on,' he invited again, noting her slight hesitation or uncertainty.

'It's all to do with that money he's been getting lately,' she said. 'All that cash, with no sign of him committing crimes to get it . . .'

'And?'

'Well, Mark, when I was in Greater Balderside Police Headquarters I happened to see the noticeboard. There was a Crimestoppers notice, highlighting a reward. £5000 leading to the recovery of some stolen jewellery . . . and then, if you remember, in the papers last week, a local businessman was offering £10,000 for information leading to the arrest of the person who'd killed one of his night-watchmen during a raid, and in this paper tonight, there's a £5000 reward . . . there's loads of them, Mark, if someone concentrated on collecting these, they could make a fortune . . . I know they're not all in one locality, but even so . . .'

'Hmm' was all he said. 'Go on.'

'Well, even before I began to think Darren might be involved in that kind of thing, I saw that the American Government was offering $25 million for information leading to the identification and arrest of the people who'd conspired to demolish the World Trade Center, and then there's that stolen painting in Italy, Bellini's *Madonna and Child*. There's a reward of £200,000 for its recovery . . . this is big money, Mark. There are lots of rewards, all there for the taking, and quite a number are very local and fairly modest by those standards. They're all waiting to be collected and I'm not suggesting Darren is trying to collect them all! But a clever and practising criminal is very likely to know who's committing crimes, or even planning crimes, in his locality, that's how we get police informers . . . I'm not talking about the big American rewards here, or the sort of funds that cause people to provide tip-offs about drug smuggling, art thefts and so on, I mean the local stuff. And if one man was picking up all, or even just some of those rewards, he'd have a nice tax-free income. All from rewards. It could explain Darren's sudden wealth.'

'So you think he's been haunting the library and police station to swot up on the latest offerings?'

'It makes sense, why else would he go there? And where else could he get the up-to-date information free of charge? Unless there's a website listing all the available rewards . . .'

'You could have a point, Lorraine. Well thought out. And do you feel it means his disappearance is based on the fact that someone realized he was informing on them? Was he determined to collect some reward? Finding out what a local villain was doing, digging deep in the hope of earning one of those rewards? Has he stumbled across something big enough to persuade him to grass on other villains? And get himself into bother? Do you think Darren has done a runner to get out of their way?' He pursed his lips. 'But, at the end of the day, do you honestly think one of Jack Mallory's lads would turn informer? Or become that kind of super-grass?'

'Maybe he's not an informer who splits on other villains, maybe he just points the way to the recovery of stolen property. Rewards often do that – they want the stuff back, no questions asked. He could be very selective and still earn good money without his criminal colleagues being arrested – and he is in the right profession to do that. He might not consider himself a grass – and, remember, a very large reward might tempt anyone to become an informer. He could cover his tracks by pretending to win money on horses – he has been spending time in betting shops.'

'So how did you come to this conclusion?' he asked.

'It's grown in my head over a day or two,' she said. 'I heard that the informers on Greater Balderside haven't been doing a very good job lately, then I saw a Crimestoppers reward poster, and heard about Darren's regular visits to that very same noticeboard. I began to wonder if Darren was nicking the goodies from under the noses of the paid informants. If he has been doing that, they might not have any new information to give to the police. It might explain why the local informants haven't been performing very well. The more I thought about it, the more it made sense. And it could be linked to his disappearance. I wondered if he'd either upset a dangerous villain or maybe stumbled across something very big.'

'I don't think anyone expected you to dig this deep, Lorraine.' He wasn't smiling now. 'Our brief was to mount a hunt for a Missing From Home, put on a bit of a show about tracing Darren, nothing more. You seem to have stirred up something of a hornets' nest . . .'

'There's more, Mark, you must listen.'

'More?'

'Jack Mallory has been attacked, we found him this afternoon, me and Andy. He's in a bad way, he's in A and E here in Rainesbury.'

'Good God!' He leapt to his feet now. 'My God, Lorraine, why didn't you tell me?'

153

'I am telling you –'

'I should have been told earlier . . . Who did it? Do you know?'

She told him how she and Andy had found Jack, adding that his handiwork had been wrecked and that they had no idea who was responsible although Scenes of Crime suggested a man called the Stonemason – or why the attack had occurred. 'It could be anybody, burglars, druggies, drunks . . . it's a lonely place, Mark, and it's on a public right of way . . . somebody passing and seeing a chance to steal something . . . disturbed by Jack . . .'

'I reckon Jack Mallory could have dealt with an ordinary attacker, even somebody younger than himself. This sounds like a beating with a purpose . . . Lorraine, you should have told me earlier, really you should.'

'I'm sorry, I thought the office might have told you, I was relating things in the sequence they happened today –'

'He's unconscious, you say?' he interrupted her.

'Yes, Andy checked with the hospital before we left the office.'

'Under guard?'

'We've a uniform constable sitting with him.'

'And who knows about this?'

'Andy, me, Andy's office, the uniform branch – Andy briefed them before we knocked off, so they could ask around Dovedale to see if anyone's been seen hanging around, being suspicious, and we wanted them to check on the breathalyser road block we discovered had been set up. Oh, and SOCO. We got them to examine the scene, they said similar attacks had been carried out in Greater Balderside, by the Stonemason. I've got to check that out and I'm aware it might become a murder scene, Mark, so we made sure everything was done. Including a search of Hill Top House, it was empty, not a sign of anyone or anything . . .'

'God, you have had a busy day. So what about Jack's relatives?'

'We asked Greater Balderside Police to try and find the

sons, to tell them. It means Greater Balderside also know about the attack.'

'There should be no need to trace the sons, word will surely reach them. If the attacker is from any of those gangs on Greater Balderside, he'll make sure everyone knows Jack's been done over. And why. That'll be the whole point of this. Now, you and Andy must both make very detailed and comprehensive statements explaining how you came to find Jack, what you found when you got to Hill Top, and what you did when you found him. You realize the Mallory Mob could accuse you and Andy of that attack . . . after all, why were you at the house? They'll want to know . . . and I think I'd better strengthen the guard in the hospital . . .'

'Mark? What is it? Why this reaction? Do you know something you haven't told me?'

'Darling, I am the Detective Chief Superintendent in charge of this sub-division and it happens that Hill Top House lies within my patch. Let's just say I was asked to keep an eye on things up there, and later I was asked to find Darren . . . Leave it at that for now. That's all you need to know.'

'You *do* know what's behind all this, don't you?' She didn't know whether to be angry or not.

'I can't reveal all my information to my staff,' he said. 'There are times when I must operate strictly on a need-to-know basis, times when not even my senior officers are aware of certain things. In this case, the Mallorys, it's all to do with them living on my patch. And we needed to mount a hunt for Darren . . . we've done that, or we're doing it. That operation must be kept going, Lorraine, keep digging, keep asking around Dovedale and on Greater Balderside, just as you have been doing.'

'You only gave us until Saturday!'

'I can always extend your time.'

'But, Mark, this attack on Jack, is it connected with what we've learned about Darren? It sounds to me as though it is.'

'It might be. It could be a warning of some kind, I can't

lose sight of that possibility. That's my immediate problem. Now, I must go and see Jack Mallory, to be sure it's him for one thing, and I must take Paul Larkin with me . . .'

'But not now, Mark, surely? Paul's on call this week, he's probably been told about this, detail him to go. He can handle it, surely? He's stood in for you before, lots of times. You've got to delegate more, Mark.'

'Not in this case. Look, it won't take me more than an hour, it's just a trip to the hospital and back, I need to brief Paul and have a look at Mallory. I'll meet Paul there. Ring him, will you, now. Tell him to meet me in the foyer in fifteen minutes. Tell him it's important – and urgent. Now, where's my mobile?'

'But Mark . . . you're off duty, you said we don't talk shop and now you're dashing off –'

'Help yourself to another sherry, and keep your eye on the oven,' he said, grabbing his jacket as he rushed through the hall and checking for his phone. 'And keep that whisky ready for me!'

Then the door slammed and he was gone. She got up and went to the window and was in time to see him driving into the street, heading towards Rainesbury District Hospital. She stood there for several minutes, looking at the space left by his departing car and feeling alternately angry and puzzled as she tried to tell herself that her relationship with Mark was purely domestic. He must keep some things from her, things to do with his duties, it was the nature of his job. His work was completely separate from her own – but sometimes she found it difficult to accept that. Or even to understand. Like now. It would be nice if he'd told her what was really happening. Or did he not trust her?

Pemberton arrived at the foyer ahead of Paul Larkin and hung around, waiting and watching.

It was busy, he noted, with families and friends arriving to visit patients but Paul was late and he was on the point of leaving to find Mallory's ward when Paul arrived, slightly breathless.

'I couldn't find a handy parking space!' he grumbled. 'Sorry I'm a bit late, boss, I seem to be parked miles away, but what's all this about?'

'The Mallorys, the old man, Jack, has been badly done over, hit over the head with a stonemason's hammer by the sound of it. He's in here somewhere. I want to look at him, to be sure it's him, and if he's conscious – or when he comes round – I'm hoping he might tell us who's behind this.'

'I heard SOCO had been called out but don't know the details. How did this happen?'

Pemberton explained to Paul, recounting Lorraine's story of events, and added, 'I need to replace the guard, which is why I wanted you here. I want you to see Mallory, and arrange for an armed guard, selected from your own officers, not from Uniform. But a uniform presence near the main entrance might be a good idea, with radio contact with Mallory's ward.'

'Right, got that.'

'Come along, let's find him.'

Enquiries from reception showed that Mr J. Mallory was in Ward 7 and that his condition had not altered since admission. There was no confirmation that any member of his family had yet been traced, and when Pemberton explained his interest, he was allowed to visit the patient. After all, it was visiting time and two visitors were permitted to each patient, although this man was under special observation due to his age and condition. Care must be taken, but Pemberton's rank and warrant card gained admission for him. He found the ward – a small one which contained six beds – and when the constable on duty noticed Pemberton's arrival, he rose to his feet in a relaxed form of attention.

'PC Hodgson, sir.'

'I'm Detective Superintendent Pemberton and this is DI Larkin. Any idea of this man's condition, and has there been a change since he arrived?'

157

Pemberton looked down upon the recumbent figure, a dark-haired and rather swarthy man with a few days' growth of whisker about his chin and cheeks. His hair was black and long, probably in need of a wash and trim, but he lay on his back and his head was bandaged about his ears, with just a hint of blood near his left ear. His hair stuck up through the top of the bandage, like a clump of black grass sprouting from a plant pot.

'No, sir, he's not moved. He's not said anything. I'm not sure of his condition but I don't think it is critical.'

'Any visitors, apart from staff?'

'No, sir, no one.'

'Who's in charge of him?'

'That's the ward sister over there, sir, behind that desk.'

'I'll have words with her. Paul, tell PC Hodgson about the Mallorys, will you, while I'm doing business with the sister. And arrange for the guard to be armed from this point onwards. I'm going to have him moved into a ward of his own, for security reasons. And while I remember, get Divisional CID to make enquiries into this attack, it'll relieve the pressure on Andy and Lorraine.'

Sister McFee was a stout matronly lady in her late forties and sensed that the approach of the very smart fair-haired man did not herald anything simple.

'Yes?' She did not look him in the eye, but continued to study what looked like a complicated form full of figures.

'Detective Superintendent Pemberton, Rainesbury CID.' He waved his warrant card under her nose, and she reacted. He now had her full attention.

'Oh, I see. Ah, so, Superintendent, how can I help?'

'Mr Mallory, the man under police guard.'

'Yes?'

'How is he?'

'He has been seen by the surgeon who feels he is not too badly injured, not as badly as we first feared. He has a depressed fracture of the skull caused by a severe blow of some kind, a single blow, but we do not believe his brain has been damaged; there was a lot of blood, so it seems, and he is severely concussed.'

'He's not in any danger then?'

'Not in our opinion, no. Emergency surgery was not required. Of course, he will have to remain here for some time under observation until we decide how to treat the depressed fracture; there is a big dent in his skull, to put it in layman's terms, and without treatment it could affect his brain . . . The surgeon will be examining Mr Mallory shortly.'

'Good. Now, sister, I need Mr Mallory to be placed in a single-bed ward, for security reasons.'

'Oh, well, I'm not sure we can agree to that, it depends on availability and his condition –'

'He's at risk of being murdered, sister, which is why we have placed a police guard over him. That head injury was no accident. That is why I am here. If you wish to take that risk –'

'Oh, no, I'm not, I had no idea . . . Yes, I'm sure we can find a suitable ward . . . You'd like to see it, would you?'

'I would.'

'Then follow me.'

Pemberton expressed his approval of a single room at the distant end of the ward, far enough from any entrances to require a lengthy walk past the reception desk and other beds; anyone attempting to reach Jack was bound to be observed by several people, staff and patients. With a police presence, it would be as secure as possible, he felt. The sister lost no time transferring Jack to his new room. The wheeled bed meant he could be moved with ease and within minutes he was lying alone with the constable nearby, Larkin nodding his own approval.

'I'll leave you in charge of things, Paul,' Pemberton said. 'Whether or not any of Jack's offspring will turn up is something I don't know, but do beware that others might try to get access to him, as visitors. Your men need to be very careful – beware of men – and women – in white coats! And you'll need to treat this as attempted murder, get some teams working on it immediately. Have words with Hansfield or someone in authority at Greater Balderside as well, tell them what's happened and ask if they know if anyone had it in for Jack. See me in the morning with any developments or results. I'm going home now.'

'Sir,' said Paul Larkin.

Pemberton left the hospital but did not go home immediately; instead he drove to his office, nodded to the constable on the enquiry counter and trotted upstairs with an impressive display of fitness. In his office he closed the door and lifted the telephone, made sure the line was secure and rang a Durham number, the home of Detective Superintendent Alistair Petrie of the National Crime Squad. Petrie answered.

'Pemberton here, Alistair. Can we talk?'

'Yes, go ahead.'

'Jack Mallory's been attacked with a hammer – the Stonemason, we believe. I don't think it was intended to kill him, it was a single blow. He's not dead but he's unconscious in Rainesbury District Hospital, condition stable. A wardrobe he was building was smashed as well, plus some things in his workshop. The scene's clean, no weapon or evidence left behind. A professional job. Seems to me like a warning. I've a police guard sitting with him.'

'Trying to get to Darren, you think? To warn him off?'

'That's my immediate reaction.'

'Thanks for the tip.'

'One other thing,' Pemberton added. 'One of my officers has got pretty close to the background of all this.'

'Good work, eh?'

'Good detective work, yes, not pillow-talk from me. You ought to know that. She's Lorraine Cashmore, my live-in partner, one hell of a good detective.'

'If she gets too close you might have to withdraw her from the enquiries, Mark. We don't want this operation scuttled, certainly we don't want any problems at this critical stage.'

'I can't curtail her too much, she'll smell the proverbial rat if I do, but I'll keep her in check,' Pemberton laughed.

'I'll depend on you for that,' said Petrie, and they ended their call.

Pemberton left the office and drove home. Lorraine was in the kitchen and the meal had not dried into a hard mess, nor was it burnt to a frazzle.

'It's ready when you are, Mark,' she said, hoping she didn't sound too cool towards him.

'I can have my whisky now,' he smiled. 'I've moved Mallory into a more secure ward, a one-bed room, and Paul is seeing to the security. He'll get Divisional CID to make enquiries into the attack, to take the pressure off you.'

She poured him a generous glass of whisky and said, 'I thought that would be part of our brief now. Clearly not! So am I allowed to know what this is all about, Mark?'

'No time,' he grinned. 'Dinner's ready. We mustn't spoil things by talking shop, must we?'

Chapter Eleven

At breakfast the following morning, Friday, Lorraine deliberately, but with some difficulty, refrained from even hinting she wished to talk to Mark about the Darren Mallory enquiry. She wanted to show respect for his wish to keep their home life as free as possible from the problems of work, especially over the first meal of the day. As she left for work, however, Pemberton called after her, 'See you for coffee as usual? With Andy and Paul? We'll talk about the Mallory business.'

'Fine,' she smiled, then hurried to her car.

During the short drive to divisional headquarters in Rainesbury, Lorraine found herself concentrating upon her driving through the streets, always busy between eight and nine on weekday mornings. As a consequence, she reached the office without her mind dwelling solely upon Mallory. She was at her desk when Andy Williams approached with a fistful of papers.

'I had a good start to the day, I got in early,' he beamed. 'I had to take my wife to the railway station, she's going to see her sister in Leeds, they're going on a shopping expedition. Now I feel as if I've been here hours! I've rung the hospital – there's no change in Jack Mallory's condition, he's still unconscious but hasn't deteriorated and the surgeon sees no cause for concern. He doesn't think Jack's life is at risk and the general consensus is that his skull fracture can be treated. He should regain consciousness given time – but how much time, no one knows. If and when he does wake up, the hospital will ring this office. None of his relatives has rung or called, though. And our police guard remains until further notice.'

'I wonder if Probert managed to inform the Mallory brothers?' she asked.

'I've not spoken to him this morning. If no one turns up by lunchtime, we might consider giving him a call to see how he fared. Now, this pile of paper is an email with a long attachment. It's from Probert. It's Greater Balderside's dossier on Darren Mallory – dates, times and places where he's been spotted by their surveillance teams.'

'We'd better read it!' she grimaced.

'It's going to take ages to wade through all that, and you'd finish up more confused than ever if you tried to absorb it all at one go,' he advised. 'I think we need to get an overview first, before we worry too much about the detail.'

'That sounds reasonable!' She sounded relieved. 'And it might be a good idea to extend our enquiries as far as we can, then we can use this record as a means of double-checking our facts.'

'Good idea,' he said. 'And apart from anything else, most of the action in this file is based on Greater Balderside anyway – routine stuff we don't really want to know about, although we mustn't forget that the clue to his disappearance might be in here somewhere. Let's hope we find it if it is!' And he plonked it on her desk.

'Has he included any information about Welch?' she asked.

'There's a note somewhere among that lot to say Probert's double-checked all his sources, including a look at the police file of the attack, but there's nothing much to add. Welch was merely a witness, he's not known to the police, his name doesn't crop up in any national or local police records.'

'Just like most members of the public!' she sighed.

'Exactly, he's never done anything to prompt the police to keep a file on him or to take any interest in him, until now. As you say, he's just one member of the great Joe Public, a victim of crime. There's no trace of him living anywhere in the district so far as anyone can tell, Scunthorpe Police have never heard of him and the only extra snippet comes from the probation officer who attended the court case.'

'Not Dent?'

'No, one of his staff. A man called Waite. Probert has tracked him down and phoned him on my behalf. Waite remembered the case and said Welch was between twenty-five and thirty years of age – the file said he was twenty-seven – of medium height and medium build with well-cut brown hair, and wore a smart dark suit when he gave his evidence. He added that Welch had no discernible accent.'

'That description could fit anybody!' snapped Lorraine. 'It could be any one of hundreds of thousands of men in this country . . .'

'It's all we've got, Lorraine.'

'So what are your plans for today, Sergeant? It's Friday, we've only got tomorrow.'

'Our final day and not a sign of Darren!' He shrugged. 'We can't do much more. We haven't to investigate Jack's attack, there must be a reason for that but it's someone else's job now – but we have got two full days to find Darren.' She sighed heavily. 'Where shall we go today?'

'We need another chat to that fellow we met in the shop at Fremingthorpe, the one who saw the vehicle check that Saturday night. I need to know exactly what he saw, and I need to contact Greater Balderside again, to see if the check was anywhere in their area. I'll ring them next, then I think we could start our enquiries with that witness. Did you take his name?'

'Yes, it's in my notebook. He's a smallholder in the village, he'll be at home during the day. His name was Seddon. Joe Seddon, he told me. I have his address.'

'Right, that's our first port of call. We'll take things from there. Now, I'll give Greater Balderside another ring, then our next job is to join the boss for coffee.'

'In the meantime,' she smiled, 'I'll start to wade through this file!'

As Lorraine began to glance through the wealth of paper on her desk, Andy went into his own office to make the call. Within half an hour he had returned.

'I've spoken to the inspector who deals with "Duties" at Sidlesbrough,' he said. 'With all their staff, they've a man working full time deciding which shift they're on. A sergeant with a mind like a computer, spending his days filling in dozens of forms to show where every copper is – or should be – at any particular time, and he assures me they did not stage an official vehicle road check of any kind on Saturday the twentieth. No breathalyser checks, tyre or lights checks, no searches for stolen property or drugs – nothing. Certainly not in our area. He would have known if there'd been anything like that. He's had words with their Road Traffic Division too, and they didn't set up any road blocks that Saturday.'

'It seems Mr Seddon was mistaken?' she suggested.

'He might have seen a road check, but not that particular Saturday. He was pretty certain when we spoke to him but I suppose he could have got his dates wrong. It happens all the time. All we can do is ask him.'

'We must do that. If we can establish that Darren passed through that check, it would help in tracing his movements after leaving the Blue Raven,' she mused. 'And if there was no road check in Greater Balderside Police area, then it must have been in our patch.'

'Inspector Dawson says not, Lorraine. He maintains no one in our force staged a checkpoint that Saturday. Somebody's got it wrong.'

'Let's hope our Mr Seddon can shed a little light on it!'

Twenty minutes later they were sitting in Mark Pemberton's office along with Paul Larkin, and all had a cup of coffee before them.

'Andy,' Pemberton addressed the sergeant. 'What's the latest?'

Andy Williams gave a coherent account of everything they had done yesterday and concluded with the outcome of this morning's phone calls to Greater Balderside and the hospital, plus a mention of the dossier on Darren, adding

165

that he and Lorraine were going to visit Mr Seddon to establish precisely what he had seen. Pemberton nodded his agreement while issuing the reminder, 'If you do find Darren, don't forget to tell him about his father.'

Paul Larkin then added his comments. 'I've fed Darren's name, and Dylan Welch's, into all our computer records. There's a bit on Darren, but nothing more than Greater Balderside has told us. And nothing at all about Welch.'

'Like a tourist, eh? Passing through.'

'There's nothing odd about that. I can't see we need to make a mystery about him. I've had some feedback too, from Uniform. They've already been to some of those locations you mentioned yesterday, Andy, routine enquiries but all without success.'

'Another dead end!' sighed Lorraine.

'Their enquiries suggest no one's seen Darren out on those moors, but they've a few more places to visit today. They're starting at the Dovedale end of the road. I'll keep you informed if there's any result.'

'We'll be in that part of the world today,' Andy pointed out. 'We might be able to visit some places too – we'll begin at the Greater Balderside end of the road, that should ensure we don't call at places already checked out. We've about thirty miles to cover.'

And so it was that Andy Williams, with Lorraine at the wheel, set out once again across the moors to interview Joe Seddon. Lorraine had brought the thick dossier on Mallory with her, thinking it might prove useful if they needed to check any facts in view of any information hopefully gleaned today. A forlorn hope perhaps, but a probable time-saver! They descended into Fremingthorpe village and asked at the post office for directions to Seddon's smallholding. It lay to the west, they were told, along a track called Back Lane. Every moorland village seemed to have a back lane, Lorraine thought, and most of them – like this one – were unsurfaced.

She turned down the rough lane with its narrow hawthorn hedges, pot holes and deep gutters. Soon, they crossed a small moorland beck in which ducks and geese abounded and drove into an array of tumbledown sheds, henhouses and outbuildings; there seemed to be hens everywhere and a black-and-white sheepdog barked a welcome as it strained on a long lead. Its noise brought a man into the open as their car eased to a halt, Lorraine endeavouring to park in a place devoid of wet mud. She spotted a patch of concrete near the house and eased to a halt upon it. The man they'd seen earlier in the shop now came towards them.

'Now then,' he said as they emerged.

'Good morning,' said Andy. 'Mr Seddon, isn't it?'

'Aye, we met yesterday. You're those police asking about that missing Dovedale lad?'

Seddon was a stocky man clad in overalls and wellingtons, and he had a woolly hat on his head; in his late forties, he had the ruddy complexion of a man who spent his days in the open air and appeared cheerful and welcoming.

'That's us,' smiled Lorraine, making the introductions. 'We'd like to ask you some more questions about the road block you noticed.'

'Aye, well, ask away. If I can answer, I will. I've nowt to hide.'

Andy took up the questioning. 'Can you tell us exactly what you saw that night, Mr Seddon?'

'Well, I didn't take a right lot of notice, but this police car was parked with its blue light flashing and two bobbies with torches were waving cars into that lay-by . . .'

'Which lay-by?'

'Well, that 'un near Hangdale lane end, like I said.'

'A considerable distance out of Greater Balderside?' suggested Andy.

'Oh, aye, twelve miles or more, I'd say.'

'Thanks. Now, they were directing cars into the lay-by, you say?'

'They were. Not every car, mind, because I never got waved in. They just waved me on past, indicated I should keep going.'

'What was the reason for the check, have you any idea?'

'Nay, lad, not really. I reckoned it must have been for breath tests, being that time of night, I don't think they'd be checking tyres and brakes at night, although they might have been doing lights. They do sometimes, have purges on duff car lights and that reminds me, there was a low-loader or breakdown truck in the lay-by, parked up. Probably nowt to do with the road check, unless they found a car which was unfit to be driven . . . so it could have been a safety check, eh? I mean, if they found a car that's unfit, they might have to cart it away somewhere.'

'Was it a police low-loader?'

'How should I know that?'

'Well, we do have some low-loaders, they've got police markings on the cabs, sometimes we have to collect our own broken-down vehicles and carry them into our own garage.'

'I can't be sure, I never really took much notice. I only spotted it because it had one of them orange lights flashing, like breakdown trucks have.'

'It was flashing at the time, was it?'

'Oh, aye, there was lights everywhere. Blue, orange, white, red . . . like Blackpool Illuminations, it was. And bollards, making a lane into the lay-by. You couldn't help but see the bobbies, they have to do that, eh? Make themselves easily seen. To stop accidents happening?'

'They have to be very careful when pulling cars up on a busy road, yes. Now, is it possible the police car was broken down, and was in the process of being recovered? Maybe it wasn't a road check after all?' Andy suggested.

'Oh, I don't think the police car was broken down, Sergeant. It was parked across the road, like they do for road checks, and all lit up with a blue light and headlights on, and two bobbies waving torches. It said Police on the doors. They waved me through, like I said, not that I was worried. I'm not a drinker, you see, never touch a drop so a breath test wouldn't have worried me. But they were definitely waving cars into that lay-by because the chap following me got pulled in. Don't ask me how they selected the cars . . . mebbe summat to do with faulty lights or noises they make or summat.'

'Were they faulty? The lights on that car?'

'Not so far as I know, he'd followed me most of the way from Greater Balderside, and I never noticed owt wrong with 'em. He had 'em dipped most of the time, to stop dazzling me from behind, considerate chap, I thought. Anyway, he was the one that got pulled in.'

'What sort of a car was it?' asked Lorraine. 'And how many people were in it?'

'No idea, sorry. I mean, it was behind me all the time, with its lights on so I never really got a good look at it . . . it wasn't owt special, not like a Jag or a sports car, I think I'd have noticed that, even at night. I'd say it was an ordinary saloon and I got the impression it was light-coloured, silvery grey I'd say, but really I can't be certain. And I don't know how many folks were in it. I saw the driver's face sometimes, in the lights of other cars coming towards us . . . in my mirror, it was, but I'd never know him again.'

'Him?' asked Andy.

'I'm fairly sure it was a chap, yes. Short dark hair, and he drove fast, I drive fast . . . he kept up with me.'

'Thanks. Now, the policemen. Were they wearing uniforms?'

'Oh, aye, helmets, the lot. Two of 'em.'

'Was there anything distinctive about them? Old or young? Fat or thin? Beards, distinguishing features of some kind?'

'Not that I'm aware of. They were just a couple of coppers doing their job, to my mind. I never took much notice, I was only too glad not to be stopped. Not that I'd been drinking, like I said, but you never know what they'll turn up if they start checking tyres and brakes and things.'

'OK. Now, back to the low-loader for a moment. Which way was it facing? Was there a car on board? Or was one or perhaps more waiting in the lay-by?'

'No, there was nowt there. The lay-by was empty, except for the low-loader and it had nowt on board. It was facing the same direction as traffic on that side of the road. You could just run a car straight up on to it, the ramp was down.'

'And was there a driver with the low-loader?'

'Now I can't be sure about that, Sergeant. I was past in a moment or two, you see, so I didn't get chance to have that close a look.'

'And were there other cars behind you, Mr Seddon?'

'Not just then, no. But a few minutes later a chap caught up with me, just before I got to our road end, going like a bat out of hell, and he whizzed past me as if I was standing still. A red racer of some sort.'

'Not the car which had followed you?'

'No, I'm sure it wasn't. It was a young buck showing off . . . but they didn't pull him in, did they? And he must have passed through the check not long after me.'

'Any idea who it was? It would be nice to talk to him.'

'Sorry, no idea. I can't say I recognized it, it wasn't a local car.'

'And were you alone?'

'I was. I'm not married, never had the time or inclination to get myself tied down with a wife. I'm past forty-five so I reckon I've passed my best-before date!'

'That's not too old for romance!' laughed Andy. 'You might meet the woman of your dreams one day . . .'

'I can't imagine who'd put up with me or want a seven-day-a-week job and not much money, to say nowt of smelly pigsties and having to muck the hens out.'

Lorraine tried to bring the conversation back to business. 'Mr Seddon, we need to know the exact time and date you saw the road check.'

'It was a week last Saturday, like I told you.'

'The twentieth?'

'Right.'

'This is very important to us,' Lorraine said. 'So how can you be sure?'

'It's my mother's birthday, the twentieth, we'd had a

party for her. Seventy, she was. The whole family. Me, being the eldest, had to give a speech –'

'So what time would you come through that check-point?' she continued.

'Oh, about quarter to one, I'd say. Maybe ten to. Sunday morning by then, of course. We packed up mother's party at midnight, it was in an hotel, and my sister went home with her in the taxi. I got to my car, it was just round the back in the hotel car park, and I had a bit of chat with a cousin, then I came home. Yes, quarter to one or there-abouts.'

'When we saw you yesterday, we were asking if you knew Darren Mallory from Dovedale, that's the lad in the photo we showed you.'

'Aye, I know. I remember you asking. I asked around the village after you'd gone, but folks there don't know him.'

'I know you said you couldn't get a good look at the man in the car behind you, but I was wondering if it might be him?' Lorraine eased a photograph from her handbag. 'Have another look at his photo.'

Seddon took it, studied it carefully and shook his head.

'Sorry, I'd like to help but I couldn't say if he's the chap who was behind me. Like I said, I'm pretty sure it was a man . . . you sometimes get flashes of light from other cars, lighting faces up, sometimes you can see through the mirror who's driving the car behind . . . but I never got a good enough look at him. He had dark hair, though, like that photo and he was about that age, I'd say.'

By this stage, they had exhausted their enquiries and, after a courtesy chat about his smallholding and the joys of earning a living in one's desired way, they left.

'We must have a look at that lay-by,' said Andy Williams. 'Maybe there's a house nearby, or a farm or something?'

'But Andy, if Mr Seddon is so sure he saw the road check that Saturday, why have two police forces denied any part in it?'

171

'Because it might be the truth, Lorraine. Perhaps they weren't real policemen,' suggested Andy. 'Just think about that. The timing is about right to catch Darren on his way home that night, we know he would use that route, he used it most Saturday nights. It means others would know that. In most cases, he's a bit like the Scarlet Pimpernel – they seek him here, they seek him there – but this is one place they could almost be sure of catching him. I think the car following Seddon was driven by Darren, Seddon said it was a young man with dark hair. And it's easy enough to get hold of a blue rotating light and stick it on the roof of a car – there's some in a café near us, a former police station but the lights are modern. You can get realistic-looking uniforms from any fancy dress supplier, certainly good enough to fool the public on a dark night.'

'You're suggesting someone was lying in wait for him?'

'What else?' He shrugged his shoulders. 'Everything fits, Lorraine. It seems to me that Darren drove straight into some kind of ambush. And who's going to question the sighting of a police road check at night? Most of us are only too glad not to be pulled over.'

'And you think Darren would stop, even for a police check?' she asked.

'I don't think he'd make a dash for it, unless he suspected something was amiss or if he had a car stuffed with stolen goods or something worse. Or he'd been drinking. I get the impression Darren was too careful to let himself be caught like that. So, yes, I think he would pull up for a road block if he had nothing to lose, especially if he thought it was genuine.'

'We've no proof it wasn't genuine, have we?'

'Apart from the fact neither police force will admit to setting it up,' Andy reminded her. 'I appreciate that a road block could be set up almost anywhere at any time by a couple of bobbies out on patrol, but how's that explain the presence of the low-loader? That implies advance planning of some kind. And, I would suggest, the knowledge or approval of a senior officer.'

'I don't know what to think about this,' Lorraine

admitted. 'It seems all rather too far-fetched. I mean, Andy, if he was ambushed and spirited away that night, where is he now? And his car? Worse still, could he be dead?'

'That's what we have to find out. Come along, we've got work to do. The lay-by's next. If that road block was there for a while, which it would surely have to be, whether legitimate or not, then others must have seen it. I'm sure that road must carry lots of revellers home to the sticks after a night out on the tiles of Greater Balderside. And there might be others who use it at that time of night, lorries, for example, shift workers. You know, this gets more intriguing by the day . . .'

'Hangdale lay-by, here we come!' smiled Lorraine, putting down her foot.

The drive across the moors was glorious but they had no time to spend on enjoying the scenery and some thirty-five minutes later they passed the junction leading to the hamlet of Hangdale. A mile or so beyond, they saw the lay-by on the offside of the road; they drove past until they found a convenient place to turn around and were soon drawing to a halt beside the road. It was a narrow lay-by, able to accommodate perhaps four articulated lorries one behind the other, or eight or nine cars. The only adornments were a waste bin and a wooden notice forbidding overnight camping.

Andy climbed out and Lorraine followed. A brisk, sharp breeze was blowing and they had extensive views over the moorland below where the landscape dipped away from the road and the lay-by, while at the other side the moors rose higher than the carriageway. In effect, this section of the road ran around the side of a hill. Lorraine found her map and spread it on the car bonnet, asking Andy to hold it down before the wind carried it away.

'We're here.' She stabbed the map with her finger. 'Greater Balderside is over there, to the east – you can see the murk which covers the conurbation – and Hangdale is over that hill. There's a road up to it, and a couple of farms along that road. I think we should ask there, to see if anyone saw the road block . . .'

'It can't be seen from the village.' He waved his hand to indicate the vast open space all around them. 'This lay-by can't be seen from anywhere, except the road itself. It's hidden from below and blocked by the hill above.'

'If your theory about them being false police officers is correct, you can see why it was chosen,' she pointed out. 'But I wasn't thinking about that, I was wondering if anyone from these villages or farms along the road had travelled this way on the twentieth; if they had, they might have seen the road check.'

'It's worth a diversion along the lane to Hangdale!' he smiled. 'Come along, let's sample some country air and it'll soon be lunchtime. I wonder if there's a decent pub in Hangdale?'

The first farm – High Cragside – was owned by J. and J. Marshall, according to Lorraine's list. As they drove into the premises, a middle-aged man wearing a flat cap, overalls and wellies was sweeping muck from the cowhouse. He paused to watch them park and find their way through the mire towards him.

'You need wellies if you're coming to see me,' he chuckled. 'Not selling insurance, I hope, or cattle medicines . . .'

'Police,' Andy called to him.

'Not the local bobby, though? It must be serious.'

He leaned his broom against the door jamb and ambled across to them. 'Marshall,' he said, extending his hand. 'Jim Marshall. So what can I do for you?'

'Williams, Detective Sergeant,' returned Andy. 'From Rainesbury, and this is Detective Constable Cashmore.'

'A bit out of your territory, aren't you? Up here?' The farmer had a bemused expression on his face.

'It's all in our division,' returned Andy, 'but I must admit we don't get up here very often. Now, this man,' and he produced his photograph of Darren. 'Darren Mallory, from Dovedale. He's missing and we're trying to find him. We know he comes past your road end every day to work in Greater Balderside.'

Marshall shook his head. 'Can't say I've seen him, sorry. What's he done?'

'Nothing that we're aware of, we're just trying to find him, he's been missing for almost a fortnight now.'

'Well, he's not come to this farm, I can tell you that.'

'There was a police road check on that lay-by,' Lorraine said. 'On the night of Saturday the twentieth, actually it was probably in the early hours of the Sunday, the twenty-first. Did you see it, or were you aware of it?'

'We can't hear a thing from that road, which is mebbe as well, but no, I never saw it. You could ask my son, though, he's out and about at all kinds of daft times, chasing women in Sidlesbrough and such. Joe's his name, he's in the hayshed. Over there.'

Joe was a younger version of his father, even down to the way he dressed, and Lorraine thought he'd be around thirty. A sight of Darren's photograph produced a vigorous shaking of his head: although he spent a lot of his free time on Greater Balderside, going clubbing with a group of pals, he had never set eyes on the handsome dark-haired man in the photo. Then Lorraine mentioned the road check.

'A week last Saturday, you say?' He frowned. 'On that lay-by just at our road end?'

'Right,' said Andy. 'Two police cars and a low-loader, they were there about quarter to one.'

'They weren't there at quarter past, I can tell you that,' he said. 'Me and my mates got back from the Double Six about then, and they came in here for a nightcap. Six of us. There was no road check then.'

'And what about when you set off to go clubbing?'

'No, we left here about half-past seven to drive into town, there was nothing then.'

'Darren went to the Blue Raven that night,' Andy told him. 'We know there was a road check and we're trying to find out if he went through it, or got stopped. If he did, then we know he got this far on his way home.'

'Sorry, I can't help, but you could ask my mate Steve Thorburn, he was with us in Sidlesbrough at the Double

175

Six but he left a bit earlier than us. He had to get up for milking next day, so he said he wouldn't come back to my spot, he knows we stay up late on Saturdays!'

'And where can we find him?' asked Andy.

'Birch House, next stop down our lane. He'll be there now.'

'Thanks, that's useful.'

Birch House was a tidier holding and looked better cared for, and as the police car came to a halt in the stackyard, a young fair-haired man with a collie dog at his heels emerged from a building. Some six feet tall and burly, he had film star looks and a smile which revealed a wonderful set of white teeth. Lorraine thought he was gorgeous . . .

'Hello!' There was a warmth in his greeting. 'Is it me you want, or my brother?'

'Steve Thorburn,' said Andy.

'That's me. So how can I help?'

Yet again, Andy explained their mission, showed the photograph of Darren and asked if Steve had seen him or knew him; the answers were all negative. Then Lorraine mentioned the road bock and Steve smiled.

'Oh yes, Joe's right. I left earlier than the rest and there was a road block near the end of this lane, using that lay-by.'

'What time was that?' asked Lorraine.

'Half-past twelve or thereabouts.' He frowned as he tried to recollect events with more clarity. 'I left the club about quarter to twelve so yes, by the time I'd got my car and driven out here, it would be half-past, or as near as dammit.'

'Did you get pulled up?' asked Andy.

'No, I was quite surprised. I was waved through. I'd had a drink or two, I must admit, but I wasn't over the limit I don't think. I don't mind admitting I was worried . . . anyway, they waved me on and I came straight here.'

'Was anybody being checked when you drove through?'

'No, there were cones making a lane into the lay-by, and

176

a police car across the nearside lane, and two bobbies with torches, and a breakdown truck in the lay-by. As there was no car in the system, I was sure I'd be pulled in.'

'And you are sure that was the evening of the twentieth?' asked Lorraine.

'Absolutely. The Saturday before last. Last Saturday I could stay later, it was our Graham's turn for milking.'

'The truck in the lay-by - what sort was it?'

'A breakdown of some sort, it had a flashing amber light. I didn't bother to look at it closely, I was only too glad to get away, I can tell you!'

'Which way was it facing?'

'It had its back end towards the traffic, facing towards Dovedale. And I recall its ramp was down, as if it was expecting a car to drive straight on to it.'

'And how many vehicles would it carry, do you think?' asked Andy.

'Oh, just one. It wasn't one of those big low-loaders that carry several cars, more like one from a local garage, a breakdown truck with an amber light.'

'Did you notice any insignia on it? Name of the garage? Colours?'

'It was a lightish colour, I'd say, white mebbe, but I can't say much else. I was past it in seconds, glad to get away,' and he chuckled.

'Now, another angle. Those youngsters who go into town on a Saturday, we've talked to Joe Marshall and he mentioned his pals – but the road block wasn't there when he came past, not long after you. Do many people go into Greater Balderside on a Saturday night?'

'A few from hereabouts, yes, concerts, meals, theatre and so on, not a great number, I wouldn't think, due to the drink-drive business. Not many youngsters come home as early as us. The older folks might come past about the same time we did, but clubbers might be as late as three or four in the morning or later. We're farmers, we come home early because we've got to get up for work next morning.'

'Would you know who they are? Those people who

drive into town? We'd like to find out who was using this road at that time of night. We'd like to know when the road block was set up, how long it was there.'

'Sorry, no, they come from all over these moors. But if you want to know about the road check, you could always ask the police!' He grinned.

'Believe me, it's easier asking passing witnesses,' retorted Andy.

'Well, to be honest, I don't know who goes into town regularly on a Saturday. We've our gang, Joe's pals and me, eight or nine of us and all I can say is you can ask about the villages, in the pubs, to see who goes into town on a Saturday and comes home late.'

They questioned Steve about any sounds he might have heard, or any sightings of the road block earlier that evening, but he couldn't help any further.

They left in the certain knowledge that someone had established a road block at that point on the Saturday night when Darren had disappeared. But if none of the local police had done so, then who? And why?

Chapter Twelve

Hangdale was a tiny hamlet of rugged stone houses clustered together for shelter against the bleak northern weather and it boasted a population of some two hundred. It was tucked deep in a cleft in the moors, sheltered from the winds by the surrounding hills and almost invisible in its saucer-like hollow until one climbed high on to the circling moors to gaze down upon it. Its isolated location meant it had to be self-supporting, and so it was in that it boasted a small public house, a shop-cum-post office and a garage which probably spent more time dealing with agricultural implements than cars. Lorraine parked outside the shop as Andy looked at his watch wondering whether it was time to eat – and then he spotted the twin green petrol pumps a few yards away.

'Tell you what,' he said. 'You go to the pub and order our lunch – I'll have a steak pie and chips or something similar, and a pint to go with it – and while you're doing that, I'll pop along to that garage to see if they know who's got a low-loader hereabouts. If those were fake cops, they must have borrowed it from somewhere fairly local.'

She agreed and decided to take the Mallory file with her. If Andy took longer than expected, she could usefully occupy her time checking Darren's more recent known movements.

The pub was small and ancient, with a stone floor and a few battered tables occupying the bar area. Dark with small windows, and made even darker by the plentiful dark brown paint, it had a deserted and even damp air and it also smelt of beer and tobacco smoke. This was purely a drinking place, she realized, it hadn't kept pace with the modern idea of serving bar meals. She was thinking of leaving so they could go elsewhere when a stout grey-haired lady, who must have been seventy, appeared behind the counter.

'Yes, miss?'

'I was wondering if you did meals . . .'

'Nowt cooked, but I can do a sandwich if you want. Home-cured ham, home-made chutney and home-made bread. Brown. All fresh. And I've got some apple pie and cream, home-made, that's if you'll want a pudding.'

'Er, well, yes,' smiled Lorraine. 'Two sandwiches, please – my friend's just gone to the garage. And while we're waiting, I'll order a pint of bitter for him and I'll have a dry white wine.'

'We don't do wine, no call for it in Hangdale.'

'Oh, well, in that case I'll have half a bitter.'

'I'll get them for you now, then you can enjoy it while I'm doing your sandwiches, it'll take a few minutes,' and the landlady reached for the necessary glasses and prepared to pull the drinks. 'Holidaying, are you?'

'No, I'm a police officer, CID.' Lorraine placed the Mallory file beside her on the bar as she eased Darren's photograph from her handbag. 'We're looking for this young man, he's from Dovedale. Darren Mallory. He's gone missing, we're trying to find him.'

The lady took the photograph and held it up in the light from the small windows then shook her head. 'Sorry, can't say I've ever seen him in here. How long's he been missing?'

'Nearly a fortnight.' Lorraine then explained her concern. 'We're asking in all the villages between Greater Balderside and Dovedale.'

'Well, I'll keep my ears and eyes open, miss, you could always give me a ring later. Marjory Ibbotson, Fox and Hounds, that's me. Everybody calls me Marj.'

She was now heaving on a beer pump handle and producing a handsome-looking pint for Andy and so Lorraine took the opportunity to ask about the road check;

it would have been about a mile and a half from this village and on the main road and she added that none of the local police knew about it.

'I've a few regulars on a Saturday night,' the landlady told her. 'Not just from here, they come from the farms hereabouts. If there'd been any police about, they'd have told me.'

'We know it was operating around one in the morning,' Lorraine explained. 'What we can't be sure is when it began.'

'Well, I'm allus closed and locked up well before one, I don't have late drinkers because I close on time, I need my sleep at my age, but I'm open till eleven. It's generally about half-past before everybody's gone and I do have one chap – Alex Rogers from Low Mires, that's a house along the main road towards Mireholm, well, Alex allus comes in at quarter past ten and goes home when I shut.'

'So he might have seen something?'

'If anybody did, it would be him. He's been in here every night since, of course, regular as clockwork is Alex, but he's never said owt about a road block or police being about that night. He would if he'd seen anything. Go and have a chat with him, tell him Marj sent you.'

After she had pulled the drinks, she placed them on the counter and Lorraine carried them to a corner table to await Andy and the sandwiches. Alone in the bar, she opened the Mallory file and decided to begin with Saturday the twentieth, the day Darren vanished. The contents had been assembled in chronological order and she had no trouble locating the section she wanted to study. Soon she was reading about Darren's day that Saturday, the last to be recorded – it was far from being a complete account and comprised little more than a few sightings by police observers. Darren was known as Target in the notes. She found: '10 a.m. Target arrived in Sainsbury car park. Parked in Row F. Left car, carrying black hold-all. Entered store, dressed in jeans, green sweater, trainers. Target did not talk to anyone, did not collect trolley. Followed into store. Entered Gents. Three minutes later Target emerged wearing a pale blue anorak and baseball cap. Ran into restaurant area and vanished after leaving via restaurant delivery door. 12 noon. Target seen to enter William Hill's bookmakers. Did not emerge after ten minutes but when observer entered the premises, there was no sign of Target. Thought to have left through rear door. No further sightings until 8.30 p.m. when he entered the Blue Raven, dressed in smart dark suit, tie. He was alone upon entry but struck up friendship with young woman, later identified as Julie Carver, employee of Sidlesbrough Building Society. Spent time talking to her, left premises with her and they went their separate ways. Midnight, Target seen to board his own Vauxhall car and drive towards the outskirts. This is his usual practice on a Saturday night; it is known he always goes home at this point.'

She turned to the previous page, Friday, and it was in similar vein, recording his arrival in the town at 8.30 a.m., his subsequent dodging antics, a sighting in Sidlesbrough police station foyer at 11.05 a.m., a chat to a female traffic warden at 12.15 p.m., a visit to William Hill at 2 p.m. from where he went straight to the central library at Sidlesbrough and spent three-quarters of an hour reading the daily papers. Then he went to an exhibition in Sidlesbrough Art Gallery, a display of Giovanni Bellini's works. What on earth was a man like Darren Mallory doing in an art gallery? Planning a robbery perhaps? Or another trick to confuse his watchers? When he emerged, he dodged his observer and was not seen again that day.

Lorraine realized Darren must have – or must have had – some kind of base in town, somewhere he could relax, put his feet up, store his personal belongings or even do his deals, whatever they were. She wondered if such a place had ever been sighted during these observations, Probert had not mentioned it. She began to think that this log might not provide any clues of value to her, particularly anything relating to the reason for Darren's disappearance, and then Andy arrived.

'I got delayed,' he said. 'By the chap at the garage. He didn't see the road block but when I mentioned the breakdown truck or low-loader, he said he could give me the names of garages hereabouts who've got such a vehicle. He had no idea where it might have come from, not that I could give a very detailed description. However, there's some kind of mutual aid system between a dozen or more garages in this part of the moors. He says in summer when the tourists are about, they get lots of breakdowns, folks failing to top up their radiators or oil, or running out of petrol, or getting punctures and not having a spare tyre, the sort of daft things that tourists do, going out unprepared. Sometimes a garage gets more than one request to turn out in an emergency and so they run this mutual aid system, one calls another if he needs another breakdown truck in a hurry. So the chap here explained it to me and rang every one of his contacts, just to see if their vehicle had been borrowed that Saturday. And none had! I offered to pay for the phone calls, but he wouldn't hear of it. And he doesn't know Darren or the Mallory brothers. I called at the post office-cum-shop, too, they can't help. Ah! That looks a good pint, I hope it's not had time to go flat!'

Lorraine told of her chat with Marj, warning him he'd not get a cooked lunch, and then the lady herself arrived carrying two dinner plates, each containing a huge doorstep of a sandwich with a luscious ripe tomato sitting beside it.

'Grew those tomatoes myself. Now, if you want more chutney, shout, or more drinks, I'll be through the back,' she said, and vanished to go about whatever business she was doing.

'Crikey! You could use this as a doorstop!' smiled Andy, taking a bite and then saying, 'Wow, taste this ham . . . and the bread . . . now this is proper food . . .' and he licked his lips and then began to wolf down his meal with liberal sips from his pint glass. Lorraine told Andy that her initial perusal of the Mallory file did not produce much hope of leading to a breakthrough in her enquiries, but that she would persist, adding, 'I'd like to talk to Alex Rogers before we leave here. So what's our next plan?'

'I was toying with the idea of calling at every garage

between here and Greater Balderside, to ask about low-loaders and breakdown trucks, but there's no need now. I get the impression there are thousands of the things, so how do we find that particular one? Unless there's one been stolen . . . now, there's an idea! I haven't checked that . . . that's for after lunch. By jove, Lorraine, this is a crackingly good sandwich . . .'

'There's apple pie and cream to follow if you want it,' she smiled.

'Home-made like this?'

'Yes.'

'Right, I can't miss that . . . and coffee?'

The lunch was memorable for its simplicity and cost – Marj charged only £1.50 per sandwich – and when they left, they drove to a hilltop site from where Andy could ring Inspector Larkin on his mobile. Reception in the hollows on the moors was very poor.

When he'd established contact he explained his growing suspicions about the road check and the breakdown truck, and asked Paul Larkin if he would check both within their own force area and with Greater Balderside, to see if there'd been any reports of stolen breakdown trucks on or around Saturday the twentieth; and he asked for a further check on the likelihood that either force had staged that road block. If it was genuine, there must have been some incident to precipitate it, even something simple like bringing a stolen car to a halt.

When he'd finished, Larkin said, 'I'm glad you rang. We've had two developments since you left this morning. One – Joseph Campion has turned up safe and sound. Greater Balderside rang to tell us in view of your enquiries on their patch, you've got him down as missing. He's been travelling in the UK, so he told Greater Balderside when they spotted him, touring Cornwall in recent days. Wanted to get away from it all, he told them, a break from family and other pressures. They don't believe that, they think he's been abroad. So we can cross him off our lists. And two – Jack Mallory's recovered consciousness, but he's not

184

spoken yet. The boss is going to visit him this afternoon, when he gets the all-clear from the hospital.'

'Any sign of a family visit?' asked Andy.

'Nothing,' confirmed Larkin. 'And no word from any of them. I did a check with your contacts in Greater Balderside – they've spread the word among the villains on their patch and they're confident the news will reach the Mallorys. Like we thought earlier, the Mallorys might suspect some kind of trap, even if there isn't one, and might not turn up.'

Andy relayed that news to Lorraine; she was pleased Mark had decided to visit Mallory in hospital, but she found the news about Campion somewhat puzzling.

'He's been touring this country?'

'That's what Larkin said but Greater Balderside seem to think he's been abroad.'

'So why didn't anyone know this? His wife, family, friends? Why was he reported missing if that's all he was doing?'

'For the same reason Darren's been reported missing?' suggested Andy. 'Someone wants to know where he was, wants to keep tabs on him.'

'Yes, but why would they want to know that?'

'Perhaps he was suspected of something . . . who knows,' Andy suggested. 'We'll never know – besides, it's nothing to do with us, Lorraine. It's all out of our force area!'

'I'd like to know more about his supposed holiday!' she snapped. 'He's been away for six months, some holiday! And when did he get back? How long has he been home?'

'I'm sure you would love to dig into that one, but I repeat – it's nothing to do with us. Now, we've got to call on your Mr Rogers at Low Mires.'

Alex Rogers, probably well into his sixties, was a tall and very thin man with a thatch of straw-like fair hair; dressed in a warm sweater and corduroy trousers he greeted them at the door of his lonely cottage.

Low Mires, a single-storey stone house with blue slate

185

tiles, stood alone beside a moorland track, and like many such places it had hens running all over, a couple of sheep dogs behind a gate and a few ginger cats sleeping in the yard. They opened the gate and went towards him as he waited at his back door.

'Visitors!' He seemed pleased to see them. 'It's not often I get visitors here, I'm not on the proverbial beaten track. I'd have said you were hikers if you'd been wearing the right gear, or tourists looking for bed and breakfast, or maybe someone who's got lost.'

'Wrong each time!' smiled Andy. 'Police. We're detectives,' and he made the introductions, adding that Marj from the Fox and Hounds had sent them.

'Alex Rogers, retired gamekeeper of this parish,' said their host. 'So how can I help you? I wouldn't have thought there was much crime to detect up here!'

Andy showed him Darren's photograph and Rogers shook his head, saying he did not recognize the young man, nor had he noticed him in this area. Then Andy turned to the road block, explaining his interest and adding that none of the local police forces had established a formal road check that Saturday.

'It might have been spontaneous,' he admitted to Rogers. 'Two bobbies out on their own being warned about a stolen car or something suspicious heading their way, and they decide to stage a checkpoint to try and halt it. There was a breakdown truck or low-loader nearby – whether or not that is connected to the incident is something we don't know. But both the road check and the truck were seen there at the same time.'

'And what's your interest in it? Am I allowed to be nosy?'

'We're trying to establish the time it was there, we're interested in the possibility that Darren Mallory might have driven through it, or been stopped there for some reason. If he was stopped there, it's the last sighting of him that we know about – so we need to establish that, and then we want to know who were the police officers who

186

set up the block. They should have a record of everyone they halted.'

'Clearly, your own people aren't much help?'

'They've tried, but there's no record of an official road check, that's why we think it might have been done on the spur of the moment. There's always a possibility that the breakdown truck was not connected with the road check and it's a mammoth task tracing every officer who might have done it, if it was established at very short notice and only for stopping one car.'

'Well, I can help, but not a lot. Being a former game-keeper, I'm used to wandering around these moors at night, and I still do it, even if I am retired. Force of habit, I suppose, the need for a bit of fresh air before bedtime. I like to be nosy, I'll admit that, I like to see who's dumping litter on the moors, stealing sheep, poaching, having it off with someone else's wife, that sort of thing. You'd be amazed at what I see on my nightly walks, I've a wonder-ful collection of car numbers . . . anyway, the road block. It wasn't there when I went to the pub – I always walk to the pub and take a roundabout route which takes me over the moors right above that lay-by, I get a grandstand view.'

'You've a reason for going that way? It seems a long way round,' commented Andy.

'It is a long way round, yes, by no means a direct route for me, but cars often park up there, you see. I like to know who's about, years of doing it in my job, I suppose, like you. Anyway, I left Marj's pub at quarter past eleven, like I always do, and came back by the same route, a long walk, taking in the lay-by and other spots where rogues tend to gather. I know them all, Sergeant . . . but yes, I came past the lay-by, walking high above on the moors, and saw them actually setting it up.'

'Good, good,' beamed Andy. 'Wonderful. So tell us about it.'

'Well, there's not a lot to tell really. Once I saw it was a police matter and they weren't poachers, it didn't really concern me – other than a spot of natural curiosity as to what they were doing. First to arrive was the breakdown truck.'

'From which direction?' interrupted Andy.

'From Greater Balderside. It drew straight into the lay-by. I saw it pull in and stop, it was a dull white colour, then the driver lowered the ramp at the rear, as if getting ready for a car to be hauled or driven aboard straightaway.'

'Was the amber light flashing?' asked Lorraine.

'Not just then, no.'

'Did you see the driver? Or a mate if he had one?'

'Yes, there were two of them, in overalls. Orange overalls, fluorescent, for easy sighting at night, I suppose.'

'Not police officers?' asked Andy.

'No, they looked just like any other breakdown service. I thought someone might have broken down nearby and was being towed by friends into that lay-by, using it as a pick-up point or something. You know, a pre-arranged collection point.'

'Possible, I suppose. Now, was there a name on the truck? Did you see its registration number?'

'Sorry, no, I was too far away to see it. And I can't recall a name. I mean, it was of no real concern to me. They weren't shooting sheep or poaching so I didn't try to take details.'

'Fair enough. Now, the police.'

'Well, yes, they came a few minutes later. A police car with two officers, in uniform. They got out and spoke to the mechanics, then placed their car at an angle across the road, in the nearside lane facing Dovedale that is, with all its lights on, and blue light flashing. They laid cones out as a route into the lay-by, directly to the rear of the breakdown. Then the breakdown put its amber rotating light on and they all settled down to wait, with the bobbies standing on the verge, waiting.'

'And what time was all this?' asked Andy.

'Midnight as near as dammit. It wasn't a complete blockage of the road, and I stood in the darkness and watched for a while, but they just waved everybody past. I could see it wasn't a routine breath test check or for expired excise licences or lights, that sort of thing, otherwise almost everyone would have been pulled in, but they weren't. Nobody was pulled in while I was watching. I thought they were waiting for something in particular, but when nothing was stopped by about twenty past twelve, I decided to go home.'

'So you never saw them draw anyone into the lay-by or on to the low-loader?'

'Nope, nothing.'

'And could you hear any conversation?'

'Not a thing. I was too far away – and anyway the wind up there would have made it impossible to hear anything. Sorry.'

'Was there anything odd about the appearance of the policemen?' Andy was still convinced this was not a genuine police road check. 'Their uniforms, behaviour, anything really?'

'You mean they might have been filming for a television programme or something?'

'Who knows?' Andy said. 'Some of those drama productions can recreate police scenes very realistically. Or they might have been fakes. I just wondered if you had any reservations about what you saw, being a trained observer.'

'Fakes? You mean they might not have been real policemen?'

'That's between you and me. It's something I have to consider. It's odd there is no record of that check in any of the logs in either Greater Balderside Police or ourselves. And that breakdown truck, low-loader or whatever you call it, must have come from somewhere.'

'Well, blow me!' Rogers looked amazed at this. 'Who'd have thought it, and here's me ignoring it, thinking it was all above board when I might have been able to help you if I'd watched a bit longer or got a bit closer and taken numbers and things . . . it just goes to show you can't be too sure.'

'So it didn't register in your mind as something that wasn't quite right?' Andy persisted.

'Well, no, it didn't. If it was fake of any kind, it fooled me.'

'Thanks,' said Andy. 'You've been most helpful . . .'

'I haven't, though, have I? I've missed an opportunity to help solve a crime but honestly, Sergeant, if it was a set-up, it was a very, very good one. But why would anyone want to set up a fake road check? Were they stealing cars, do you think?'

'We've not had any reported stolen by that method,' Andy confirmed. 'But as to the real reason, well, your guess is as good as mine.'

'People round here know me, Sergeant,' Rogers told him. 'And if I start asking about that road check, I might just learn something. I'll not say you think it's a fake, that's between you and me, and I know how to keep my mouth shut. I can ask the locals if they saw it . . . and if I get anything extra, I'll call you.'

'A pair of extra ears and eyes around here would be useful,' agreed Andy, passing his card with the Rainesbury telephone number on it. 'If you do call, ask to speak to me or Detective Constable Cashmore in person.'

'I understand.'

And so they left Alex Rogers, a man of the moors, and they knew he would ask lots of questions of the local people, if only to regain the self-respect he felt he'd lost by letting that big fish go! If only he'd taken the number of that breakdown truck . . . or even the police car . . . or gone closer to listen . . . he'd have done that, in his younger days working for the estate . . .

'Where now?' asked Lorraine.

'I think we should stop in every village to ask around, to try and find anyone who might have driven past that lay-by between midnight and one o'clock that Saturday.'

'You're convinced they were fakes, aren't you?' Lorraine put to him.

'What else can I think? It seems to me that they set themselves up deliberately to ambush Darren on his way home. And they succeeded. That's what I think. But how can I convince anyone? How can I prove the breakdown truck was part of the set-up?'

'Its amber light was flashing,' said Lorraine. 'It wouldn't have been doing that if the driver was merely parked up resting, or waiting for someone.'

'That's possible, I suppose.'

'Come along, we've no other avenues to explore, so let's invade these peaceful villages,' she smiled. 'Look what we turned up through our visit to Hangdale.'

'All right, off we go,' he said. 'There's only tomorrow left for us.'

'And still no sign of Darren!' Lorraine sighed.

Upon receiving the call from the hospital, Mark Pemberton went immediately, and by three o'clock he was marching into the secure side ward in which Jack Mallory lay. The uniformed constable at the main door acknowledged Pemberton, but did not salute – one did not salute plain-clothes officers – and the CID man inside the ward stood up as Mark entered.

'Anything?' Pemberton asked.

'No, sir.'

Mark pulled up a chair and placed it close to the bed so that he could sit and look into Mallory's face. He was rewarded by a dark scowling expression and heavy angry breathing from the still-bandaged face and head.

'Hello, Jack.' Pemberton spoke quietly. 'My name is Pemberton, Detective Superintendent. Your doctor says you're fit enough to talk to me, for a few minutes.'

No reply.

'My officers probably saved your life, Jack, you could have lain there undiscovered for days. They made sure you got here after someone hit you, and I just wondered if you would tell me who attacked you. And why?'

No reply.

'We're looking for your Darren, we think he's come to some harm. He's been missing since a week last Saturday

. . . I wonder if you have any idea where he might be, or what's happened to him.'

No reply.

'We're trying to trace your other lads, so they know you're here. So far, no one has called, but I wanted you to know we're doing our best to find them, to tell them about you.'

That comment was rewarded by the tiniest of lip movements, the merest hint of a smile.

'So, Jack, once more. Who did this to you?'

The lips closed tight and Pemberton did not remain any longer. He rose to leave the room and said, 'He's noted for not talking to the police, but we'll not give up . . .'

And then they were aware of a tall, dark young man walking towards them. When the CID man challenged him, he said, 'My name's Garry Mallory. I think my old man's in here.'

Chapter Thirteen

Without another word, Garry, a powerful man with the swagger of a confident aggressor in spite of being the youngest of the Mallory family, went straight to the bedside, sat on the chair which Pemberton had been using, leaned over to look at the bandage work around Jack's head and said, 'Hi, dad.'

'Hello, son.' The voice was croaky and faint.

'We've come to take you home,' were Garry's next words.

The result was a rueful smile, but no comment from Jack.

'We'll get the bastard who did this, don't you worry about that.'

Again, Jack merely smiled and nodded his head.

Then Garry turned to Pemberton. 'Who are you? A doctor?'

'Pemberton. Detective Superintendent Pemberton,' and before Garry could interrupt, he went on, 'My officers found your father and had him brought here, he's been very badly injured.'

'So you've done your bit. Where's the doctor?'

Pemberton turned to the detective on guard and nodded. 'Can you find a doctor and bring him here?'

'Sir,' said the officer.

'We want to know who did this to your father,' Pemberton said to Garry.

'So do we,' grunted Garry. 'And we'll find him. You needn't bother any more, we'll find him and we'll deal with him. We're not making a police case out of this, this is our show, Mr Pemberton.'

'It's not as simple as that, we can't allow people to take the law into –'

'You can't stop us, Superintendent, he's coming home with us. We have our own way of doing things. I said we'll deal with his attacker, and we will, didn't you hear me? Now get out, I want to talk to my father. It's personal, family business.'

Pemberton knew he had no alternative and so he left the ward and closed the door. Moments later, the detective returned with the doctor.

Pemberton explained, 'I've left them alone, father and son, they want to talk. I shouldn't intrude. Now, doctor, Garry wants to take his father home.'

'I wouldn't recommend that, Mr Mallory's condition is still finely balanced, his injury needs treatment with constant attention and assessment, very professional care, if I may say so. If he leaves here now, that wound could present problems.'

'Perhaps you'd explain to his son?'

'I will, but if he insists . . .'

'He will insist, his family are accustomed to getting their own way, doctor. They're a criminal gang, you ought to know that. A violent criminal gang.'

'I'm tempted to say I don't care who they are, but if they do insist, I can't hold the patient without his consent – and I mean his consent, not that of his son.'

The doctor went into the ward and closed the door. Through the glass, Pemberton could see some animated conversation and then the doctor emerged, red-faced and flustered, saying, 'He's leaving. Now.'

'Where's he going?' asked Pemberton.

'Home, that's all his son would say, no address, no word of who'll be caring for Mr Mallory. Really, I do need to know so that I can establish some kind of support . . .'

'Don't even try, doctor, but there'll be procedures won't there? And forms to complete, Jack's signature to obtain, absolving the hospital . . .'

'In that young man's words, Mr Pemberton, he said stuff your forms and stuff your procedures, just get me a stretcher, then he said his brothers are outside, waiting. If we cause problems, they'll come and sort things out, so he said.'

'If they won't sign anything, make a record of it anyway, I'll be your witness,' Pemberton told him.

As he spoke those words, Pemberton saw Garry speak into a mobile phone, and then he went to the locker beside the bed to find his father's outdoor clothes. At that point, he realized he was being observed and closed the curtains. The doctor went to speak to the ward sister and arrange a stretcher, then three men arrived, all with the dark hair and surly features of their father. Without a word, they marched into the ward and closed the door.

Even if it was against hospital rules to use mobile phones, Pemberton moved out of earshot and found a quiet corner in the corridor near some parked wheelchairs, pulled his mobile from his pocket and rang the hospital's own number – he'd ensured he had a note of that in his records. Moments later, he was speaking to reception.

'Detective Superintendent Pemberton here. Is my constable there?'

'He is, Mr Pemberton, in the foyer. Shall I call him to the phone?'

'Please.'

When the constable responded, Pemberton said, 'Jack Mallory's leaving, his sons are here. I'm sure you saw them arrive . . .'

'I had no idea who they were, sir, they could have been anyone's visitors . . .'

'That's not my concern, they're no danger to him. Look, watch them leave. Find out which vehicles they use, get registration numbers. They're taking the old man with them, on a stretcher, so you can't miss them. Get yourself outside now, don't make it obvious you're watching them. I'll follow them down . . .'

'Sir,' and that was it.

Pemberton then rang his own office and Paul Larkin answered.

'It's Pemberton, Paul, I'm at the hospital. The whole Mallory Mob is here, except Darren, they're taking Jack home. On a stretcher. Can you arrange a surveillance operation, I need to have them shadowed all the way to wherever they're going. I know it's short notice, but I want to know where they're taking Jack, and where their own base is. Have words with Greater Balderside, see if they can help at their end. I've a constable waiting to get the numbers of any vehicles they use . . . the minute he's got those, I'll ring again . . . keep 450707 free, I'll call on that line.'

And then he went back to the ward. The doctor was chatting to the detective and two hospital porters waited nearby; they'd brought the stretcher and it had been taken into the ward without them. Nonetheless they waited outside, expecting to have a task to perform.

Then the door opened and two of the brothers struggled out with a stretcher bearing the heavy form of their father. At that stage, the porters stepped forward.

'Leave it, we'll see to him,' snapped one of the brothers, and they made for the lift. Garry and the other brother followed behind. As Garry passed Pemberton he paused briefly and said, 'I don't know how or why your lot came to be at dad's house but if they saved his life, thanks. And don't waste your time trying to blame the Clarksons, this isn't their work. And don't try to follow us now.'

Suddenly, they were gone. The lift descended with the stretcher on board and so Pemberton, the detective at his side, hurried down the staircase to the ground floor, three flights away. He arrived as the Mallorys were crossing the floor of the foyer and he saw an ambulance outside the main door. The rear doors were open; there was a black Mercedes in front of it and a red BMW behind. In a very smooth operation, Jack Mallory was placed in the rear of the ambulance by two uniformed attendants. Moments later, preceded by the Mercedes driven by one of the brothers, the ambulance pulled smoothly away from the hospital entrance and made for the exit. The BMW followed driven by another brother; the remaining pair had climbed into the rear of the ambulance to be with their father.

Pemberton managed to get the registration numbers of all the vehicles, noting that the ambulance bore the word AMBULANCE across the front and rear, that it had a blue light on the cab roof, but that it did not appear to bear the insignia of any organization or hospital. As it vanished into the traffic outside the hospital gates, the constable emerged; he'd been standing in the hospital's bus shelter.

'Sir, I got the details you wanted,' and he passed a piece of paper to Pemberton. 'The ambulance had some small writing on the nearside, down near the base of the nearside door. It said, "Westholme Hall Hospital, Sidlesbrough", and there were two attendants, both male, in their thirties, I'd say.'

'Great stuff! Thanks.' Pemberton eased his mobile phone from his pocket and rang Paul Larkin on 450707; even if Paul was on the other line, he'd answer this call. 'Hi, Paul.' He was soon speaking to his deputy. 'I've got details of the Mallory vehicles,' and he provided the inspector with the necessary information. 'Don't try to follow them, they'll stop you with one of their own road blocks, they've got two cars they can use to stop you, but try and shadow them. We want to confirm where that ambulance is really based, and where they're taking Jack. And where their own base is – this might be the chance for us to find out. Get cracking on that straight away. Oh, and where are Lorraine and Andy?'

'Somewhere on the moors, sir, calling at villages asking about Darren.'

'Get them to call at Hill Top House in Dovedale before they come home. Just as a check to see if Jack is taken there. I doubt it, but we ought to be certain.'

'Right, sir.'

Pemberton thanked the detective and the constable for their patience, each saying that no one else had called upon Jack Mallory. Now it was time for him to return to his office and make a few private phone calls.

Lorraine and Andy worked their way along the roadside communities between Hangdale and Dovedale, ignoring Huttondale as they'd already been there. There were a handful of farms whose entrances emerged on to that road and they called at each, but none of the occupants knew Darren or the Mallory brothers, they hadn't seen the road block and they didn't know anyone who habitually visited Greater Balderside and returned home late on Saturday nights. Some of the villages had no central point such as a shop, pub or post office, which meant knocking on doors, and in Howekeld this produced a result. They were told of a young couple, a local youth and his girlfriend, who always went to the cinema in Sidlesbrough on a Saturday evening and then went on to a club.

They traced the lad; he worked for the family's slaughterhouse on the outskirts of Howekeld, his name was Adrian Evans and he had come home that Saturday night, passing the lay-by about quarter to twelve. There was no road check at that time, he assured them, and no breakdown truck parked there. The lay-by was empty, and he did not know the Mallory brothers.

As they steadily and methodically worked their way towards Dovedale, they encountered the village constable of Fremingthorpe whose patch included Dinnsby, Howekeld, Lammergate, Huttondale as well as Dovedale. He was PC Roy Dickenson, a lively thirty-five-year-old, who was undertaking similar low-key enquiries into Darren's absence, but who'd had no luck. Personally, however, he did know Darren Mallory by sight and other members of the family because they lived on his patch. And he knew of their reputation.

'I was told all about them when they arrived,' he explained. 'I've been keeping tabs on them but, to be honest, they've not given me a moment's worry and the old chap seems happy to spend his days in his work-shop.'

He went on to say he'd received the circular about Darren but had not seen him for several weeks and could not help with any sightings since a week last Saturday. The presence of the road block was news to PC Dickenson but in the light of what they told him, he could not suggest anyone else who might have staged it. He would ask around the area, however, for indications of the ownership of the breakdown vehicle and for any sightings of the checkpoint by local people. It was while chatting to PC Dickenson that Andy's mobile phone bleeped.

'Andy, it's DI Larkin,' said the familiar voice. 'Where are you?'

'Howekeld, between Greater Balderside and Dovedale,' he responded. 'With DC Cashmore, and we've PC Dickenson, the local policeman, with us.'

Larkin explained about Jack Mallory and his unexpected departure from hospital, adding a description of the ambulance and accompanying cars. 'You'd better acquaint PC Dickenson with the latest developments too, tell him to ask his boss to pass the word around. Mr Pemberton wants you to visit Hill Top House, we want to know where Jack Mallory's being taken. He won't have had time to get there yet – give it another hour – but can you put that on your agenda for today? We need to find out where he goes – and if it's not Hill Top House, it might give us a clue to Darren's whereabouts, or where the rest of the Mallorys have their nest.'

'No problem,' agreed Andy who then acquainted Larkin with the outcome of his own actions to date, emphasizing the puzzle about the road block and low-loader.

'Good, keep up the good work – and let me know if there are any developments.'

Before PC Dickenson left them, he assured them he would pay frequent visits to Hill Top House and the immediate vicinity in the hope he might catch sight of Jack and members of his family, and then he went off to continue his own enquiries. The affair of Darren Mallory had given him a new purpose, something to add spice to his rather mundane daily routine, and he would do his utmost to find answers and to keep Andy informed.

For Andy and Lorraine, the rest of the afternoon passed in an unproductive series of interviews. Eventually, before heading back to Rainesbury, a drive of almost an hour, they made for Hill Top House. As before, they drove along the cinder track and parked outside the heavy wooden rear gate before entering the curtilage. But the house was deserted. There was no indication anyone had been to the house or workshop since Jack's departure, and Andy satisfied himself that the keys were still where he had left them.

'We'll ask around the village on our way home,' he told Lorraine. 'Someone might have seen the ambulance and its motorcade.'

But no one had seen it, or Jack and his family, and in particular, no one had seen Darren since their last visit. It was Friday afternoon and time to go home – and they had not found Darren Mallory. They had not even managed to trace the source of that low-loader/breakdown vehicle.

'Another dead end,' sighed Lorraine. 'We've not done very well with this enquiry, have we?'

'There's always tomorrow.' Andy tried to sound optimistic. 'Come along, it's time we went home.'

As the motorcade smoothly crossed the moors between Rainesbury and Greater Balderside, frantic efforts were being made to monitor its progress. In attempting to establish a surveillance operation, Larkin was acutely aware that any hint of a police presence in its wake would result in the Mallorys either establishing a temporary road block with their cars or adopting some other diversionary tactics; to block the road for only a few minutes would ensure the ambulance took an alternative route or that it was able to out-distance any pursuing vehicles.

At very short notice, unmarked police cars from several units – the Road Traffic Division, Criminal Investigation

Department and Criminal Intelligence Unit or indeed any-where else – had to be found and directed towards the route – or routes – likely to be taken. They must be placed under strict instructions not to follow the motorcade and not to let themselves be seen, but to monitor its progress in a covert operation by making good use of lay-bys, junc-tions, roundabouts, parking areas and even by travelling towards it from the opposite direction or making use of constables on foot, always passing ongoing information from one observer to another, and from one police force to another, in the hope they could observe the ambulance, particularly as it neared the end of its journey.

Greater Balderside Police offered every assistance, say-ing they would position observers on all the roads into town, with particular attention to those entering from the south and east. Once the motorcade was sighted entering that force area, and especially as it crossed the town boundaries, then it would be easier to monitor its progress. Surveillance cameras, established for the purpose of catch-ing thieves, burglars and other law-breakers, could be utilized too. During those discussions, Paul also ascer-tained that Westholme Hall Hospital was indeed genuine – it was an upmarket private hospital in its own grounds on the outskirts of Sidlesbrough. An observer would be posted there to check whether or not the ambulance returned to that address.

Meanwhile, Paul Larkin had already set about establish-ing true ownership of the ambulance. He began with a computer query to the DVLA via the Police National Com-puter link; he entered the registration mark of the ambu-lance and the computer told him that it was listed in the name of Westholme Hall Hospital in Sidlesbrough on Greater Balderside. It was taxed too. That was the first surprise for Paul – he had thought the number plates might have been false or that Westholme Hall Hospital might have been a fictitious address placed on the vehicle for criminal purposes. But so far, things seemed genuine. He decided to ring the hospital.

'Westholme Hall,' said the well-spoken receptionist.

'My name is Detective Inspector Larkin from Rainesbury Police,' he introduced himself. 'My officers have just had cause to check a vehicle whose registration mark indicates it is owned by your hospital,' and he provided details of the number and a description of the vehicle and its attendants. 'I'm just ringing to establish that you are the true owners and that it's not been stolen or misused.'

'Is there a problem?' asked the voice.

'No, no problem. Just a routine check,' he said. 'We just want to be sure the vehicle is legitimate.'

'Well, yes, it is,' she responded. 'It is ours and it is hired out at the moment.'

'To a Mr Mallory?' he asked.

'I'm not at liberty to discuss private matters over the telephone,' she responded. 'But I can confirm the vehicle does belong to this hospital.'

'A private hospital? Not NHS?'

'Yes, we are private.'

'And its hire to a private individual, with professional attendants, to convey someone home from hospital is quite routine, is it?'

'Yes, it is. We don't often receive requests of that kind, but yes, if an ambulance is available we will always consider any legitimate request with due sympathy.'

'Can I ask whether it is expected back at the hospital today?'

'Yes, it is. By seven this evening. Can I ask the reason for this enquiry, Inspector? I hope our vehicle has not been involved in an accident.'

'No, it hasn't,' he assured her. 'But just as you cannot reveal details of a private and personal nature, I cannot reveal details of a police operational nature. But you have solved one problem for me, thank you.'

Immediately after replacing the phone, he rang Ted Probert in Greater Balderside Police.

'Larkin again, Ted,' he said. 'That ambulance. It's legitimate, hired out by Westholme Hall, a private hospital. You might like to ascertain whether Jack Mallory's been taken there for treatment or whether he's been taken somewhere else. The ambulance is expected back by no later than seven this evening.'

'Thanks, sir, we'll attend to that.'

Paul Larkin hoped the army of police vehicles somewhere out there would be able to trace every stop by that ambulance before it returned to base. After completing that call, he prepared a statement on his computer and included all the action he had taken. All that information would go into the Darren Mallory file and it might help, even in a small way, in determining what had happened to him.

When Andy and Lorraine returned to Rainesbury, Pemberton and Larkin were still working; there was no early finish for them this Friday. Larkin was waiting for a call from someone, somewhere, to tell him what had happened to the ambulance and Pemberton was waiting for Larkin to update him.

'Ah, our moorland explorers are back!' smiled Pemberton as Lorraine and Andy walked in. 'Any news?'

Andy provided an up-to-date account of their day's results with particular emphasis upon the significance of the timing of the road check, whereupon Pemberton nodded and said, 'Well, you did what you could. No news is good news, someone once said. So it looks as if Darren vanished into thin air? Ambushed and kidnapped by a cleverly staged road check?'

'In the absence of anything else, it does seem to be one explanation, sir. In an attempt to find who's responsible, I've got local officers enquiring about likely sources of that breakdown truck,' Andy assured him.

'There's no report of one being stolen,' Larkin chipped in. 'Neither in our area nor Greater Balderside. On top of that, I've done a second ring-round to see if there is any record of police officers setting up the check – and hiring, begging or borrowing the low-loader – but I've come up with nothing.'

'Dead end after dead end,' sighed Lorraine. 'Any news of Jack Mallory?'

'Only that he has discharged himself from Rainesbury Hospital and he's been whizzed off in a legitimate private ambulance, never to be seen or heard of since. Using a real ambulance is exactly what the Mallorys would do, knowing we'd keep them under surveillance. Now, we're waiting to hear the latest from Greater Balderside,' Larkin added. 'The motorcade was seen to cross their boundaries about thirty-five minutes ago, and the last we heard it was being monitored through the rush-hour Friday night traffic. Without blue lights flashing, I'm told, it's all been done in a very careful and steady way, a gentle and smooth run with consideration for the patient, it's not rushed at all.'

'Look, there's no point us all hanging about here,' Pemberton said. 'I'd better stay in case there's some big decision to make. Lorraine, you go home, I'll see you there before too long, I trust. And Andy, you go to your beloved too.'

'I don't mind hanging on, sir,' Andy said.

'I know you don't, but I'll bet your wife has your meal all ready and waiting and I know you'd hate to miss that! In any case, it's Saturday tomorrow, so let's see what turns up before we decide tomorrow's strategy. But thanks for today, all of you.'

And so Lorraine and Andy left; Lorraine would make a nice meal for Mark, one which would keep without spoiling if he was likely to be late.

It was quarter to six when Greater Balderside Police rang Pemberton's office.

'Detective Chief Inspector Noakes, sir, Sidlesbrough CID.'

'Ian, delighted to hear from you. How's it gone?'

'The ambulance has discharged its passenger, sir, and returned to Westholme Hall Hospital.'

'Good. And where did it discharge Jack Mallory?'

'At the Thornbush Hotel, sir, in Sidlesbrough. It went

directly into the hotel's underground car park, our cars couldn't have followed if they'd wanted to, not without a bit of fuss. There's a guest-only ticket system with a barrier, the ambulance must have used that. It emerged from the car park and returned straight to the hospital. Our observer at Westholme Hall confirmed it was empty when it returned, he was able to look into the rear when the attendants were checking it over.'

'So what happened to Jack?'

'There's a lift to all floors, sir, from the car park, our man managed to gain access on foot, Jack wasn't in the car park by then and must have used the lift.'

'And what about the two accompanying cars? Containing his sons?'

'They split up in traffic, sir, before arriving at the hotel, we don't know where they went. With the personnel available at that point, we could only shadow the ambulance.'

'They knew we would follow them, that's evident. Was there a watch on the front door of the hotel?'

'No, sir. We were lucky to have someone in the vicinity at all, a plain-clothes man on foot, he stayed with the ambulance.'

'So Jack could have been wheeled into the lift, up to the reception and out through the front door before anyone realized?'

'Our man asked at reception, sir, no one answering Mr Mallory's description passed through reception. Certainly, no one on a stretcher.'

'And if he was put into the lift, he must have had some kind of help, especially if the ambulance drove away. He couldn't manage that alone, not in his condition. Somebody must have been waiting for him, his sons, perhaps? Got there ahead of the ambulance perhaps? Were their cars already in that basement car park, do you think?'

'No, sir, we checked. And they weren't at the front entrance either.'

'And Darren's car? Did your man think to check for that as well?'

'He did, sir, it wasn't there.'

'Fair enough. I suppose one or two of the brothers could have got there ahead of the ambulance, parked nearby and walked. Can anyone – the general public, I mean – get access to that underground car park on foot?'

'Yes, sir, on foot's no problem, it's vehicles that can't enter.'

'So the Mallorys have done it again . . . lost us . . .'

'We believe they may have a suite at the hotel, sir, booked for Jack.'

'You've spoken to the manager?'

'Yes, he has no knowledge of the name Mallory and it does not appear on the hotel register or booking lists. But we appreciate they could be using a false name, and that the booking could have been done at the last minute.'

'That manager needs to be interviewed, Ian – or he might be in cahoots with the Mallorys. I wonder if he's paying them protection money? And that makes me wonder if they're also "protecting" that private hospital.'

'Word has it, sir, among the local CID, that they use hotel rooms when they're in town, for sleeping, meetings and so on, under other names. We've tried tailing them, but they always lose us . . .'

'Same old story, eh? That's where Darren's learned his skills, I'll bet. OK, Ian, thanks for everything. So what are your people doing now?'

'We're maintaining a watching brief on the hotel, sir, to see if any of the Mallory Mob are noticed coming and going. We'll keep it up for twenty-four hours for starters, we can find the personnel for that – we think the old man will need a doctor or some form of medical treatment, so we'll keep our eyes open for signs of that happening.'

'Well done,' said Pemberton. 'Keep in touch.'

He told Paul Larkin the outcome of that call and Paul asked, 'Does that mean you want someone to pay a visit to the hotel?'

'No, we can safely leave that side of things in Greater Balderside's hands. I don't want us to get too involved in what happened to Jack – after all, we've had no formal complaint about the assault – although I did think we might find some clue as to the whereabouts of young Darren. Maybe he's in the same hotel?'

'Shall we raid it?'

'On what grounds? We can't go raiding hotels just because we think a man's there who's voluntarily left hospital, and who won't make a complaint about another villain. Darren's not wanted for crime, either, even supposing he is there, and neither is Jack. Sorry, that's a non-starter. We need evidence of a crime before we can even think of doing that.'

'But we might have found their operating centre! A nice hotel for which they provide protection in return for a secure suite of rooms? We could conduct covert enquiries first, speaking to chambermaids, night porters and so on, and then persuade the manager or owner to tell us whether the Mallorys are "protecting" the place.'

'No, Paul – after all, it's not on our patch, is it? It's Greater Balderside's problem, they're aware of events so let's leave things to them. I think we can go home now. Let's see what tomorrow brings, shall we?'

Chapter Fourteen

There was coffee as usual in Pemberton's office that Saturday morning. Detective Inspector Paul Larkin, Detective Sergeant Andy Williams and Lorraine Cashmore were all present. As they waited for Mark to begin, Lorraine studied him in his chair behind the desk; he was as smart and outwardly self-assured as always but, because she knew him so well, she detected the faintest hint of some underlying stress. He'd not been very talkative at breakfast, as if brooding over some problem, and now he was fiddling with a round glass paperweight, moving it from hand to hand like a ball, something he rarely did. She watched him tossing it backwards and forwards, his hands awaiting each short lob as if he was pre-programmed. He'd not shown his usual drive in pursuing criminals either, he'd been quite content to let Greater Balderside take over matters which she felt she ought to be pursuing, like that business with Thornbush Hotel. And last night at home, he'd been rather more silent than usual. When she asked if he was all right, he'd shrugged his shoulders and said, 'Yes, fine. Why?' She knew he did not want to talk about work but remarked that he was quiet. He said, 'Well, it's been a funny week, I'll be glad when the weekend's over. We can have Monday and Tuesday off! Maybe we can go out somewhere, for a walk on the moors?' She had greeted the idea with genuine enthusiasm.

Now he was going to consider today's duties for Andy and Lorraine.

'As I said at the outset of this enquiry,' he began, 'I was prepared to give it until Saturday, although I wanted you to give it your best shot. And you've done that, so thanks.'

'You mean it's all over, sir?' asked Lorraine, remembering to address him formally.

'Yes, there's nothing more we can do, other than maintain a watching brief. The uniform branch is doing that.'

'We've put a lot into this!' piped Lorraine.

'So you have. Now, from this time onwards, Darren's name will feature in our records until we know he's safe. We'll make sure his name appears under all the appropriate headings and so this investigation will revert to a routine Missing From Home enquiry. Our somewhat intense efforts will therefore come to an end as of now.'

'But sir . . .' Lorraine now found herself torn between her wish to discuss this on equal terms with her lover, and her need to remember her role as a subordinate police officer. 'I thought, in view of yesterday, we would be pressing for enquiries in Greater Balderside, from that hotel, or even making our own enquiries. Darren might be there. I know the hotel's not in our police area, but on top of everything else we do need to find the man who attacked Jack Mallory – and that attack *did* occur in our area. Then there's that low-loader or breakdown vehicle and the road block – that was in our area as well. We need to trace those vehicles, the low-loader and the police cars. There's such a lot we could be doing.'

'Greater Balderside Police are conducting enquiries into the business of the hotel and the possibility that it houses Jack Mallory and even his sons. It might even be their permanent base. I'm happy to leave that to them. They will keep us informed – and remember, there has been no formal complaint from Jack about the attack, and his sons don't want us to take action. We can forget that, I've told CID to ignore it. With no official complaint, and a family who won't talk to the police, we'd never get the evidence for a prosecution anyway.'

'This isn't how things should be done –' she began to say.

Pemberton ignored her. 'Jack is not going to die from his

injuries, and my view is that it was a gangland warning of some kind, someone telling the Mallorys to keep their noses out of something or other.'

'I know, sir, but –'

'Lorraine!' He looked at her with a hardness in his eyes and at that moment she realized she was out of order. Pemberton spoke her name as a rebuke; she was being over-familiar with a senior officer. After all, Mark was the boss, he made the decisions and she must respect that. This was work, not some private domestic issue.

'Sorry, sir.'

He nodded to acknowledge her apology and continued. 'Now, so far as Darren is concerned, we have put rather more effort into tracing him than we would normally do for such an absence, and in spite of that we have not found him. I accept he was in the Blue Raven two weeks ago tonight, alive and well. I am also aware of the theory he could have been abducted in a well-staged ambush but I think we can forget that. Take a more realistic look at it . . .' and he paused for effect. 'Consider the low-loader or breakdown truck for starters. It might have been there by pure coincidence, nothing more than a breakdown truck operating some distance from its base. It could have been active all day, or during the whole of that evening, and perhaps its attendants were taking a rest after having delivered a car, a broken-down vehicle perhaps, some-where in the locality.'

'Sir.' She spoke before she could stop herself. 'Three witnesses said the breakdown truck was flashing its amber light . . . if it was merely resting in that lay-by, it wouldn't be doing that, surely? There'd be no flashing lights.'

'That's a good point but not proof.' Pemberton glowered at Lorraine for daring to interrupt. 'Next, consider the road block. Two police officers and a police car. Who were they and where were they from? No police officer has admitted being present at that road check and there is no official record of it being conducted. Why? Were they fake officers? Think about it. Isn't that a little far-fetched? Sup-pose a pair of genuine policemen on patrol that night, and rather bored, decided to pull up a car for, shall we say, unofficial reasons? To chat up a pair of girls perhaps? A couple of good-lookers who weren't afraid to show interest in the officers. That sort of thing happens, it's done, I know it's done – you're on nights, you see a couple of lovely women by themselves in a car, they wave at you, they give out the right signals and so you overtake it, flash your blue light and show off, then you get some distance ahead and stage a road block, you pull them up for a chat and a laugh, it's all a good joke. You take their names and addresses and promise to meet them at some other time . . . now, you tell me a police officer who's never done that? And then tell me one who'll admit to doing it – especially when the top brass is trying to discover who might have set up a road block without good reason . . . I know you can check the duty sheets for that night, but who's going to own up to such behaviour?'

'All right, sir, I can understand that, I think we all know that sort of thing happens but there are other things to consider.' Lorraine felt compelled to state her case. 'We can't ignore Darren's secretive behaviour, the source of his money, the rewards he might have been claiming –'

'They were all in Greater Balderside area, Lorraine,' Pemberton reminded her. 'They're not our concern.'

'I know, sir, but it's possible they were relevant to his disappearance,' she persisted. 'And there was his attack on that man, Welch . . .'

'That was in Greater Balderside's area too,' smiled Pemberton.

'So it's more dead ends?' She sighed heavily. 'And this is another to add to our list. We've come to another dead end, sir, thanks to you. I get the impression no one's interested in finding Darren . . . why did we do all that work?'

'I'll ignore those remarks,' he said without smiling. 'Having considered our actions and heard Lorraine's comments, I believe we can go no further with this enquiry. So, Andy and Lorraine, what I need from you now is a very detailed report to finalize things.'

Andy nodded as he glanced at Lorraine, who issued a large and audible sigh of frustration.

Pemberton continued, 'Everything must be put down on paper in considerable detail. I want you to record everything you have done, every person you have interviewed, every angle you have explored both in our area and in Greater Balderside and I should welcome any opinions you might have, any conclusions, like the theory of his abduction. In short, the lot.'

'It might take a while, sir,' conceded Andy Williams.

'I wouldn't expect otherwise, Andy, it has to be done properly. Today it's Saturday when most of the admin offices are deserted. Find yourselves a very quiet office, pick one well away from telephones, and begin to compile your report. I shall expect it to be concluded by the end of your duty today. Five o'clock or so, then you can have Saturday night off!'

'No problem, sir,' said Andy, speaking for both.

'Good. Now, it's important that every fact is included. I need a chronological account of your week's work, the pair of you, with names, places, dates and times. I need a copy for my records and it's always wise to keep copies for yourselves. Then, when you've finished, you can go home – you've put in some extra time this week and I'd like you to take advantage of that by taking time off today if you finish early, but I don't want a rushed and shortened report . . .'

'Sir,' said Lorraine, rising with a feeling that somehow she had been defeated and that all her hard work had prematurely ended. She'd had no opportunity to conclude her enquiries. 'I'll honestly feel we're failing to take advantage of some important new leads –'

'Come along, Lorraine,' Andy interrupted her with as much cheer as he could muster. 'It's over, Mr Pemberton knows what he is doing. The sooner we get our report done, the sooner we can go home.'

With a backward glance at the stern Pemberton, who did not look her way, Lorraine reluctantly allowed herself to be led out of the room by Andy Williams. When they had gone, Pemberton smiled ruefully at Larkin. 'I feel as if I've watched them build a lovely house only for me to knock it down, but we had to end it now, tomorrow it should be all over,' he said. 'A pity really, they put a lot of work into this one – as I expected.'

'They're a good team, sir,' acknowledged Larkin.

'They are. We're lucky having such dedicated officers. Now, Paul, I shall be working late tonight, all night probably and well into Sunday. After hearing Lorraine just now, I'm not sure I dare tell her!' he laughed.

'She does put a lot of effort and emotion into her work, sir, but she'll come to terms with the idea that you really are the boss!'

'I hope so. Emotion's a funny thing, it can sometimes override common sense. But come on, Paul, we've work to do and I could do with another coffee.'

Lorraine, still smarting from Pemberton's apparent disregard for the commitment she had shown during the enquiry, found a comfortable office downstairs equipped with a computer. Andy found another along the same corridor – they had decided to work separately on their notes at the outset, and then check the facts together before producing the final computer-generated document.

Using her official notebook as an aide-memoire, she found the work relaxing and even therapeutic, so much so that whilst she worked she forgot about Pemberton's dismissal of her recent efforts and found herself mentally weaving together all the strands and snippets of information gleaned since Monday. She began with a heading for each day and then split the day into morning and afternoon, then went further back in time to the day Darren had last been seen, and further back still, to the time Joseph Campion had vanished. Eventually she produced a modest time-chart.

To that she began to add the other factors – the assault on Welch, the attack on Jack Mallory, sightings of Darren in town which she gleaned from the file given to her by

Greater Balderside Police, including his visits to book-makers, libraries, the art gallery and police stations. Then she made columns for the names of the key personnel – Campion, Darren, Dylan Welch and Jack Mallory – and, using the dates known to her, she watched to see whether any of them overlapped in time or place. At this point, she realized she was treating it as a murder enquiry.

It was not on the scale of a murder investigation of course, but she felt she could apply the same principles, the cross-referencing of facts and names, the double-checking of the movements of key personnel, the impressions and observations of the few witnesses they'd found, like that retired gamekeeper. Quite unexpectedly, what she had initially regarded as a chore and a device to keep her occupied this Saturday morning, had developed into a means of reviving her memory and enabling her to gain a greater understanding of Darren's disappearance. Although it was extremely unlikely she would actually find him, it might help to explain the mystery of his absence and she found herself growing increasingly enthusiastic.

When she studied her notes relating to the disappear-ance of Joseph Campion, she realized her file was incom-plete. Inspector Larkin had, almost casually, told her of his return from a supposed holiday in Cornwall but he had not mentioned a date; Lorraine therefore picked up the telephone and rang his extension.

'Larkin.'

'DC Cashmore, sir, ringing from some far-flung outpost of an office downstairs. It's about Campion. You told me he'd returned home.'

'Yes, I did, but I don't think we need worry about him, he's not come into the frame for this enquiry. He's not our problem, Lorraine, Greater Balderside will have him under scrutiny.'

'I appreciate that, but I'd like to round off my entry, sir, so when did he return? Do we have that information?'

'I'm sure we do – hang on, Lorraine,' and she heard him begin to rustle a pile of paper. There was a pause of a few moments, then he said, 'He was seen in Port Haverton on Tuesday, 30th July. Last Tuesday in fact. The officer who spotted him had words with one of the locals who knows Campion, and it appears he'd returned only that morning.'

'Thanks, sir,' she said, jotting down the date.

'How's it going? You sound very cheerful!'

'Fine!' She now sounded enthusiastic. 'I'm just tidying up all the loose ends, like this bit.'

'It's nearly lunchtime, that sergeant of yours will be getting his daily hunger pangs. Don't work too hard!'

'I won't, sir,' and she replaced the phone.

While concentrating upon her notes about Campion, she recalled that when Probert and Baxter had first briefed them, they'd said Campion had a link with the Mallorys; that link had never been fully explained, although it was connected with car thefts. Did all or some of the Mallorys steal cars for Campion? There was more to find out about that – and about Darren's role. One interesting fact about Campion's return, however, was that he was now back in the country, or in this part of the country, and he'd returned *before* Jack Mallory was attacked. Was that significant or not? As she pondered this, she continued to compile her report. At that stage, the name of Dylan Welch assumed further importance. He had been dismissed by Greater Balderside Police and indeed by her own colleagues as nothing more than a travelling rogue who'd met his match, and then merely a victim and resultant witness, but Lorraine began to wonder if he was more than he had appeared. Was it relevant, for example, that Joseph Campion had disappeared a few days after the arrival in Port Haverton of Dylan Welch?

The key to the true role of Welch might lie in the fact that he had telephoned the Crown Prosecution Service to find out the date of his court appearance and had then turned up to give evidence. That was not the behaviour of a travelling villain or even an innocent victim, especially one who might be using a false name; such a person could have easily vanished without trace and therefore made the hearing void. But Welch had not done that. He'd rung to enquire about the date and he'd turned up to give evidence after a period of absence. In Lorraine's opinion, that was the action of a professional – a police officer, security services agent, Customs official or some other official working undercover. And afterwards, he'd vanished; there was no police record of Welch, he was not known to anyone and had provided a fictitious home base of Scunthorpe. In her view, Welch was an undercover agent who'd been watching Darren. Was it significant that Welch had disappeared following the assault, disappeared because he feared his true role might be recognized? In establishing his alter ego, however, he'd taken low-key lodgings near the docks, complete with laptop computer, and had paid regular visits to the docks – so was his story true? Had he been looking for work on the docks or was that a pretence to explain his presence? Lorraine favoured the latter.

And that led to the next question. Why would he be shadowing Darren Mallory? It was while contemplating this puzzle that Lorraine grew to realize that much of the action in this scenario had taken place on, or very close to, the docks at Port Haverton. To help her, she studied the file given to her by Greater Balderside Police and it was evident Darren had regularly taken jobs on the docks, usually short-term appointments of a manual kind. Was that to gain knowledge of how things functioned there? Furthermore, Welch had taken digs very close to the docks and had spent time seeking employment there, or so he had told his landlady, and Joseph Campion relied on ships to conduct his illicit trade in stolen vehicles, drugs or whatever scheme he was currently involved in. And, she realized, docks, and Port Haverton in particular, featured in her recent enquiries. Not prominently, but always there, always in the background. She jotted the words 'docks' and 'ports' on a notepad near her computer, then programmed it into the 'find' mode. As the cursor scanned the document she was preparing, the words appeared on several occasions, both as part of the name of Port Haverton and in other contexts. Ports and docks were somehow important to this investigation.

As she scanned her entries for Darren Mallory – using the very scant information available – she felt that he had not disappeared voluntarily. He'd told Julie Carver he hoped to see her again at the Blue Raven the following Saturday and he'd told the petrol pump attendant in Huttondale he wanted a full tank on Saturday 20th July so that he had enough to run around at the weekend. Those were hardly the words of a man who knew he was going elsewhere. Darren was a skilled liar but even so, Lorraine believed his disappearance was neither voluntary nor planned. The fact that his toilet requisites were left behind added to that belief. And in spite of his antagonism to police enquiries, Jack Mallory had expressed concern about his son. Perhaps he had reason to do so? The attack on him might reinforce that. In Lorraine's opinion, Darren had fully intended staying at home that weekend – the twentieth – and into the week which followed. This week, in other words – but he'd been forcibly removed. Then there was Darren's rather odd habit of sitting in the pub in Dovedale, reading newspapers. It was hardly the action of a virile young criminal but it did tie in with his trips to Sidlesbrough library and even the police stations in Greater Balderside where he'd studied posters, advertisements and notices. And there was his visit to the art gallery. Lorraine felt sure he was studying the latest high profile monetary rewards and as there was no website which consolidated them, he had to rely on wading through every newspaper, every day . . . a chore, but one with its own rewards. So if Darren was claiming rewards, how did he go about it?

This thought led inevitably to the realization that Darren might have stumbled across something far bigger than he had anticipated. She wondered if he had read about some reward, some huge reward, but had the perpetrators of the operation discovered his unwelcome interest and got rid of him?

As she pondered this, her mind flitted to Joseph

Campion and his activities, the proximity of the docks, the huge profits from smuggling drugs into the United Kingdom, the absence of Campion and his return, the attack on Jack Mallory, the disappearance of Darren, the likely kidnapping of Darren who might have been seeking the reward for informing on the drugs importation if in fact that's what it was . . .

Then her door opened and Andy Williams walked in.

'There you are! I thought you must be hiding in some old castle or dungeon – or of course, you might have gone out for lunch without telling me!'

'Would I do that? No, this is just a junior clerk's palace,' she laughed. 'It's ideal for me right now.'

'My stomach tells me it's time for a break,' he said. 'The canteen's shut today but I know a nice little tourist café which does wonderful chips.'

'Say no more, Sergeant!' she laughed. 'I'll be with you in just one second!'

Half an hour later, as they sat behind Andy's massive plateful of haddock and chips and Lorraine's more sedate prawn salad, he asked, 'So, how's it going? You've not finished yet?'

'No,' she admitted. 'It's taking longer than I thought.' And she explained her curiosity about the factors thrown up by the morning's work.

Andy listened intently and nodded. 'I agree with you. You've convinced me that Darren's stumbled on to something bigger than even he expected, and whatever it is, it's going to happen this weekend. The signs are all there, even to the point of halting our investigation. Clearing the decks ready for action, in a manner of speaking! And I'll bet it's going to happen on the docks at Port Haverton.'

'Without Darren?' she said.

'Right. By some means, fair or foul, he's discovered what it is. Like you, I think he's after a reward of some kind, but he's been ambushed to keep him out of the way until it's all over.'

'So the exercise, whatever it is, can go ahead without the risks he might have created by being around?'

'Something like that, I'm sure. I'd expect police partici-
pation and observers – and HM Customs and Excise . . .
This one's not for us, Lorraine. It's all down to our friends
in Greater Balderside Police. Our job is to finish our report
and go home, we've done our bit, although I'm not sure
what it was or how relevant it was to the affair as a whole,
but now we keep our noses out . . .'

'I've quite a lot to do yet,' she admitted. 'It's taken
longer than I thought.'

'Me too, but I'm happy I've done a good job. Now, enjoy
that salad.'

After lunch, and alone in her temporary office, Lorraine
rang Sidlesbrough Art Gallery to learn a little more about
the current exhibition. After convincing the curator of her
bona fides, she was told it was a collection of the works of
the Bellini family – Jacopo (1400–1470), his son Genile
(1429–1507) and younger son Giovanni (1430–1516). The
works had been assembled from galleries, museums and
churches across the world and included all five of Jacopo's
surviving works: four versions of the *Madonna and Child*
and a Crucifixion. After this weekend, the exhibition
would move to Edinburgh, and then on to Paris. In fact,
today was the exhibition's last day in England. She asked
about the value of the paintings and was told some were
worth a great deal of money but that rigid security measures had been taken to protect them. 'One's already gone
missing, that sharpened our senses,' admitted the curator.
'A *Madonna and Child* by Giovanni, it was stolen in Italy en
route to the first of these exhibitions . . . sloppy security by
the Italians. I can't confirm it's worth a fortune, no one
could put a true value on it, but it could reach £1 million
or even £2 million at auction in the right circumstances,
more even, if a keen collector wanted it . . . but these
pictures don't usually come on to the market so any figure's pure speculation.'

'There's a reward out for its recovery,' said Lorraine,
recalling the notices in the police station and elsewhere.

'There is. Art dealers around the world have stumped up an offer of £200,000,' he told her. 'It's high because they feel if anyone does find it, they could be tempted to keep it . . . there's a big market in stolen works of art! They feel the cash will persuade any thief to hand it over to the authorities.'

Having chatted to the gallery, Lorraine then telephoned DS Probert at Sidlesbrough to ask about Campion's links with the Mallory Mob and he said there was no close connection; occasionally Campion might ask one of them to steal a car to order, or help with the disposal of stolen goods, but, added Probert, such links were not very strong. Casual was the word he used, although in recent weeks he'd noticed a cooling off between them. He had wondered if it was in any way linked to Darren or his disappearance, but he had no evidence to support that theory.

Lorraine did not finish her report until four o'clock. She and Andy produced a final version together and put it in Pemberton's in-tray, under a 'Confidential' cover. Then she went home and by the time Mark returned – he said he'd been to a briefing at police headquarters – she had produced a lamb hotpot, a savoury casserole with lamb chops, potatoes, vegetables and seasoning all in one dish. It smelt delicious. When he came into the house, Mark took her by the shoulders, kissed her and wrapped his arms tightly around her.

'I'm sorry about this morning, I couldn't help it.' She snuggled deep into his embrace. 'It was rude of me, I should have shown more respect. I was out of order . . .'

'Forget it, it's only work,' and he tightened his arms and held her for a long time. 'We love each other, Lorraine, that's permanent, it's something for ever. Work is ephemeral, what's dreadfully important one day can be a mere hazy memory the next. We can't let such things come between us.'

'No,' she sighed. 'No, we mustn't but all the same, it's wrong of me to expect you to make exceptions.'

'Darling . . .' He maintained his strong armhold. 'There's more . . .'

'It's Saturday, Mark, and you're not on call this week. Saturday is when people have time off to relax, I hope you're not going to talk about work, we have rules, remember?'

'I know, but time off when you want it is a luxury denied most police officers, darling, especially at weekends. And especially when they're of my rank. We don't work normal hours.'

'Oh my God . . . are you saying you've got to work? Tonight?'

'I've time for a meal,' he said. 'I've been to a meeting at headquarters, a very important meeting. I have to work tonight, but I don't have to report at Control until ten o'clock. That means no alcohol . . .'

'Oh, Mark, I'm sorry . . . I've done it again . . . I mustn't criticize you, it's not your fault . . . It's a very late start, but you've time to eat?'

'I've time to eat,' he said.

'So what is it?' she asked as she went into the kitchen to make sure things were ready. 'Why do you have to work late on a Saturday like this? You're a superintendent, for God's sake, you can delegate duties, you've a staff of keen young underlings who can stand in for you. What about Paul Larkin? I thought he was on call this week?'

'Paul's working as well, he'll have been told by now.'

'And us? Me and Andy?'

'You've done your bit, Lorraine. You can enjoy your evening off!'

'Done our bit? You're now admitting that all that running around after Darren Mallory was part of this?'

'I'm not saying anything like that. All I'm saying is that you've had a busy week and you're not required for tonight's exercise. You can relax now.'

'How can I relax without you, Mark? I'll be all on my own on a Saturday night while you're God knows where! Doing what? I'll be worried sick about you.'

'I'm not really sure where I'm going to be. I'll get my

orders at ten, like the rest of us. Come on, let's have our supper. At least I can enjoy that before I leave. I'm not sure when I'll be back, so lock yourself in.'

'You mean you'll be working through the night? I thought you'd finished with night duties years ago, plodding the streets at all hours! It's times like this I wish I wasn't in the police service.'

'It would be a mighty boring life otherwise!' He seized her and kissed her full on the lips. 'Listen, I might not be back tonight, I might have to work into tomorrow too. I'll try to keep in touch, it's all very hush-hush. I'll bet council office clerks and assembly-line operatives don't have this kind of excitement. And I do love you, Lorraine Cashmore, I really do . . . Come on, it's time to eat.'

'You're making fun of me!' she chided him.

'Would I dare?' he laughed.

Their dinner tasted as delicious as it had smelt, and he enjoyed the sticky toffee pudding with custard followed by cheese and biscuits, and then coffee.

'Am I allowed to know where you're going?' she asked as they shared the chore of washing the pots.

'Sorry,' he said. 'To be honest, I don't really know myself. All I'm told is that I must report to my own divisional headquarters at ten o'clock tonight for a preliminary briefing. Briefing on, as they call it. Then I go to Greater Balderside.'

'Greater Balderside! I'm getting sick of that name!'

'It's a joint operation, an all-night exercise,' he said. 'All north-eastern police forces are taking part, as well as the National Crime Squad. The man in charge is James Craig, he's an ACC from Durham – so there you are. You know as much as me – and not a word to anyone!'

'Mark, I can't talk to anybody tonight, can I? How can I reveal dreadful secrets from here? Especially when I have no idea what's going on. But I do recognize the expression on your face, you're holding something back, I know you are. You're not telling me everything. How long's this exercise likely to go on?'

He shrugged his shoulders. 'All night and possibly into

tomorrow, there's no stated time for it to end. And it's not an exercise in the true sense of the word, it's the real thing.'

'Oh, God, there are times I wish I was a secretary or a mousy clerk somewhere . . .'

'It should be all over very quickly, the tide's in our favour.'

'The tide?' she cried. 'You mean it's something to do with shipping? You know nothing about shipping, Mark, or smuggling or drugs running or illegal immigrants . . . this is out of your league . . . why you?'

'Maybe it's because I'm in charge of the Criminal Investigation Department at Rainesbury, which is a seaside resort and a port, and also because our division borders Greater Balderside – and because Darren and the other Mallorys live on our patch.'

'So this has to do with Darren Mallory, has it? I was thinking you brought our enquiry to a rather swift and sudden halt, Mark, you must admit you ended it all a bit prematurely.'

'Look, I'm sworn to secrecy. All I can tell you is that it's a joint operation involving police forces whose area includes the north-east coast – ourselves, Durham, Cleveland, Northumberland and Greater Balderside – and we've a long stretch even if we don't have a major port. I won't know my role until I am briefed, and most certainly, I shall not have any idea what this is all about.'

'I don't believe you, Mark Pemberton!' she cried. 'You do know what's going on . . . We've been set up, haven't we, me and Andy Williams, floundering in the dark on some pretended Missing From Home enquiry . . . God, Mark, there are times I wonder where the police service is heading.'

'Don't even think about it,' he said. 'Just do as the boss tells you!'

'And you are my boss?'

'I am, so come here! And I must leave in ten minutes.'

Chapter Fifteen

When Mark had gone, Lorraine settled down to listen to music while reading the daily papers. There were three – they took *The Times*, the *Yorkshire Post* and the local *Rainesbury Evening News* – and in them she came across five references to rewards. *The Times* featured a huge newly announced reward of £175,000 offered by an international firm of jewellers for information leading to the recovery of £4 million worth of diamonds stolen in transit in London, and it mentioned in passing the £200,000 reward for the still-missing Bellini *Madonna and Child*. A pair of more local rewards were announced in the *Yorkshire Post*: one for £1000 offered by a Harrogate garage for information leading to the arrest of the thief or thieves who had stolen a valuable second-hand sports car from their forecourt, and another for £1000 from a businessman who'd left £10,000 in a bag on his car roof as he'd driven away and lost it. And she smiled at the Rainesbury local paper's item highlighting the reward of £50 for the recovery of a lost cat. In contemplating these, and the characters who might be tempted to try and claim them, she recalled that the FBI had offered $25 million for information leading to the capture of an al-Qaeda terrorist in the wake of America's September 11 atrocity. With the announcement of three new rewards in just one day, she wondered how many were offered throughout the country in the course of, say, one year. And how much money was offered – and claimed – in just one year?

There was very little publicity about those who successfully claimed rewards; claimants usually demanded anonymity and probably insisted on cash too, and she realized that a person with criminal contacts could make a very useful income by claiming these tax-free monies – and with much less risk than actually committing crime. It was while contemplating this scenario that she wondered whether there was any central source of information about rewards currently on offer, and a quick search on her personal computer suggested there was not. Her mind turned to Darren Mallory and his visits to libraries along with his scrutiny of police noticeboards bearing details of current rewards – it seemed that regular and determined checking of newspapers, along with the Crimestoppers advertisements, was probably the only sure way of learning about unclaimed or new rewards.

And as she considered those points, she wondered whether any of the major rewards still available had any bearing on the events about to unfold on Greater Balderside. Clearly, it was something connected with shipping, probably drug smuggling, so had there been publicity about a large reward leading to the recovery of a drugs shipment? Illegal immigrants perhaps? Or stolen cars? She felt sure that if there had been, she would have recalled it – certainly, over the past weeks there'd been lots of local rewards, from £50 for the recovery of a lost cat to sums of £250, £500 or even £1000 for information leading to the arrest of criminals or the recovery of precious or sentimental objects stolen during burglaries.

She remembered one elderly gentleman offering £5000 for the recovery of a brooch which had belonged to his late wife – he wasn't worried about the thief being caught, all he wanted was the return of his own special treasure. And as her mind began to recall similar offers, she remembered a criminal scam of some four or five years earlier. To effect the scheme, thieves would raid art galleries or stately homes and steal high value paintings and other works of art. In such cases there was always speculation about the ability of the thieves to dispose of such well-known and identifiable properties – stories circulated about fanatical collectors who would encourage and even finance such crimes solely to acquire a famous work of art which would then be hidden from public view within their prized collection. But there was another angle. Specialist thieves would steal a famous painting and then await the announcement of a reward for its recovery. And then the thief, claiming to be an informer, would reveal its safe whereabouts and claim the reward money – anonymously.

Sitting alone with her thoughts, Lorraine wondered how many rewards might involve something as large as a shipment of goods to this country, drugs for example, or some other commodity like illegal immigrants . . . but who would know? Crimestoppers was very localized – she could ask them but she felt she might be looking for something larger. The newspapers themselves might have some kind of filing system – but it was Saturday night and none of those papers would be functioning now, there being no Sunday editions. But there were Sunday nationals . . . and the more local *Sunday Herald* published on Tyneside. Their offices would be staffed . . . it was worth a phone call, surely?

She rang the *Sunday Herald* first and asked if the crime correspondent was available; he was, and his name was Luke Crawford. Her call was put through to the crime desk.

'Crawford, crime,' came the response in a strong Tyneside accent.

'This is Detective Constable Lorraine Cashmore from North Yorkshire Police,' she announced herself. 'I wonder if you can help me?'

'You've a nice story for us, have you then?'

'Not at the moment, but it's advice I'm seeking,' she said.

'Then you've come through to the most helpful reporter in the whole world, Miss Cashmore – or is it Mrs Cashmore or Ms Cashmore?'

'Miss,' she laughed.

'Well, that's a good start. So how can I help?'

'It's to do with rewards for information about crimes,'

she began. 'I wonder if you keep records of rewards currently available?'

'I keep a file, yes. Cuttings from other newspapers mainly, Crimestoppers circulars, letters from local businesses and individuals who offer rewards, that sort of thing. We've one on the go right now, in Newcastle. A city centre shop's offered £500 for information leading to the arrest of the yob who mugged an old lady right outside the store and made off with her handbag. A good local tale.'

'That's the sort of thing I'm interested in,' she told him. 'Now, would you know if there's a big reward outstanding, say for big-time crime, drug smuggling, stolen car rackets, illegal immigrants, exotic birds, that sort of thing.'

'Do I sense there might be a story in this for me?' he countered.

'If there was, I'd gladly give you first crack at it,' she returned. 'But at the moment, it's just a bit of research on my part.'

'There's that big jewellery theft in London, but that's miles away from here, man, I canna see our local villains'll know owt about that, and that FBI offer, the al-Qaeda thing, that's still unclaimed. And that picture nicked in Italy, a Bellini. I can't recall any other major ones, not in this country, not on offer right now.'

'I know about those you've just mentioned –'

'Do I sense you've got some specific crime in mind, Miss Cashmore?' he interrupted her as his journalistic instincts began to dominate the conversation.

'I am thinking of the sort of thing which might lend itself to smuggling through the docks . . .'

'Ah! You're back to drugs, then? I can't say I know of any big drugs reward – the trouble with that is, it's international, all sorts of countries involved, all sorts of ships travelling the world, so there might be some reward somewhere, lurking unclaimed and even unrecognized . . . but, I'll be honest, if there was one in this country for information about drugs, or any other dodgy imports for that matter, like immigrants, I think I'd have known about it.

It's a subject I keep at the back of my mind, I'm fairly clued up about it and write articles about it from time to time.'

'There's no central list of current rewards, is there?' she put to him.

'There isn't. I did consider compiling a rewards website but it would be very time-consuming and almost impossible to get up-to-date information. There are simply too many rewards, most of them very small and very localized. By the time you've got the thing updated, it'll be out of date, it would always be out of date in fact. Even if we concentrated on the bigger rewards we'd still have the same problems, especially if there's international connections. We thought about doing a weekly list in the paper but the snag is you'd get all kinds of time-wasters calling in and making silly claims – same with a website. As things are, it's usually folks with specialist knowledge who can produce the right sort of information to receive the reward – or very alert criminals, of course. A lot of criminals milk the rewards system, you'll realize that? And likewise, lots never get taken up because the claimants can't satisfy the necessary conditions. We do mention them sometimes, and we repeat the better ones on occasions, and we like to build a story around them. Now, if you've a good story . . .'

'I know about those art thefts, where criminals were stealing paintings and then claiming the rewards for returning them.'

'Well, there we are, that's a good example.'

'Thanks, you've been a great help.'

'I said I was the most helpful reporter in the world, Miss Cashmore. It pays dividends . . . Now, if you need publicity for something, we do circulate in your part of the world, you know.'

'I'll bear you in mind,' she said. 'And I mean that.'

'You could always try the *Sunday Messenger*,' he added before closing the conversation. 'I've a mate down there in London doing the same as me, he's into rewards for big-time crime, more of the nationwide type of stuff than the local things I deal with. We swap notes. He wonders if big rewards are a good thing, he reckons criminals commit crime simply to claim the rewards . . . but call him. He'll be there now, working the Saturday late shift. Name of Trevor Brooke with an "e" – give him my regards. Nice to talk. Bye.'

'Bye.'

Never one to waste an opportunity, Lorraine rang the *Sunday Messenger* and asked for Trevor Brooke. He listened as Lorraine outlined her query and then, in a fine Home Counties voice, he explained things in much the same way as Luke Crawford. He did say that a large American charitable foundation used to have an ongoing reward system for information leading to the arrest of drug peddlers around the world – it was a million dollar reward – but that had been dropped a few years ago.

'Currently, Miss Cashmore, there are no large rewards which are linked to the international drugs trade, nor indeed do I know of anything connected with illegal immigrants, exotic birds or even the stolen car trade. I often think the rewards from such crimes are far greater than any reward that can be offered –'

'Much the same as those rewards for stolen works of art,' she interrupted his flow of words. 'The criminals themselves were claiming the rewards.'

'Indeed they were and some were saying they'd damage the paintings if the rewards weren't handed over. That, of course, is blackmail. But it's funny you should mention paintings. There is one large reward on offer at the moment, and it's for a stolen masterpiece. I did a feature in the paper after it was stolen. The reward's still up for grabs, Miss Cashmore, it was mentioned only recently because no one's claimed it and the painting has never been found. It was one of the Bellini *Madonnas*, Giovanni Bellini that was, son of Jacopo. It was kept in a church at Arezzo in Tuscany – it had been there for centuries, well secured but almost forgotten. It's a small work painted on panel, only fifteen inches by twelve. It was stolen during transit to an exhibition in Florence. It's a bit like that diamond that went missing, the Mirror of Portugal. It was stolen in 1792, you know, and has never been seen since. Did you know it was part of the English Crown Jewels until 1644, there's a fascinating story behind that diamond . . . but I digress. Back to the *Madonna*. It vanished on its way to an art gallery in February, the vehicle in which it was being carried was hijacked by two fake police officers near Pratantica –'

'There's a substantial reward?' she asked, attempting once again to stem his flow of words.

'Oh my word indeed there is. That's what I'm getting around to. Art dealers across the world raised money for its recovery undamaged . . . £200,000 in English money, it's on deposit in an Italian bank. They refuse to put a value on the painting because it will never come on to the open market, but guesses range from £800,000 right up to £4 million. Pure speculation though. However, it's one major reward not yet claimed – and you'll know about the FBI's massive reward for September 11th – '

'I do, yes. Well, Mr Brooke, you've been most helpful . . . sorry to have taken up your time.'

'And don't forget *Crimewatch*,' he managed to begin before she could put down the telephone. 'I'm sure you watch that and I am sure your force will have featured in the programme. I watched it recently and you'd be amazed at the number and variety of rewards on offer – seven in one programme, Miss Cashmore, seven! Three of them were for £10,000 – a murder in the Midlands somewhere, a rape in the south-east and a load of cigarettes stolen in Middlesbrough. A computer shop was offering £5000 following the theft of some hardware, and there was another £5000 offered by the family of a man who'd been attacked outside the pub he owned – and another £5000 offered by the police themselves, that was for information leading to the arrest of a man who'd murdered a pensioner. And there was that diamond theft as well, they're probably overseas now, they'd be out of the country within hours . . . money for someone, Miss Cashmore, lots of money, easily earned, no income tax . . . ideal for crooks, would you say?'

'I had no idea there were so many rewards.'

'That's only scratching the surface.'

'I must do some more digging, I can see, and I do appreciate your help.'

'My pleasure, and if there's a story behind your query, Miss Cashmore, I'm always pleased to hear it.'

'Thanks, I'll bear you in mind.'

And so Lorraine settled down with her own thoughts, trying to link the activities of Darren Mallory with the rewards on offer in his locality. It did seem, she felt, that if there was a big shipment of drugs or some other illegal commodity about to be landed at Port Haverton sometime this weekend, then there was no reward in prospect for Darren. If he wasn't involved from that aspect, why was it necessary to ensure he was kept out of the way, if indeed that's what was happening? And was the attack on his father another warning to keep away? And, she recalled, Joseph Campion had been away recently, probably overseas, so had he been somewhere to finalize the arrangements to bring something – to smuggle something, someone – into England? He was known to be involved in drugs among other things . . . Had Darren discovered his plans, and was Darren threatening blackmail if he did not receive some reward for keeping his mouth shut? This, she realized, was probably the most likely scenario, and if Darren did make such a threat to Campion, perhaps the rest of the Mallory Mob would lend their support . . . and that might explain why they'd been warned off through the attack on their father . . . and what about a raid on the art gallery? Was that a possibility? The curator had assured her that strong security measures were in force.

But there was nothing she could do now.

From snippets she'd gleaned recently, it seemed that a reception committee was awaiting the arrival of a ship at Port Haverton this weekend, and even though Darren might be remotely connected to those events, it was nothing to do with her.

She decided to have another glass of wine before she went to bed. And then the telephone rang. It was twenty minutes to ten. Lorraine picked it up and gave her number.

'Mark here,' said the distinctive voice. 'I need your help. DC Newton's gone sick, broken a leg of all things, we were told only an hour ago. Can you come?'

'Mark, I have no idea what's going on . . .'

'You'll be briefed when you arrive. I wouldn't have recommended you if I didn't think you were up to it and we do need a secure pair of hands for this, someone capable of quick thinking with good powers of observation.'

'So what are my orders?'

'Be at Rainesbury Divisional Headquarters as soon as you can, I'll brief you there. Take a taxi if you've had a drink or two. Bring sandwiches and a flask of coffee, it might be a long night. Then we're all going to Greater Balderside.'

'Oh, Mark, what have you got us into now?'

Chapter Sixteen

When Lorraine arrived at divisional headquarters, only ten minutes from home by taxi, she was directed to the canteen which at that time of night was closed to customers wanting hot meals and sandwiches. On this occasion, it was being used as an assembly point. She walked in to find Detective Inspector Larkin, a small contingent of ten CID personnel, a pair of uniformed dog handlers and a further two officers whom she recognized as trained firearms officers. All were members of her own force. There was a vending machine in the corner from which most of them had obtained a paper cup full of coffee, and some had bought bars of chocolate from another vending machine. Pemberton allowed them to enjoy a few minutes' relaxation during which they gossiped and speculated as to the nature of tonight's task, and then he called them together.

'I'm sorry to spoil your Saturday night,' he began. 'But there'll be time and a half off in lieu. You'll all be wondering what this is about – all will be revealed in due course but first we shall travel to Greater Balderside in convoy. We'll use our personnel carrier for the CID contingent, while the dog section and firearms team will use their own vehicles. I'll be in the personnel carrier, so just follow me. We shall travel initially to G Division Headquarters of Greater Balderside Police, that's at Challonford on the southern outskirts about six miles out of the centre of Greater Balderside. There we shall transfer to disguised vehicles, all radio-equipped. They'll look like building site vehicles – building is in progress at our eventual destination. So there we are. Any questions?'

Although everyone was curious to know what lay in store for them, they knew it was pointless asking questions at this stage.

'Fine. Then we'll set off in ten minutes, just time to finish your coffees.'

The drive to G Division Headquarters took just under an hour, and the exchange of vehicles a further ten minutes after which Lorraine found herself alongside Pemberton in what looked like a battered yellow minibus of the kind used to transport workmen to and from construction sites. It had the name JOHNSTONE CONSTRUCTION in large black letters along each side plus a telephone number – she knew that if a member of the public happened to ring that number, they'd get an answering machine which would ask them to leave their own details to be contacted later. Some suitable diversionary story would be forthcoming. The other vehicles were small vans with dirty windows, and they bore the same legend – even the one used by the dog section looked like a builder's van – but these were all undercover police vehicles fully equipped with radio and other essentials.

Pemberton checked that everyone was ready and said, 'Right, follow me,' then settled in the seat beside the driver. In the back of the vehicle was a selection of yellow plastic jackets with JOHNSTONE across the backs, and a pile of yellow hard hats also bearing the name on the front. Pemberton told everyone to don a coat and hat, exhorting those in uniform to make sure their uniforms were hidden, especially when they left the vehicles. And so the procession of pseudo-shift workers made for their destination.

It was almost 12.45 a.m. as Pemberton's vehicle led the way into the maze of roads and mass of ugly hangar-like buildings which comprised the docklands of Port Haverton; the whole place was ablaze with lights and noisy with activity, giving it the appearance of a huge factory or thriving industrial complex. They ignored the signs pointing to a range of berths numbered 1 to 9, and drove along concrete roads lined with warehouses, offices, container lorry parks, offices and car-parking areas, all basking under brilliant lights, until they were following signs pointing towards 'Ferry Terminal'. It was as they drove slowly along that road, and long before the arrival at the ferry terminal, that Lorraine spotted arrow-shaped signs saying 'Johnstone' and soon they were approaching a high green-painted wire boundary fence bearing an array of signs such as 'Johnstone Construction', 'Construction Site', 'All drivers report to reception', 'Authorized Personnel Only', 'This site is patrolled by guard dogs', and 'Call 776677 for assistance'. Behind the fence lay a large area of bare earth most of which had been subjected to bulldozing and hole-digging on a massive scale – long lines of piles of what looked like concrete drain pipes and concrete pillars occupied one part with builders' huts elsewhere, and there was a large sign in the centre saying, 'Site of new ferry terminal – due for completion in 2004'.

'In here,' said Pemberton to the driver, and their personnel carrier turned towards the gate which led into the site. An attendant stood in the sentry-style hut and stepped out to halt the convoy. 'Identification, please,' he demanded.

'Pemberton from Rainesbury, and officers from North Yorkshire,' and he showed his warrant card.

'Thank you, sir.' The fact he was a superintendent was sufficient assurance that the others in the vehicle were bona fide police officers, but the vehicles following him were stopped and checked. Satisfied that all were genuine, the guard – in reality a police officer – said to Pemberton's driver, 'Over there, sir, follow the road that leads in front of that building. There's plenty of parking space around the side. Then report to the site office.' He closed the gate behind them.

Ahead, and some distance from the main thoroughfare, was a long low prefabricated building with lights burning at its windows, all of which were covered with drawn blinds, and at one end there was an entrance over which the name JOHNSTONE appeared, followed by the words 'Site Office'. Pemberton's convoy followed into the parking area and he led all his officers into the site office. A young woman clerk – a policewoman in plain clothes – was sitting at the reception desk and asked for proof of identity. This was produced and she said, 'Down the corridor and into the room at the end. There's food on the tables, help yourselves. Toilets are along the corridor.' She pressed a series of numbers and showed them a doorway which led into a short corridor. 'It's open, you can enter now.'

They entered what looked like a small lecture room. It was full of police officers, men and women, most of whom were in civilian clothes of varying degrees of tidiness, some looking like mud-stained site workers and others looking more like builders' management. A few uniformed officers were among them, their uniforms now visible beneath their yellow Johnstone waterproofs.

Metal-framed chairs were arranged in rows across the room with an aisle between them, and a large screen stood on a tripod at the far end; a projector was standing in the aisle. Alongside each long side wall were trestle tables full of food, each table bearing urns of tea and coffee. Those already assembled were helping themselves on to paper plates and the building was filled with chatter as officers, male and female, plain-clothed and uniformed, from four different police forces became acquainted with one another, all still wondering about tonight's operation. Pemberton excused himself and left his party to join the group of senior officers, some of whom he recognized, and a few minutes later, a small contingent of eight more officers entered the room. At this, the reception clerk came in and spoke to one of the senior officers; Lorraine heard her say, 'That's it, sir, everyone's here.'

'Thanks, Angie. Lock the door now, I'll give them fifteen minutes to get something to eat, then we'll start.'

It was now twenty to two on Sunday morning. It was evident that the presentation was about to begin because a man went to the projector and switched it on, testing it with a few slides operated from a portable computer. So many projectors failed at this criticial point, no matter how carefully one had made preparations, but this one seemed

236

to be functioning correctly. At the sight of something on the screen, the assembled officers finished eating, discarded their plates and cardboard mugs into waste bins, and began to select their seats. Lorraine found herself seated next to Paul Larkin while Pemberton was with six senior officers who sat apart from the others.

Moments later, a tall, powerfully built man in his late forties, with a good head of sandy hair and healthy-looking skin and clad in a sports jacket and flannels, shouted for silence. He looked like a country doctor but had a voice like a town crier, a most effective asset because everyone in the room stopped talking and began to listen. He picked up the control box for the projector.

'Good evening,' he began in that booming voice. 'Or to be correct, good morning. I'm glad you could all join us.' A ripple of good-natured laughter momentarily filled the hall. 'My name is James Craig and I am an ACC in County Durham. I have overall responsibility for the operation which is soon to begin – it is codenamed Operation Snowgoose.'

And at that point, the coloured picture of a snowgoose appeared on the screen at which Craig continued, 'It is a rare visitor to this country but if it does arrive it will usually be alone and it will attempt to mingle with other species of goose. Trained observers will easily recognize it, but most of us would not know a snowgoose from a mongoose. We are trained observers, ladies and gentleman, but we are not looking for a snowgoose – we are looking for snow, however, or cocaine or coke or whatever it is called in smart circles. And our attention is focused on the activities of this man – Joseph Campion,' and a photograph now appeared on the screen. Lorraine began to experience a tingle of anticipation as Craig continued.

'He is known to be actively engaged in the drugs trade, not to mention car smuggling and other criminal activities both here and overseas. But it is his drug smuggling that interests us today. Campion lives in Dunthorpe which is part of Great Balderside but his empire is worldwide. I am now going to hand over to Detective Superintendent Alastair Petrie of the National Crime Squad.'

A thick-set man with jet black hair and more than a few days' growth of beard now took the stand. He was dressed in blue denim overalls and large yellow boots with steel toecaps; Lorraine thought he'd have looked perfect in the seat of a dumper truck.

'Thanks, Mr Craig,' he smiled. 'Joseph Campion. A local man, a hard man, a man whose entire life has been spent as a criminal. Very successfully, I might add. A man who travels a lot, spending time in Italy, Greece, Spain, most European countries in fact, and who's been known to visit various places in South America and the Far East. All to do with his criminal activities – drugs, cars, cigarettes, booze, you name it, he's been involved. We are in regular contact with overseas police forces about him because he has flashy houses in Italy, France, Turkey and Colombia, not that you'd think he was wealthy judging by his terrace house not a million miles from here. He is wealthy, very wealthy, and he's much more than a local villain. He is part of the international crime scene, a very big fish in other words. He's our target in Operation Snowgoose – or rather, the result of his latest expedition overseas is our target.'

Petrie paused to allow them to study the man on the screen; he produced several shots of him in different clothes and even in different countries.

'Take a good look at this man, and those who follow. You'll be expected to recognize them later today.'

At times, it was difficult to appreciate that the pictures of Campion were all of the same person – a man in his late forties perhaps, tall and powerful but with different clothes, altered hair-styles, the growth of a beard or moustache or the use of dark glasses. All combined to create new images of him.

'On 19th January this year, Campion left his home in Dunthorpe here on Greater Balderside and travelled by train to London, then across to France by Eurostar. He was alone and was using a false passport – it was in the name of Raymond Michael Hudson – and he stayed at his French

238

house near Amiens. His route was monitored by ourselves, our French contacts and HM Customs and Excise. He owns a French car, a Citroën, and after a week he drove away in it, heading south. We lost his trail, but eventually he turned up on the Italian border, still alone and still in the Citroën.' A photograph of the car with Campion at the wheel was shown at a border crossing to the west of Torino.

'From there he drove down the west coast of Italy. We know he spent time in Tuscany – his credit cards tell us that – and it seems he spent almost six weeks in a rented house near Arezzo. During that stay, he was visited by four men – Englishmen from Greater Balderside, men with whom he has worked on previous occasions, and they all stayed at the Arezzo house.'

Four photographs were now shown as Petrie provided their names: 'Michael Goodwin, Joseph Noble, Oliver Cooney and Mark Currey. These are all colleagues of Campion in his criminal activities, they've worked with him for years and he trusts each one of them. He tends to make use of other people in his operations, people he can trust.'

He allowed their photographs to linger on-screen so they might recognize each man, as he continued, 'They travelled separately to Arezzo but they all arrived at his house to spend time together. They were there a week, ostensibly on holiday, then they left. Each then found his own way to Bogotá in Colombia and Campion remained at his house. We know that Campion drove north, still in his French car, to Genoa – that was three days after the men left Arezzo – and we also know the four men visited Genoa before leaving for Bogotá. At that point, we lost contact with Campion until he turned up in Greece two weeks later where he rented a villa near Athens – still using his false name. In the meantime, the four men had arrived in Colombia and there they collected a pair of Range Rovers; these were driven by the men through Peru and Chile to Rio de Janeiro and then shipped from there to Genoa. They were driven from Genoa up through France and into Holland.'

239

Now he showed photographs of the two light grey vehicles, both in pristine condition with a spare wheel on the rear.

'The Colombians are perfectionists when it comes to concealing drugs, and they have already shown remarkable skills at their ability to hide them in the wheels of Land Rovers and motor cycles. Only last year, a gang of Englishmen were caught with £22 million worth of cocaine concealed in the wheels of two Land Rovers. Think of that – twenty-two million pounds. In drugs. Hidden in just two vehicles. Men will do a lot to get their hands on that kind of money. And as we speak, two Range Rovers are heading this way, the work of our friend Campion. He owns them.'

There were pictures of a cut-away section of a Land Rover wheel used in a 1999 attempt to smuggle cocaine into England, and of a motor-cycle wheel showing a similar cut-away compartment – in all cases, the tyres were utilized to aid the concealment.

'A fifth man, Leo Winters, had also been seen with the four in Colombia.' Another photo was screened. This showed a smiling fair-haired man standing beside a Suzuki motor bike. 'He has also been spotted in Genoa and France but never in the company of Campion or the other four; he's known to be a drug runner but we don't know whether he's in league with Campion.'

He paused to allow them all to study that picture, flicked back to photos of the earlier four and of Joseph Campion and the vehicles, then said: 'We know that those five men are aboard the ferry which is due to berth here at seven this morning. It has sailed from Rotterdam. It left at eight last night, Saturday that is – and it will probably arrive off-shore by 5 a.m. or earlier today, Sunday, hence our presence. It will wait off-shore until seven before it enters the terminal. On board are the two Range Rovers and one Suzuki motor cycle, the ones you've already seen. The four men with the Range Rovers are also on board, as is our friend Leo Winters – who, remember, might be operating totally independently of the others.

'Now, with their wheels doctored to accommodate drugs, none of those vehicles can drive very far – but they *can* be driven for a short distance on the roads; the Range Rovers might be carrying their own genuine wheels, alternatively a low-loader or breakdown truck may have been recruited to collect them once they get beyond the limit of the docks. It could be waiting somewhere nearby as we talk – local Crime Intelligence Units are searching for such a vehicle. We will be warned if they find one. And the same applies to the motor bike, it might be destined to finish its journey on board another vehicle. Our operation this morning, ladies and gentlemen, is to catch those men – all five, we hope – in possession of drugs and arrest them, and also to arrest and detain any members of a support party and their vehicles who might be awaiting their arrival. And there is a possibility that Winters and his motor cycle might be a decoy. Campion is skilled at setting up decoy operations but if that is the case this time, we've rumbled him. Perhaps it was thought we might pursue the bike while ignoring the Range Rovers, and certainly a bike can out-manoeuvre us in traffic. We shall be deploying drugs dogs in the Customs areas, by the way. It will not be too difficult detaining any of those vehicles before they leave the dock – HM Customs are prepared for that – but we want to catch the helpers who will be waiting, including any who may be on shore. One of those will be Joseph Campion, he might be unable to keep away! He has masterminded this operation, so we want him. I am sure he will be somewhere around, even if he's hiding somewhere in town.

'So that is our brief this morning. Find Campion, find those five men, find all the helpers, seize all the evidence. We need to link Campion with the shipment, that's going to be the difficult part. Look out for decoys, beware of firearms or other weapons. There is one other vital factor to remember in all this – we are talking about a product which might be worth millions on the streets and we must beware that if the organizers of this run suspect it might be seized – by us or by other criminals – then they will have their own protectors waiting in the wings. If they realize their very precious cargo has been wheeled into the Customs shed for the vehicles to be searched, they might decide to rescue it – with guns, explosives or whatever. That is another reason for our heavy presence. Contemplate that scenario for a moment or two. And while you're doing that, I will hand over to Detective Inspector Martin Coxon who will outline the operational element of our plans. He will explain your individual deployment and personal responsibilities. Martin.'

As a map of the dockland area appeared on the screen, a youthful police officer stepped forward. With the help of maps and photographs of buildings, roads, docks and disembarkation points, Coxon went through the plans in meticulous detail, making sure everyone knew his or her responsibilities, where they were to be deployed and to whom they were answerable. Those with responsibilities outside the docks, where they'd have to stop and detain suspected supporters in the town, would be given a further briefing as would the specialist firearms teams. Their role would be vital in the event of an attempted armed heist of the cargo. And so those early morning hours progressed, with everyone seeing photographs of the suspects yet again before being issued with small personal files containing written orders.

When Coxon had finished his presentation, Petrie asked, 'Any questions?'

For a few moments, everyone sat in stunned silence as they contemplated the enormity of their forthcoming role, and then the questions began. They were mainly simple operational matters such as the likelihood of meal breaks, toilet breaks, the use of relief staff, rest periods, easily explained by one or other of the presenters, then Lorraine decided to raise her hand.

'Sir,' she asked. 'I have two questions. First, we have not received any information about the possible role of a man called Darren Mallory in all this. I just wondered, in view of his coincidental disappearance and his links with this area and with one of the personalities just mentioned, whether he should be considered as part of this operation?'

'I should clear that up straight away.' It was DCC Craig who responded. 'For the information of those who don't recognize the name, Darren Mallory is a local villain, a member of a family gang, who in recent weeks has been showing an unhealthy interest in activities on the docks of Port Haverton. We have every reason to believe he had managed to work out why Campion was absent and what he was up to – he even attacked an undercover Customs officer with a brick while he was under surveillance near the docks. Mallory has been collecting large rewards recently, using his criminal knowledge to gain the necessary information, and we feel he was sniffing around in the hope of gaining something from this importation of cocaine – hush money, we feel, a dangerous game with Campion I might add, but of some nuisance value to us. We felt he had to be kept out of the way during our operation, and so he has, he's been kept safely away from all this, partially for his own safety and partially so that he did not jeopardize our operation. He got rather too close for our comfort – and for Campion's comfort too.'

'Kept out of the way?' asked Lorraine. 'But, sir, how? I mean where?'

'He's in a safe house,' said Craig. 'That is all you need to know. He will not jeopardize this operation and he is perfectly safe. That is all.'

'But sir –'

'That is all, young lady. Now, you had another question?'

'I'm not sure I need ask it now, sir, but you mentioned rewards. I was going to ask if there was a reward for information leading to the arrest of this drugs gang, the one we're all waiting for.'

'You couldn't claim it if there was!' laughed Craig. 'Police officers cannot claim rewards! But no, there's no reward. It's not the kind of crime that attracts rewards, is it?'

'Thank you, sir.'

There were one or two further questions, chiefly concerning the division of responsibilities between the police and HM Customs and Excise, and then Craig dismissed everyone.

'Help yourselves to some sandwiches and things, you might need them with you, it could be a long night, and have another coffee before you leave. You'll be called to your duties in fifteen minutes, you know to whom you should report. Section leaders, please collect your throat microphones and earpieces before you leave this room. The ferry is about an hour away at the moment, but it will remain off-shore until the scheduled berthing time.'

Lorraine, with Inspector Larkin at her side, went to the coffee urn and filled herself a paper cup. Larkin did likewise but Lorraine was deep in thought, so much so that she did not acknowledge Paul for a few moments. Then he said, 'I'm glad we're with Mr Pemberton.'

'I think they've put the operational officers with commanders they've worked with previously,' she said. 'But, sir, this business about Darren. What did Mr Craig mean when he said Darren's in a safe house?'

'I think it means we needn't worry about him any more,' said Larkin.

'No, it's more than that, sir!' she almost snapped. 'They've done something with him, haven't they?'

'You'd better ask the boss about that, he's heading this way now.'

Pemberton had spotted them in the crowd and came to join them for a coffee, saying, 'I'm pleased they've allocated my own force teams to me. We're in the foot passenger lounge, the foot passengers disembark first. We'll wear our Johnstone coats. If Customs spot those five men walking through and leaving their vehicles behind, perhaps to be driven by substitutes who are already on the ferry, we'll be alerted, we'll have to identify them and halt them . . . There's a back-up as well, in case we miss any.'

'Sir,' she said. 'I've got to know this and I'm sorry if I'm

244

banging on about Darren, but what did Mr Craig mean? He said he's in a safe house.'

'I've asked him about that,' Pemberton said. 'Darren was becoming a threat to this operation, always poking his nose into events on the dock, snooping around, asking questions in offices where he should never have been allowed entry and even looking at papers when the clerks' backs were turned. He became a very real danger to the undercover police operation, he could have scuppered things, so he was removed.'

'Removed?' she cried.

'By Crime Squad officers. They dressed up as uniform bobbies and staged that road block, they caught Darren and his car and he's now in a safe house somewhere in Northumberland with every facility he wants, except he's under guard and completely incommunicado until this is over.'

'I don't believe this . . . and all the time I was trying to find him –'

'We had to put a show on, we had to make the villains believe we were looking for him – and we had to make Darren's family think we had nothing to do with his disappearance . . . They all wondered why he had vanished, what he knew, who'd done it and so on.'

'But, sir, all that time we put into that enquiry –'

'Your enquiries in our area, and those on Greater Balderside, were all done to provide a smokescreen, Lorraine. Believe me, it was necessary. But by finding out about the road block, you almost let the cat out of the bag . . . That was a pretty good piece of police work.'

'Why didn't you tell me all this?' she cried.

'How could I?' he retorted. And then someone banged a fist on a table.

'Time to go,' shouted the man with the big voice.

Chapter Seventeen

The Johnstone personnel carrier carried them around the site still dressed in their yellow plastics and hard hats, and concluded its journey on the brightly lit public car park at the passenger terminal. The place was about half full of parked cars belonging to passengers who had earlier left England on this ferry line, perhaps for a short break in Holland or perhaps for a longer stay; by the time of the ferry's scheduled return, this park would be crowded with more cars meeting incoming passengers or left here by outgoing travellers. Across to their left lay the docks, dominated by rows of towering cranes and the bulk of moored cargo ships, while all around were more unglamorous buildings ranging as far as the eye could see, many with protective high fences and surrounded by bright lights. At the edge of the car park was a smaller complex of buildings, all brilliantly lit, and above the large glass doors was the legend 'Ferry Passenger Area'. Outgoing passengers congregated here each evening for the 8 p.m. outward sailing by the sister ferry, *Snow Leopard*, but unlike an airport, incoming passengers also came through the same lounge after disembarking. This was where they met families and friends who had come to collect them, and every foot passenger had to come this way after passing through Customs. For them, there was no other legal route from the ferry.

Having received his own briefing, Pemberton knew that officers, some armed, were located at strategic points around the passenger terminal and all continued to wear their yellow coats and hard hats. It was 5.15 a.m. and the ferry, named *Snowgoose*, had now arrived in the estuary and was moored at sea. Under close surveillance from the shore, it was awaiting the call to complete its journey. By seven, it would have docked and by half-past the foot passengers, who always disembarked ahead of the vehicles, would be making their way into that lounge. It was time for Pemberton and his team to familiarize themselves with their area before events began. Leaving the security of the personnel carrier, he led his team of six across the tarmac and into the spacious passenger waiting lounge.

'Our code is Sierra Six,' he told his teams. 'I'll be receiving constant updates on progress through my earpiece.'

At this early hour the lounge was empty – or appeared to be so. They checked the toilets, wheelchair alcoves, corridors and one empty office. Satisfied that it was deserted, they settled down on the chairs and tried to look like building workers taking a break – there were coffee machines, chocolate vending machines, juke boxes, game machines and one-armed bandits all around, enough to occupy them as they awaited the arrival of the ferry. There was a two-hour wait now, unless something dramatic occurred in the meantime – after all, the ferry was stationary less than a mile away. Pemberton went into a corner and reported to Control via his throat microphone: 'Sierra Six in position, no problems. Over,' and his call was acknowledged on the earpiece hidden beneath his hard hat.

Outside, in the brilliant lights of the car park, Pemberton could see the movements of other 'Johnstone personnel', bringing vehicles on to the park, walking around to make this appear normal and, in one case, starting to erect some scaffolding near a wall. A normal sight – except that they were all police officers.

After a few minutes, one of the constables in Pemberton's team indicated a juke box and asked, 'Sir, do you mind?'

'Not if you keep the sound reasonable!' he laughed, realizing this would increase the façade of normality while not interfering with their work. 'I don't want to leave here with damaged eardrums . . .'

And so, as the long wait got under way, Lorraine went and sat beside Pemberton. At first they didn't speak, not quite knowing what to say to one another partly because of their surroundings and partly because of their difference in rank, a factor which had always to be considered when in public places. Then, with the booming music making his words inaudible to the others and his microphone switched off, he said, 'I knew very little of this, Lorraine, until we got here.'

'I know, I shouldn't have been so critical about you keeping me in the dark.'

'We're involved chiefly because the main players in this game won't recognize us. They know the local police and Greater Balderside CID, they'd spot them a mile off, even if they are dressed in these builders' jackets.'

'I don't mind doing this,' she said. 'It's a welcome change from my usual duties.'

'At the start, I had no idea Darren was a red herring either,' he admitted.

'It's one way of keeping him safely away from things while the action's going on,' she laughed. 'But is it legal? Isn't it kidnapping?'

'He'll never know who carried him off that night,' Pemberton said with conviction. 'I understand he went quite peacefully, no force was used. He was led to believe it was a gang trying to muscle in on the incoming drugs, trying to keep him out of the way, and keeping him safe in case he became bolshie . . . that's why we launched that search with you and Andy, to make it appear we had no idea where he was and who'd whisked him away.'

'So his pals, his contacts, his enemies, his family and the police were all trying to find him?'

'They were. Some thought he was involved in whatever Campion's up to, and Campion wanted him out of the way too, so the Crime Squad discovered. They didn't want him snooping about, but once he'd vanished, they had no idea where he was or what he was up to, hence the attack on his father. That's Campion's way of warning Darren, the Stonemason is one of Campion's heavies. In some ways, Darren was removed from the scene to save his own skin, although he'll never appreciate that, but if he'd been allowed to continue he could have ruined the whole operation. In the unlikely event of us being challenged, we can claim it was protective custody.'

'Surely, though, he will eventually realize what's happened?'

'Perhaps in time, but right now he thinks it was a band of fake policemen and he'll have no idea where he's being held. He'll not be harmed – in fact, he'll have every need catered for.'

'Every need?' she smiled.

'Every need,' he nodded.

They lapsed into silence as the music boomed and echoed about them; the clock ticked away the long dark minutes and daylight began to make its appearance as more people began to arrive. As six o'clock approached, dock workers and Customs officials were coming on bikes or by car and vanishing among the buildings as others departed for home after their night shift, an empty coach arrived and parked on the coach park, awaiting its complement of incoming foot passengers, one or two cars pulled into the car park and no one climbed out. They were people coming to meet friends and family off the ferry. A milkman on his float and then a newspaper boy riding his heavily laden bike went towards the Customs offices and ferry company offices. It was a place coming to life, an absolutely normal beginning to the day, but in the eyes of the hidden police officers, every one of those people was a suspect. Every person was under surveillance, however briefly, until their bona fides were established, usually without those subjects knowing they were being observed.

Then Pemberton's earpiece sounded, with only him able to hear it.

'Sierra Six,' he responded.

'Control to all units. Campion has arrived, he's in a blue

249

Ford Mondeo, a very modest car, not his usual style,' and the registration number was provided. 'He's sitting in the car park near the passenger terminal, alone. Third row from the front, sixth space from the side nearest the docks. Do not approach him, do not apprehend, do not show any interest in him. Repeat – do not approach, do not apprehend, do not show interest. Also for information, the ferry has now resumed its journey, it will berth on time. The first foot passengers are expected to disembark at seven. All units please acknowledge, over.'

'Roger, Sierra Six,' said Pemberton who then told all members of his team, adding that Campion would be closely observed by another team; his presence had been anticipated and although it needed to be known to Sierra Six, it should not directly concern them. They had to concentrate on the flow of passengers which would soon be coming this way.

During this long and uneventful wait, Lorraine found herself thinking of Darren Mallory and trying to work out his part in all this. To some extent, she found it odd there had been no reference to him during the briefing – his photograph had not been featured and there was no hint he might be involved once the cargo had arrived. Nonetheless, he had clearly been a nuisance to Campion who'd done his best to warn him off at the expense of poor old Jack, but it was also evident the Crime Squad had wanted him out of the way too. Perhaps he had learned something of Campion's plans and had intended to attempt some kind of hijack of the cocaine shipment? Maybe his visit to the docks had been to solicit information from dock workers or ferry staff . . . but the Mallorys did not do drugs, so she'd been told. And she doubted if Darren's interest in these events had been a means of blackmailing the perpetrators – a man like Joseph Campion would never allow himself to be blackmailed, she was sure of that.

There was no reward for information leading to the recovery of this shipment or the arrest and conviction of its perpetrators, and yet Darren had been the proverbial thorn-in-the-side to more than one person. He'd been snooping about Port Haverton, spending time on the docks, assaulting a man who'd apparently been an undercover Customs official. And it was during these ponderings that she had a thought, a thought which suddenly sent a cold shiver down her spine . . .

Lorraine tried to concentrate on her newest theory but the repetitive thump of the base booming from the juke box made it so difficult . . . She was trying to work out and establish all the links between Darren and this morning's operation and yet, during her enquiries and efforts to trace him, there'd been no hint of an involvement with drugs. That suggested his links with today's events must have been very slender, very tentative indeed, perhaps something very much on the periphery? In fact, she recalled, he'd not really been actively committing crime or getting involved in it during recent months, and although he'd shown he had access to a rich source of cash, he'd not – according to police intelligence – been dealing in drugs or raiding premises for cash. His source, she was almost certain, had been the range of rewards currently on offer, hundreds of thousands of pounds' worth on a nationwide basis, and even up to a hundred thousand on a purely local basis.

But, as she told herself to the accompaniment of the repetitive thump-thump-thump of the music, someone – both the Crime Squad and Joseph Campion, through Campion's heavies – had seen fit to ensure Darren did not poke his nose into this morning's operation, not only this morning but throughout the past couple of weeks. In Lorraine's mind, one fact dominated all this speculation – this supposed incoming shipment of cocaine did not attract a reward of any kind. Short of Darren attempting to blackmail Campion for the price of keeping his mouth shut – something Darren himself might not find appealing – there seemed to be no reason for Darren to be interested in Campion's activities. Campion was cunning, she knew that because of the likely decoy vehicle, i.e., the motor bike . . . or could the Range Rovers be the true decoys? The motor bike might be the carrier, albeit in a more modest fashion.

Or even another vehicle? Something like an ordinary saloon car carrying ordinary people back home after an ordinary trip to the Continent? There was always the possibility, she realized, that Darren was using himself as a decoy. Had he spent all that time haunting the docks so that people would see him and assume he was involved in something underhand or illegal . . . so could he have also fooled Campion?

She knew that ACC Craig and the National Crime Squad would have considered every possibility and would have planned and acted accordingly, so why was she worrying? Darren was not a factor under consideration at this stage – he was securely incarcerated miles away – and besides, she was a very small cog in this huge crime-fighting wheel. Who would listen to her prattling on about nothing in particular? She didn't really know what her worries were, there was nothing positive, nothing to which she could point a finger of suspicion even if something was niggling her deep down somewhere beyond her immediate recall. She reconciled herself to the fact that her views were really of minor importance in the wider scale of things.

As she tried to dismiss her thoughts, she was acutely aware that whatever was being brought into the country was now fast approaching this dock, and this dock was swarming with undercover police officers; no doubt it was also swarming with Customs officers, both undercover and performing their routine duties. She need not, should not, worry – all she had to do was precisely as she was told. Campion and his cargo, whether accompanied by decoy vehicles or not, and whether armed or not, would be detained and searched. Of that there was no doubt. She knew that this entire intelligence-led operation would be highly sophisticated and able to cope with any eventuality, however unexpected, and she must not forget that somewhere behind the scenes there were highly skilled Customs officers who'd shadowed this drugs operation across the world. They weren't likely to let it slip through their fingers at this late stage.

She tried to assure herself that every eventuality had

been considered, every loophole had been identified and catered for, every personality checked by an array of officials here and abroad, and every vehicle, decoy or otherwise, was about to be impounded for inspection . . . but still she could not relax. Then there was Campion himself, sitting out there in the car park. Why was he here? It wasn't like him to risk arrest, was it?

If he was Mr Big, paying others to bring his cargo ashore in open defiance of the police and Customs, but always at risk of being caught, why had he taken this chance? Were the riches to be gained from this worth the risk of his capture? Why had he placed himself in a situation where he must easily be recognized and arrested if things went wrong? It almost seemed he knew the police would be watching this morning, almost as if he was drawing attention to himself in this bizarre situation. Surely he did not think he could outwit the police if things did go wrong? It seemed such an amateurish thing for a top professional to do, such an unnecessary risk – but Campion was anything but amateurish!

Lorraine's instincts and intuition told her there was something not quite right about all this. The music boomed and boomed and boomed and outside there was increasing activity as the giant ferry approached the dock. More cars were arriving, people were coming into the room where she waited with Pemberton and the others, there was a growing excitement as disembarkation time approached, more buses were coming to collect foot passengers, dockside vehicles of all kinds, large and small, were moving into their operational positions, and she saw the huge white and red gates being opened to allow ferry-borne vehicles a swift exit once they'd cleared Customs.

As she watched the activities outside, almost forgetting where she was and why she was here, her mind dwelt on Darren Mallory almost to the extent that she expected to see him walk into this passenger lounge. Suppose he'd not been prevented from coming? Would he have been here this morning? She thought he might. If so, what would he have been doing? Whatever his purpose, it would have been connected with something on this very dock, something or someone on this incoming ferry, and he would have been here to do whatever was necessary to ensure he got his reward.

If he was wanting to claim a reward, she reasoned, he'd have to ensure he was in a position to convince the Customs officials of his inside knowledge – for here, within the parameters of the docks, the Customs officers were responsible for countering smuggling attempts. They'd have to be sufficiently convinced of the value of his information to take action, to divert Darren's suspect – whether man, woman or vehicle or any combination – into their search areas to establish his or her guilt. But Darren was not here to stake his claim – he had been kept away by the police; he'd been warned off by Campion too, through the attack on Jack.

And then she realized what was probably happening . . . it was Campion who was here as a decoy! He'd put himself on show because the whole escapade of apparently importing drugs was a decoy, something done deliberately to mislead the authorities! Campion would not be arrested because, when the vehicles – the Range Rovers and motor bike – were examined, there'd be nothing illegal about them or in them. No drugs, no illegal imports, nothing. Those men would be innocent too, They'd be nothing more than paid drivers bringing Range Rovers and a motor bike into the country for Campion, a known car dealer. That's all; everything perfectly legitimate.

But, reasoned Lorraine, while that diversion was going on, the real object of Campion's interest would pass freely through Customs and out into the English countryside. It was *that* person or vehicle which carried the reward, it was that incoming thing, whatever it was, which had so interested Darren Mallory.

The more she thought about it, the more she became convinced that Darren had discovered Campion was arranging the importation of something very valuable, something which carried a reward for its recovery. Darren had discovered what it was – and had deliberately misled others, including the police, into thinking he was snooping around a big drugs deal. The police had thought they'd discovered the drugs plans . . . they'd been set up for that! So Darren had fooled everyone – except Campion! And it was *that* operation which was about to be concluded – right here, right now!

'Mark . . .' She forgot where she was for the moment, then swiftly remembered the protocol. 'Sir –'

'Not now, Lorraine, the ferry's docked. The first foot passengers will be coming through any minute now. We've got to stand by for action, remember the photographs of those four with the Range Rovers and the motor cyclist . . . five men, Lorraine, we've got to spot just five suspects. We should get the nod from Customs if they see them heading our way . . .' Tense with the pressures of the moment, he moved away to speak to the others, to direct them to strategic positions, some near the entrance doors, some near the exits, then came back to her.

'Sir,' she began. 'I need to talk to you –'

'Detective Constable Cashmore.' He spoke formally to her, out of earshot of the public but in a way that told her he was far from pleased. 'I need you to position yourself near the entrance door.'

'Yes, sir, but –'

'Now, Lorraine, and I mean now. Do it. That's an order.' There was a flash of his anger, anger he'd controlled for a long, long time – until now. 'Make sure you get a good view of the route from Customs.'

'Sir, it's important . . .' She tried to confront him with her reasoning but he was immune at the moment, getting his troops into position, making sure that if those five men did get as far as this lounge, they'd get no further . . . and he walked away. As she manoeuvred herself into the best position, she found she could look across the car park. As she tried to subdue her own anger and disappointment at his attitude, she realized daylight had replaced darkness and she could see Campion in his blue Mondeo, still sitting quietly and all alone as the first of the foot passengers were due. She knew Mark was concentrating on his task, she

255

could understand the stress he was now facing and knew it would be difficult to interrupt his train of thought. She had no desire to interfere but she did need to divert his attention for just one minute.

She *must* do it, she *must*! It was so important . . . even if he was furious with her, even if he later rebuked her. He was now standing at the corner where the wheelchairs were kept and he was talking quietly to Inspector Larkin, making some last-minute observations and issuing final orders and so, even though it meant leaving her post temporarily with the passengers due any second, she ran across to them.

Pemberton was furious. 'DC Cashmore, you have left your post . . . now get back there immediately, and that's an order, the passengers are due any minute, you're need-ed there . . . God, Lorraine, what do you think you're doing?'

'Sir, I must talk to you . . . I really must . . . I think the drugs story is a decoy,' she managed to blurt out. 'There's no reward, you see, Darren was interested in rewards . . . and Campion's out there, waiting . . . he's a decoy as well . . . I'm sure he's set us up for this, sir, I'm absolutely sure of it . . .'

Larkin looked at Pemberton, trying to assess this poss-ibility, but Pemberton merely looked at Lorraine and snapped, 'Get back to your post, Lorraine, now. I'll see you there. Paul, take over, you know what to do.'

Lorraine, almost on the point of tears, hurried back to the corridor and established herself so that she had a good view of any foot passengers leaving Customs and heading this way. So far, the corridor was deserted. She sniffed back her distress and took a deep breath or two, then Pemberton arrived, his face looking red and angry. It was another visible reminder of a temper that could erupt in a flash, but which he'd controlled for so long.

'This had better be good, Lorraine! You've seconds to explain things!'

'I'm sorry, sir, really I am, but I had to say this . . .' and all her thoughts came tumbling out, her days of researching Darren, the events of the past week, the rewards on offer . . . and he listened, albeit showing his impatience.

'All right, suppose you're right . . . whatever is really being smuggled in must be very very valuable if Campion has gone to all this trouble and expense to set up a diversion. I know he can resell the Range Rovers, I know he'll recoup some of his expenses, so, Lorraine, what could be so valuable that he sets up a fictitious drug smuggling scam as a diversion?'

'I don't know!' she cried. 'I don't know . . .'

He was glancing along the corridor, expecting the passengers to appear at any moment. 'If those men of Campion's are not smuggling drugs, he'll let them drive the vehicles off the ferry . . . which means they won't come through here. He won't do the usual switch . . . Now, if he *is* smuggling something into the country, something very valuable, he's probably hidden it in a vehicle, and it wouldn't be the suspected drugs carriers because they'll be stripped down to bare metal in the search, they'd find anything else that was there for sure . . .'

'Unless it's a diamond,' she said. 'You can easily hide diamonds in clothing and luggage, or jewellery of most kinds.'

'Customs officials are alert to that, especially on boats coming in from Holland . . . it'll be something else . . . . I'm trying to think fast. Look, if he's using another vehicle, or using a person who's driving a vehicle, where on earth is it? This ferry carries 250 cars and 400 commercial vehicles.'

'If I was bringing a vehicle ashore, and had decoys on board, I'd make sure it left the ferry either immediately behind or immediately in front of the decoy.'

'Right, let's do it. I'll arrange for the vehicles behind and in front of the Range Rovers to be diverted into Customs . . . that's no extra work . . . but, Lorraine, we need to know what they're looking for, they're bound to ask.'

'Antiques,' she said. 'Valuable furniture . . . paintings . . . paintings, Mark, paintings! There's a huge reward for a painting . . . stolen in Italy . . . a *Madonna and Child*, by an

257

old master . . . worth a fortune . . . it was painted on panel . . . not canvas, I remember . . . That's it, Mark, that's it! Arezzo, it was stolen from Arezzo, Campion was in Arezzo around the same time –'

'On panel? On wood, you mean?'

'I'm not really sure what it means.'

'Then it could be hidden in a consignment of furniture,' he snapped. 'How big was it, any idea?'

'Small,' she said, screwing up her eyes. 'Fifteen inches by twelve or thereabouts . . . I remember thinking it could easily be hidden.'

'And it could be in any of those cars or lorries . . . Wait here, keep an eye open for those five men and alert Inspector Larkin if you see any heading down this corridor. I'm going for a word with Customs about searching more vehicles, we can run both operations together.'

As he hurried along the corridor, the first of the flood of foot passengers materialized from the other direction. Hundreds of them were bustling along, hurrying to waiting families, buses and cars, carrying suitcases and hold-alls – all big enough to carry the picture, or drugs. Lorraine tried desperately to search the face of every person, most of them not giving a second glance at the tall, hard-hatted woman in the builder's coat, and then she noticed the first of the cars emerging through the red and white gate. And there was no sign of Mark.

She caught Larkin's eye as he stood in the centre of the bustling lounge and shrugged her shoulders, hoping Larkin would interpret that as 'nothing doing', and she turned her attention back to the oncoming horde. The ferry could accommodate almost 1400 passengers, although a high proportion would be in cars or even coaches yet to be released, but nonetheless the oncoming tidal wave seemed endless. By now, she had calmed a little and found the scanning of faces – male faces – somewhat easier and so, when a gaggle of fifty or so white-haired women appeared, clearly a busload heading for a coach waiting outside, she took the opportunity to look outside again. Campion was still in his car, now with the passenger window wound down. A dark grey Volvo estate car motored towards the exit of the docks and passed his parking space, having just left the ferry. It bore English registration plates, and then she saw the headlights flash on and off quickly. The driver – a woman – had signalled to someone as Lorraine instinctively read the number. Campion did not react – but he was the only person in a car at that point . . . that must be it . . . not a van or a lorry full of furniture but a private car . . . and she had its number. Dodging slow-moving passengers, she ran to Paul Larkin.

'Sir.' She ushered him aside. 'We need to stop this car, it's just leaving the docks, heading for the exit,' and she gave him the registration number. 'Don't ask why, there's no time . . .'

He hurried to the outer door and caught sight of the Volvo as it moved slowly forward in the queue of outgoing vehicles, heading for the exit.

'It can't get far . . .' and without asking the reason, he pulled a mobile phone from his pocket and rang a number.

'DI Larkin,' he said to someone. 'At the passenger lounge. We need to stop a car,' and he provided details. 'It's in the queue for the exit . . . take it out of the stream of traffic, we need to talk to the occupants and search it,' and as he said that, Lorraine was at his side, nodding furiously to confirm his rapid reaction.

'I should get back to my point,' she said.

'No need,' he said. 'I've had a call, the two Range Rovers and motor bike are all in Customs now, along with those five men, the ones we were looking out for. They'll be searched, it'll take a long time though. Our part in here's over now. So let's go and see what they're doing to this car.'

'I ought to inform the boss,' she said.

'I'll do it,' he said, and activated his mobile once again, soon saying, 'Larkin, sir, outside the passenger lounge. We've ordered a car to be halted, a Volvo. Lorraine spotted something, we're going to see what happens to it. I don't know what she noticed but even as I talk, I can see two uniformed police officers have caught it, they're on the ball, these local cops. It's being directed into a building beside the exit road. A pale blue building marked "Fletcher".'

'What's Campion doing?'

'He's still sitting in his car, sir, but from where he is, he can't see what's happened to the Volvo.'

'We're having him followed when he leaves here, and I expect that will happen the moment the traffic thins out, we've got the Range Rovers now, and the motor bike, as well as a white van and a furniture lorry which would have left the ferry immediately behind and in front of them. Customs are starting to search them now with dogs, I suspect Campion knows that, his men have mobile phones. Tell Lorraine that. So what's she up to now, Paul?'

'No idea, sir, I haven't had time to find out, but I'm going to as we head for that blue building.'

'Well done, both of you.'

Larkin told the rest of his team to stand down and suggested they make their way back to the Johnstone site office while he and Lorraine walked along the exit road to where they'd seen the Volvo intercepted. Now, it had vanished and the doors of the large building were closed; Campion was moving off and he joined the queue behind a blue Audi patiently waiting his turn as the cars inched forwards. Even now, he would have no idea the Volvo had been impounded. Lorraine knew he'd be followed. Still clad in their workmen's coats, Paul and Lorraine walked to the blue building as Lorraine explained her theories to Larkin. When they arrived, he rapped on the door and waited. A policeman opened it, saw them and said, 'Sorry, mate, this is private.'

'Detective Inspector Larkin,' smiled Paul, realizing these were two normal dockland patrol officers, not part of Operation Snowgoose. 'And DC Cashmore.' They showed their warrant cards and were admitted.

The solid-looking Volvo estate car was parked in the

middle of a huge empty warehouse and a worried-looking middle-aged couple – a man and a woman – were standing beside it. They looked even more perplexed at the sight of two building workers heading in their direction and the man, trying to be forceful and brave, said, 'Now look here, I don't know what this is all about –'

'Detective Inspector Larkin and Detective Constable Cashmore,' said Larkin as they showed their warrant cards. 'Now, to whom am I speaking?'

'My name is Stanley Patterson and this is my wife, Greta,' said the man.

'And is this your car?'

'Yes, it is, but look, we've done nothing wrong, Customs didn't stop us and I can't see why you should . . .'

'Where have you come from?' asked Paul.

'Holland,' said Patterson.

'And before that?' He looked at the travel-stained vehicle with its stickers and mass of luggage in the rear.

'We've been touring Europe, we've been away three months.'

'Did you get to Italy?' asked Lorraine.

'We did, yes, we saw most of it.'

'I have no wish to detain you longer than necessary, Mr and Mrs Patterson, which means that if you co-operate you'll be on your way very soon. Now, did anyone ask you to bring anything back with you? Into England?'

'You don't mean drugs, Inspector!' shrieked Mrs Patterson. 'Good heavens no, we're not silly enough to be caught like that, are we, Stanley, we're far too experienced travellers to do such a stupid thing.'

'I don't necessarily mean drugs, Mrs Patterson,' said Paul. 'I mean anything, anything at all, as a favour. We could keep you here until we have searched your car and everything that's in it, all your luggage, your souvenirs, even down to stripping the door panels and taking the seats apart.'

'Well, I can't honestly think why you would want to do that, Inspector, we're not criminals,' said Patterson. 'I'm a respectable person, a retired local government officer and my wife was a teacher . . . you can check our credentials anywhere you like.'

'Yes, but think again, Mr Patterson. Did a stranger ask you to bring something back to England? Either in your luggage or in your car? Anything at all?'

'We would never do that, Inspector, as I said, we are far too experienced to fall for that kind of trick. We'd never accept anything from a stranger. We know the risks.'

'So you've nothing in your car that you can't account for?'

'No, of course not!'

'Mind if we look?'

'Well, it seems a bit discourteous, but we've nothing to hide.'

Larkin asked them to unlock the boot and he began his search. After unloading most of the holiday paraphernalia and luggage, he found a plain wooden stool with an upholstered top. It looked extremely cheap and ordinary, being some two feet long by one foot wide, with legs about six inches high, and the green upholstered top looked like cheap curtain material. It was tacked in place and stuffed with something soft, like rags.

'Is this yours?' he asked.

'Er, well, no, it belongs to a friend of ours. Ernie Preston, from Greater Balderside,' said Mr Patterson. 'He was on holiday near us, he hadn't room in his car and asked us to bring it home for him. We've known him for years, Inspector, it's just an old stool, a family heirloom.'

'And have you seen him since you returned?' asked Lorraine.

Mrs Patterson responded. 'He said he would come to meet the ferry, just to be sure we were on it because our return date was some time ahead and he had to go home before us, and he said we hadn't to stop and talk to him, otherwise we'd get stuck in the queue of lorries, so he said he might follow us and catch up to us on the way home. He didn't want to hold us up at the terminal. If he missed us, he said he'd come to the house and pick it up, once we'd had time to settle in.'

'So you have seen him,' persisted Lorraine.

'Yes, he was in the car park, I flashed my lights at him, just to let him know it was us and that we'd got back home as arranged,' she said. 'I expect he'll be trying to follow us now.'

'Perhaps he will. Now,' smiled Larkin,'let's have a closer look at this stool. This is what he asked you to fetch home?'

Mr Patterson now spoke. 'He said it wasn't worth anything but as a family heirloom it had lots of sentimental value, something his father had made years ago. He used it in his Italian house but now wanted to bring it back to England. He had no room in his own vehicle so we said we'd fetch it home in our estate car.'

'It looks very interesting to me,' said Larkin as he pulled a multi-tool knife from his pocket and began to pick at the tacks which secured the cover, easing them out without causing any damage and removing sufficient to enable him to peel back a few inches of the covering fabric. It was packed with cut rags, and as he pushed them back, he could see that a painted panel had been carefully tacked to the base of the stool, neatly hidden . . .

'Lorraine, look at this!' said Paul. 'This looks like a *Madonna and Child* to me, and it's painted on panel.'

'A *Madonna*?' cried Patterson. 'Under there? Good heavens, fancy using a painting as part of a footstool . . .'

'Yes indeed, and I think it could be worth rather more than this stool,' said Larkin. 'Now, you said your friend Mr Preston was going to come to your house to collect this when you got back?'

'Yes, this morning, I expect, unless he catches up with us on the way home,' smiled Mrs Patterson.

'Then I think we should arrange a reception for him.'

Chapter Eighteen

Standing beside the Pattersons in that huge hangar, Paul Larkin radioed Pemberton with the news and then asked if someone could fetch him a conventional police vehicle as he wished to accompany two people to their home in Leathamkirk, a suburb of Greater Balderside.

Pemberton knew that Paul would not wish to leave those people alone, there was too much at stake. Now that Part One of Operation Snowgoose had concluded satisfactorily with the Range Rovers, motor bike and five men in custody pending the necessary searches and further enquiries, Pemberton decided to confront the Pattersons. He wanted to see them for himself; members of the National Crime Squad, along with armed police officers, were guarding the Customs shed where the suspect vehicles were held, so he was not needed there.

A few minutes later Pemberton arrived and Paul met him outside, leaving Lorraine to ensure the couple did not contact anyone, did not alert 'Preston' by mobile phone or try to conceal anything within the hangar. Beyond their earshot, Paul explained what had transpired and Pemberton listened carefully.

'So if this picture is the missing *Madonna*, it's worth a fortune,' he said. 'It must be if Campion was prepared to invest in an elaborate and expensive subterfuge to get it into the country, and then dupe this couple into acting as his couriers.'

'So it would seem, sir. I think we should go along with the Pattersons, covertly, to their home, to wait for Campion to collect the picture, unless they meet him along the route somewhere.'

'We've got to be very careful with this one, Paul,' cautioned Pemberton.

'I realize that, sir, but to deal with any eventuality and be on hand to get the necessary evidence, I think we must accompany them all the way home. That's the only way we're going to nail Campion for this.'

'And if he's warned in advance, he won't turn up, will he?'

'Warned in advance, sir? He doesn't know we've detained them, we were beyond his vision when we pulled the Volvo in. I can't see how the Pattersons can have alerted him from here, we've got them safely contained and Lorraine's with them, she's confiscated their mobile phone. Lorraine is certain that "Preston" is Campion, the Pattersons acknowledged him, or rather Mrs Patterson did.'

'She could be innocent, Paul. If she was in on this, it's hardly likely she'd draw attention to herself by acknowledging Campion as she did. But whatever happens now, they'll be in trouble from Campion. We can't let them go home, Paul, it presents too many opportunities for them to alert him. Once they get home, all they have to do is to draw a curtain, switch on a light or deploy some other pre-arranged signal and bingo – our quarry keeps away, we're left with the picture and the stooges while Campion gets away scot-free. He'll lose the picture, but the Pattersons will be charged with theft, smuggling it through Customs or whatever can be thrown at them. Campion will not hesitate to discard them. And if Darren's alerted us to this, I wouldn't like to be in Darren's shoes right now, not when Campion realizes what's happened.'

'So you think the Pattersons are not innocent tourists, sir?'

'Paul, if you had nicked an internationally renowned painting worth a fortune, one which is now being sought all over the world, would you entrust it to complete strangers to carry hundreds of miles across Europe, even if it was hidden in a footstool?'

'Well, no, I wouldn't.'

'Of course you wouldn't. And neither would Campion. These old folks are in on this, Paul, mark my words, although we might never prove it. Or one of them is, the old man I suspect, even though he might not know what was under the base of that stool. Perhaps we should go along with them, pretending we believe their innocent involvement. Or were you going to suggest something else?'

'I was going to suggest that Lorraine drives their Volvo to their home address, with Mrs Patterson as the passenger and the picture still on board, while Mr Patterson joins me in a police car, then we drive in convoy back to their home address.'

'In the hope Campion hasn't smelt a rat and actually turns up there to collect his prize, you mean? It won't work, Paul, he'll spot you a mile off!'

'The Pattersons said he would go to their house if they don't liaise on the way home.'

'And you believe them?'

'I'm beginning to doubt it now, sir! There's also the question of protection, especially if they are innocent. If Campion realizes we've got possession of his precious painting, he could use firearms in an effort to recover it . . . it could be worth as much as a consignment of drugs, remember.'

'And for something as valuable as that, it's worth taking a lot of risks, Paul, so it might be wiser to remove the stool from them, take it into protective custody in a manner of speaking. If things do go wrong, at least we'll have recovered the painting!'

'So how do we nail Campion without proof of him possessing it? And, sir, with every passing minute, without the appearance of the Pattersons ahead of him, or any calls from their mobile, he's going to get increasingly worried. He could arrive at their house ahead of them . . . we can't delay their arrival too long, he's bound to realize something's gone wrong.'

'I think he'll have already come to that conclusion, Paul. We've got the couple here for a start. He must have found out by now that they're not ahead of him on the road, you can bet there was some pre-arranged signal or meeting place. Probably our only choice is to take the Pattersons into custody and seize the painting as evidence, then let Campion think they've done the dirty on him. Suppose he thinks they've nicked it, what's he going to do about that?'

'He'll come back here to look for them, he'll retrace the route, or alternative routes, he'll go to their house, many times I'd say, he might even break in to search it and he'll visit all the places he knows they're familiar with.'

'He'll do all that and more, Paul, I'm sure, or get his minions to do it for him, so he's not seen associating with the Pattersons. Now, there is another problem. This affair is not within our force area, this is part of Greater Balderside, remember, and so we should really hand it over to them, or to the National Crime Squad as it might be considered part of, or an extension to, Operation Snowgoose. I am duty bound to report it to ACC Craig.'

'So Lorraine won't get any credit? Or any part of that reward for recovering the picture?'

'She can't claim any reward, Paul, she's merely doing her job. I know she's done remarkably well, I'll make sure it's all noted in her personal file. Now, let us keep the Pattersons here a little longer, for one thing Customs will want to interview them about the smuggled picture, the Crime Squad will want to search their car just in case it has drugs on board too, or they might be carrying something else of interest. But whatever happens, when they do go home, they won't be carrying that picture. We've got it, it's safe now, we're not going to risk it any further in the hands of the Pattersons, and in time it can be returned to its rightful owner, once the formalities are over. And that's all due to Lorraine's good police work.'

'I think it's a real pity she can't claim the reward, sir. If it hadn't been for her digging her heels in –'

'And what about Darren Mallory? I bet he's been working for months on this one, planning to get the reward, being devious and cunning. You know, really he had some part to play in its recovery too – a small part admittedly – even if he doesn't know about it. If it hadn't been for him snooping about the docks, this recovery would never have happened. When he hears all about this, he's going to feel cheated as well, isn't he? Two hundred thousand pounds is a lot of money, Paul.'

'You're saying that if it hadn't been for him, this picture would not have been recovered?'

'It's a very good argument, Paul, one I would support, but he'll just have to do better next time! There are other rewards waiting – and if the local police have any sense, they'll be keeping a very close eye on Darren. Who knows what else he might lead them to?'

It was some weeks before ACC Craig rang Pemberton to update him. He was told that Joseph Campion would not be prosecuted for any involvement with the *Madonna and Child*, there being insufficient evidence to proceed against him apart from the fact that the original crime was committed in Italy. The Pattersons had been charged with breaches of the Customs and Excise regulations and the Italian police wanted to talk to them about the theft of the Bellini; the question of extradition was under consideration. No drugs had been found in their vehicle, nor had any other illegal object, but their description and that of their vehicle had been recorded in all Customs records for future observations.

Mrs Patterson was thought to be an innocent party, chiefly because she had unwittingly drawn attention to her vehicle by acknowledging Campion's presence and thus leading to the recovery of the painting.

No drugs were found in the two Range Rovers or the motor bike either, and all their drivers had been free to leave. The paperwork suggested this was nothing more than a normal vehicle purchase, even if it had been done over remarkably long distances.

Darren Mallory had been allowed home after spending a fortnight in a place which was totally unknown to him. He was never told where he had been kept nor was he told why. Even when he had his car returned to him, he had no idea who his captors had been; he got no answers to any of his questions. Even though he never asked about the Bellini painting, however, he was told that it had been recovered.

Soon afterwards, £20,000 was paid anonymously into his building society account. It was ten per cent of the reward offered for the recovery of the *Madonna and Child*: after hearing the story, the administrators of the reward had felt his part should be acknowledged, albeit in a small way. The wording of the offer did say the reward should go to anyone who, by his actions or information, led to its safe recovery – and Darren's actions, not being illegal in themselves, had led to its recovery. The rest of the reward money was given to an Italian religious charity.

Darren, of course, could never tell anyone that he had received a share of the reward money; apart from branding him a grass or police informer, it could also reach the ears of Joseph Campion who would not be very pleased about it.

The man known as the Stonemason had been found in Port Haverton, severely beaten about the head, but he had refused to make an official complaint and said he had fallen while drunk. He never admitted the attack on Jack Mallory.

Oddly enough, as the Bellini exhibition had not concluded at the time of the raid, the *Madonna and Child* had been put on show in Greater Balderside, if only for half a day. Because of the security measures in place, it had been deemed the safest and most suitable place to keep it temporarily and it occupied the space it would have filled had it not been stolen. When the police and Customs had completed their work with it, it was sent back to the church in Arezzo. It transpired that Darren's visits to the gallery were a means of checking that the picture had in fact been stolen – then through his criminal contacts and his own astute work, he'd discovered where it was heading – and had worked out who'd stolen it.

It had taken some weeks for all those details to be finalized, but as Lorraine said to Pemberton one Saturday night some time afterwards, 'If Campion had really wanted that painting, why didn't he steal it from the local exhibition?'

'There was too much security,' smiled Pemberton. 'Security for such a valuable piece of art work is always pretty watertight in the UK, it was much easier and less risky to nick it during transit in Italy.'

'He must have wanted it very badly.'

'I'm sure he did, he went to a lot of effort to make sure he got it. People do collect valuable paintings as a form of insurance, and villains don't usually have pension schemes. Perhaps that's why he wanted it? As an insurance in his old age. Now, of course, the authorities in the countries where he has houses are going to search them all just in case he's got other stolen old masters hidden away.'

'I believe quite a lot are missing, from all over the world.'

'They are, so we – or you – might have done the art world a favour with this!'

'And in spite of all the security, legitimate or otherwise, and all the deviousness of Campion, Darren actually discovered the picture's whereabouts.' She smiled mischievously.

'He did, I said he was clever. And do you realize, Lorraine, he's the only one to benefit from all this – he's finished up £20,000 better off even though he can't tell anyone about it.'

'So we've come to another dead end, he's got some of the reward he was chasing and the church has got its painting back. I suppose that's our real achievement.'

'It is, so maybe we'll open a bottle of bubbly tonight, eh?' smiled Mark Pemberton.

She kissed him. 'And don't you dare answer that phone if it rings!'